CORNELL WOOLRICH

His name represents steamy, suspenseful mystery fiction . . . chilling encounters on the dark and sultry landscape of urban America in the '30s and '40s. Author of more than 100 stories, novelettes, and books—many dramatized on such classic radio shows as *Suspense*, on TV's *Climax* and *Alfred Hitchcock Presents,* and in great films like *The Bride Wore Black, Rear Window,* and *Phantom Lady*—Woolrich is in a class by himself.

CORNELL WOOLRICH

"HIS WRITING GOES RIGHT THROUGH YOU LIKE A SHRIEK IN THE NIGHT. SOMETIMES YOU EVEN WISH YOU COULD FORGET IT, BUT YOU CAN'T."

Dorothy Salisbury Davis

CORNELL WOOLRICH

"HE CAN DISTILL MORE TERROR, MORE EXCITEMENT, MORE DOWNRIGHT NAIL-BITING SUSPENSE OUT OF EVEN THE MOST COMMONPLACE HAPPENINGS THAN NEARLY ALL HIS COLLEAGUES AND COMPETITORS."

Ellery Queen

CORNELL WOOLRICH

One of the truly great and truly original American writers . . . now coming back to readers everywhere from Ballantine Books.

CORNELL WOOLRICH

Also by Cornell Woolrich
Published by Ballantine Books:

Black
Alibi

BALLANTINE BOOKS • NEW YORK

This edition published by arrangement with Simon & Schuster, Inc.

Manufactured in the United States of America

First Ballantine Books Edition: November 1982

INTRODUCTION
BY FRANCIS M. NEVINS, JR.

HE WAS THE POE of the twentieth century and the poet of its shadows. For almost thirty-five years this tormented recluse wrote dozens of haunting suspense stories, the most powerful of their kind ever written— stories full of fear, guilt, and loneliness, breakdown and despair, and a sense that the world is controlled by malignant forces preying on us. And throughout his life he felt those forces eating away at him.

Cornell George Hopley-Woolrich was born in New York City on December 4, 1903, to parents whose marriage collapsed in his youth. Much of his childhood was spent in Mexico with his father, a civil engineer. The experience of seeing Puccini's *Madame Butterfly* in Mexico City at the age of eight gave him his first insight into color and drama, and his first sense of tragedy. Three years later, he understood that someday he too, like Cio-Cio-San, would have to die, and from that moment on he was haunted by a sense of doom that never left him.

During adolescence he returned to Manhattan and lived with his mother and her socially prominent family, and in 1921 he enrolled in Columbia College, with his father paying the tuition from Mexico City. He began writing fiction during an illness in his junior year, and quit school soon afterward to pursue his dream of becoming another

F. Scott Fitzgerald. His first novel, *Cover Charge* (1926), chronicles the lives and loves of the Jazz Age's gilded youth in the manner of his current literary idol. This debut was followed by *Children of the Ritz* (1927), a frothy concoction about a spoiled heiress's marriage to her chauffeur, which won him a $10,000 prize contest and a contract from First National Pictures for the movie rights. Woolrich was invited to Hollywood to help with the adaptation and stayed on as a staff writer. Besides his movie chores and an occasional story or article for magazines like *College Humor* and *Smart Set*, he completed three more novels during these years. In December of 1930 he entered a brief and inexplicable marriage with a producer's daughter —inexplicable because for several years he had been homosexual. He continued his secret life after the marriage, prowling the waterfront at night in search of partners, and after the inevitable breakup Woolrich fled back to Manhattan and his mother. The two of them traveled extensively abroad together during the early 1930s. His only novel of the period, *Manhattan Love Song* (1932), anticipates the motifs of his later suspense fiction with its tale of a lovestruck young couple cursed by a malignant fate that leaves one dead and the other desolate. But over the next two years he sold almost nothing and was soon deep in debt, reduced to sneaking into movie houses by the fire doors for his entertainment.

In 1934 Woolrich decided to abandon the "literary" world and concentrate on mystery-suspense fiction. He sold three stories to pulp magazines that year, ten more in 1935, and was soon an established professional whose name was a fixture on the covers of *Black Mask, Detective Fiction Weekly, Dime Detective*, and countless other pulps. For the next quarter-century he lived with his mother in a succession of residential hotels, going out only when it was absolutely essential, trapped in a bizarre love–hate relationship that dominated his external world just as the tortured patterns of the inner world of his fiction reflect the strangler grip in which his mother held him.

The more than 100 stories and novelettes Woolrich sold to the pulps before the end of the thirties are richly varied in type, including quasi-police procedurals, rapid-action whizbangs, and encounters with the occult. But the best and the best known of them are the tales of pure edge-of-the-seat suspense, and even their titles reflect the bleakness and despair of their themes: "I Wouldn't Be in Your Shoes," "Speak to Me of Death," "All at Once, No Alice," "Dusk to Dawn," "Men Must Die," "If I Should Die Before I Wake," "The Living Lie Down with the Dead," "Charlie Won't Be Home Tonight," "You'll Never See Me Again." These and dozens of other Woolrich suspense stories evoke with awesome power the desperation of those who walk the city's darkened streets and the terror that lurks at noonday in commonplace settings. In his hands even such clichéd storylines as the race to save the innocent man from the electric chair and the amnesiac searching for his lost self resonate with human anguish. Woolrich's world is a feverish place where the prevailing emotions are loneliness and fear and the prevailing action a race against time and death. His most characteristic detective stories end with the discovery that no rational account of events is possible, and his suspense stories tend to close not with the dissipation of the terror but with its omnipresence.

The typical Woolrich settings are the seedy hotel, the cheap dance hall, the rundown movie house, and the precinct station backroom. The dominant reality in his world, at least during the thirties, is the Depression, and Woolrich has no peers when it comes to putting us inside the life of a frightened little guy in a tiny apartment with no money, no job, a hungry wife and children, and anxiety consuming him like a cancer. If a Woolrich protagonist is in love, the beloved is likely to vanish in such a way that the protagonist not only can't find her but can't convince anyone that she ever existed. Or, in another classic Woolrich situation, the protagonist comes to after a blackout (caused by amnesia, drugs, hypnosis, or whatever) and little by little

becomes convinced that he has committed a murder or
other crime while out of himself. The police are rarely
sympathetic, for they are the earthly counterparts of the
malignant powers that delight in savaging us, and their
primary function is to torment the helpless. All we can do
about this nightmare world is to create, if we can, a few
islands of love and trust to help us forget. But love dies
while the lovers go on living, and Woolrich is a master at
portraying the corrosion of a relationship between two
people. Although he often wrote about the horrors both
love and lovelessness can inspire, there are few irredeem-
ably evil characters in his stories, for if one loves or needs
love, or is at the brink of destruction, Woolrich identifies
with that person no matter what crimes he or she might
also have committed. Technically, many of his stories are
awful, but like the playwrights of the Absurd, Woolrich
uses a senseless tale to hold the mirror to a senseless uni-
verse. Some of his tales, indeed, end quite happily (usually
thanks to outlandish coincidence), but there are no series
characters in his work, and the reader can never know in
advance whether a particular story will be light or dark,
whether a particular protagonist will end triumphant or
dismembered. This is one of the reasons that his stories are
so hauntingly suspenseful.

So much for the motifs, beliefs, and devices at the core
of Woolrich's fiction. In 1940 he joined the migration of
pulp mystery writers from lurid-covered magazines to
hardcover books, and with his first suspense novel, *The
Bride Wore Black* (1940), he launched his so-called Black
Series, which influenced the French *roman noir* and the
development of the bleak Hollywood crime movies of the
forties, which the French have labelel *film noir*. Julie
Killeen, whose husband was killed on the church steps
moments after their marriage, spends years tracking down
and systematically murdering the drunk driver and his four
cronies whom she holds responsible for the beloved's
death. Eventually she is herself stalked through the years
by homicide cop Lew Wanger, and when their paths finally

converge both hunters find themselves in the presence of the malignant powers. This Woolrich classic was followed by *The Black Curtain* (1941), the masterpiece on the overworked subject of amnesia, in which Frank Townsend recovers from a three-years' loss of memory, becomes obsessed with the determination to learn who and what he was during those missing years, and finds love, hate, and a murder charge waiting for him behind the curtain.

The third book in the cycle, *Black Alibi* (1942), which you are about to read, is a terror novel about a killer jaguar menacing a large South American city, while a lone Anglo hunts a human murderer who may be hiding behind the jaguar's claws. This time Woolrich dropped his quintessential themes of loneliness and despair and concentrated exclusively on pure suspense. The result is another masterpiece, with a sense of menace breathing on every page. The five long setpieces, in each of which a vividly characterized young woman is stalked through the landscape of the night by unspeakable horrors, are among the finest sequences Woolrich ever wrote.

The novel is an expansion of one of the longest and least known of Woolrich's dozens of pulp crime stories, "The Street of Jungle Death" (*Strange Detective Mysteries*, July–August 1939). The earlier version was set in Hollywood and described the carnage following the escape of a leopard in the film community. In the novel, Woolrich kept almost all of the story structure of the pulp tale, added much more vivid characterizations and infinitely more suspense, and moved the action from California to the South America he remembered from childhood travels with his father. The only major plot change he made was to convert Jerry Manning, the press agent and grotesque murderer of the pulp story, into the hero of the novel.

Like most of his books, *Black Alibi* sold almost at once to the movies. RKO bought the rights and assigned the project to the production unit of the legendary Val Lewton (1904–1951), who in the early forties was responsible for some of the most poetic low-key horror films ever made.

The Leopard Man (1943) was produced by Lewton and
brilliantly directed by Jacques Tourneur, another visual
poet whose talents were akin to Woolrich's own. Dennis
O'Keefe starred as Manning, with Margo as Clo-Clo
(transformed from a semi-prostitute into a castanet dancer
in order to clear the censors), and Jean Brooks as Kiki.
Ardel Wray's screenplay moved the plot to New Mexico,
cast a new character as the murderer, and climaxed at a
procession of blackhooded monks whose like will not be
found in the book you are holding. But despite divergences
from the letter of the novel, Lewton and Tourneur kept the
movie faithful to the Woolrich spirit with (to quote critic
Joel E. Siegel) its "artful images of fear." Thus, it's still
well worth seeing today. There was also a radio version of
Black Alibi, broadcast October 11, 1946, on *Molle Mystery Theater*, but neither a list of cast and credits nor a
tape of this adaptation seems to have survived.

The fourth novel in Woolrich's Black Series, *The Black
Angel* (1943), deals with a terrified young wife's race
against time to prove that her convicted husband did not
murder his girl friend and that some other man in the dead
woman's life is guilty. Next came *The Black Path of Fear*
(1944), in which a man runs away to Havana with an
American gangster's wife, followed by the vengeful husband, who kills the woman and frames her lover, leaving
him a stranger in a strange land, menaced on all sides and
fighting for his life. The series ended four years later with
Rendezvous in Black (1948), a creative reworking of the
avenging-angel motif from *The Bride Wore Black*, but with
the sexes reversed: A grief-crazed young man, holding one
among a small group of people responsible for his fiancée's
death, devotes his life to entering the lives of each of that
group in turn, finding out whom each one most loves, and
murdering those loved ones so that the person who killed
his fiancée will live the grief he lives.

During the early forties Woolrich continued to write
stories and novelettes for the pulps, and dozens of his huge
backlog of earlier stories were adapted for dramatic radio

on series like *Suspense* and *Molle Mystery Theatre.* As the
novels increased his reputation, publishers issued numerous
hardcover and paperback collections of his shorter tales,
and many of his books and stories were made into *films
noir* of the forties (although the most famous Woolrich-
based film, Alfred Hitchcock's *Rear Window,* was made in
1954). As if all this activity were not enough, Woolrich
continued to write more novels, too many for publication
under a single byline, so that he adopted the pseudonyms
of William Irish and (his own two middle names) George
Hopley for some of his most suspenseful books.

The Irish byline debuted in *Phantom Lady* (1942), in
which an innocent man is sentenced to die for the murder
of his wife, while his two best friends race the clock to find
the apparently nonexistent woman who can give the husband an alibi. The second Irish, *Deadline at Dawn* (1944),
is another clock-race story, with a desperate young couple
given until sunrise to clear themselves of a murder charge
and escape the web of the city. In *Night Has a Thousand
Eyes* (1945), as by Hopley, the suspense rises to unbear-
able pitch as a simple-minded recluse with uncanny powers
predicts a millionaire's imminent death by the jaws of a
lion, and the doomed man's daughter and a sympathetic
cop struggle to avert a destiny that they suspect, and soon
come to hope, was conceived by a merely human power.
Waltz into Darkness (1947), also written as Irish, is set in
New Orleans around 1880 and tells of the hopeless love
affair between an unbearably lonely man and an impossibly
evil woman. And in the last Irish novel of the forties, *I
Married a Dead Man* (1948), a woman with nothing to
live for, fleeing from her sadistic husband, is injured in a
train wreck, is mistaken for another woman with everything to live for who was killed in the crackup, grasps this
heaven-sent chance to start life over with a new identity,
falls in love again, and is destroyed by malignant powers
along with the man she loves.

Despite overwhelming financial and critical success,
Woolrich's personal situation remained as wretched as

ever. His mother's prolonged illnesses seemed to paralyze
his ability to write, and after 1948 he published very little:
one minor novel under each of his three bylines in 1950–
51 and a few short stories. That he was remembered at all
during the fifties is largely due to Ellery Queen (Frederic
Dannay), who reprinted a quantity of Woolrich's pulp
tales in *Ellery Queen's Mystery Magazine.* But Woolrich
and his mother continued to live in comfortable isolation,
for his magazine tales proved to be as adaptable to televi-
sion as they had been to radio a decade earlier, and series
like *Ford Theater, Alfred Hitchcock Presents,* and *Schlitz
Playhouse of Stars* frequently presented thirty minute
filmed versions of his stories. Indeed even the prestigious
Playhouse 90 made use of Woolrich, turning *Rendezvous
in Black* into a feature-length teledrama (broadcast October 25, 1956) starring Franchot Tone, Laraine Day, and
Boris Karloff.

When his mother died, in 1957, Woolrich cracked. Di-
abetic, alcoholic, wracked by self-contempt, and alone, he
dragged out the last years of his life. He continued to write
but left unfinished much more than he ever completed, and
the only new work that saw print in his last years was a
handful of final "tales of love and despair." He developed
gangrene in his leg and let it go untended for so long that
when he finally sought medical help, the doctor had no
choice but to amputate. After the operation he lived in a
wheelchair, unable to learn how to walk on an artificial
leg. On September 25, 1968, he died of a stroke, leaving
unfinished two novels, a collection of short stories, and an
autobiography. He had prepared a long list of titles for
stories he'd never even begun, and one of these captures his
bleak world view in a single phrase: "First You Dream,
Then You Die." He left no survivors, and only a tiny
handful of people attended his funeral. His estate of nearly
a million dollars was bequeathed in trust to Columbia Uni-
versity, where his literary career had begun, to establish a
scholarship fund for students of creative writing. The fund
is named for Woolrich's mother.

"I was only trying to cheat death," he wrote in a fragment found among his papers. "I was only trying to sur-

mount for a little while the darkness that all my life I surely knew was going to come rolling in on me some day and obliterate me. I was only trying to stay alive a little brief while longer, after I was already gone." Trapped in a wretched psychological environment and gifted, or cursed, with an understanding of his own and everyone's trappedness, he shaped his solitude into stories that will haunt our descendants as they haunted our forebears. He could not escape death, but the world he imagined will.

1. THE ALIBI

SHE WAS SITTING THERE at her glass, at the fashionable going-out hour, trying to decide between a cluster of crystal grapes and a live gardenia as a shoulder decoration, when someone knocked at the suite door, outside across the adjoining reception room.

Whatever her decision was in the matter, she knew it would have a city-wide effect. It meant that for the next few weeks hundreds of young women would either all be wearing clusters of crystal grapes or live gardenias.

It was hard to believe that just a couple of brief years ago no one had cared a rap what she stuck on her shoulder. Nor anything else about her, for that matter. She'd been wearing her heels down to the quick and getting consistently laid off in an endless string of third-rate Detroit roadhouses. And now— She turned her head and gave it another look through the windows; she couldn't resist it. That was the testimonial, the badge, of her importance, however transitory it might turn out to be; that out there.

CASINO EXCELSIOR
KIKI WALKER
en la gran revista de arte
"TRIC-TRAC"

The biggest spectacular in the city, rearing against the cobalt late-afternoon sky. And when the current was shot into it next week, for the opening, you'd be able to read her name after dark all the way up at the other end of the Alameda.

They were already naming perfumes and nail polishes after her, and of course paying for the privilege, and the newest concoction at the smart Inglaterra Bar was the Kiki Walker Cocktail (fiery-red at the top and stunning, the barman explained to everyone). For the whole of the last "winter" (June-September) she'd been queening it over the third largest city south of the Panama Canal, with her own car and chauffeur, personal maid, hotel suite. Not bad for a run-of-the-mill roadhouse entertainer from Detroit, stranded down here when a traveling show blew up. Not bad at all.

She still wasn't quite sure how it had come about herself. A little dancing talent, a little singing talent, and a great deal of luck had done it for her. It was mostly a case of happening to be in the right place at the right time, and of having no competition to speak of. In Detroit her lyrics had been shoddy; down here they couldn't be understood, so they sounded witty. In Detroit her red hair had been a commonplace; down here it was a rarity. And then Manning and his crazy stunts might, just might, she was willing to admit, have played some small part in attracting the public eye to her.

Their first meeting was not a thing she cared to be reminded of. He'd been sitting at a table at a sidewalk café, needing a shave and a clean collar, and she'd stopped in to find out if they couldn't use a cashier—or even a waitress. He'd bought her a cup of coffee, because he was still good for a cup of coffee at that particular place and she looked as if she needed one. When they got up from the table half an hour later, he was her press agent. Two weeks later she had her first job and he had a clean collar.

"I *made* him," she used to end the unwelcome reverie at this point.

That he might have had something to do with making her was unthinkable, not even to be considered for a moment. Whoever had made whom, one thing was certain: now she had the place put away in her pocket.

The knock had been repeated. "It's probably Señor Manning, Maria," she called out to her maid. "Let him in."

She heard the latch go back, but then instead of the maid's usual little welcoming remark, there was a shriek of mortal terror, a scurry of footsteps, and the fling of a chair, as though somebody had dropped down behind it.

Kiki turned quickly on the bench she had been occupying, rose questioningly. Before she could do more than that, it was upon her, she had seen it herself. It was one of those incredible images that the mind disbelieves in even at the moment of apparition. It was a head, down there on the floor, coming through the open doorway at her from the outside room. The head of *something or other* was the best she could do to identify it at that first awful moment; some member of the cat tribe; leopard, panther, were the successive labels flashed before her shell-shocked mind.

It was black, spade-shaped, ears wickedly flat, muzzle to carpet, coming in fast with an impression of zigzag undulation. That was all she waited to see. Her own scream slashed out to join the maid's and she turned and vaulted lightly, and with an instinctive agility that betrayed the dancer in her, to the top of her own dressing table. Perfumes, powders, and knickknacks rained down all around her to the floor, including a little toy music box that promptly began to sound off a tinkling little tune. She stood there aloft in flurried motion, skirts clutched nearly at her thighs and waving them defensively to and fro to ward the horror off.

It was only then that she became aware of the muzzle gripping the jaws, the taut leash, and the familiar Middle Western face of Jerry Manning peering blurredly at her from the background. Her outcries only became more verbal, not less vocal. Between them was the graceful, sinuous, almost snakelike body of the thing, straining forward belly-low against the leash; powerful shoulder muscles rippling under the seal-smooth black fur, tail twitching feverishly, in the attempt to get at the flutelike music box.

"Get it out of here!" Kiki wailed in high C. "Manning,

what's the matter with you, bringing anything like that in here?"

"It won't hurt you," Manning tried to reason with her, pushing his Panama farther back on his brow. "There's nothing to be afraid of. I rode all the way in with it just now in a produce truck myself. It's perfectly tame; it was raised from a cub by a guy lives outside of town."

"Well, what do you bring it to me for?" She had stopped screaming, at least.

"I thought it'd be a good idea for you to show yourself with it, when you take your daily outing along the Alameda."

"With *that*? Never! Not from here downstairs to the front door, much less driving along the Alameda! Now listen, Manning, I'm getting tired of your brain waves—"

He had taken time off to light a cigarette, using one hand. "Think of the splash you'll make. Just step out of the car with it, sit down at the Globo for a Martini for a few minutes. What's there so hard about that? I've planted photographers all around there, to take you with it. I can get you the whole inside spread of next Sunday's *Gráfico* on it; I've got an in with old man Herrera. Two whole pages of green rotogravure all to yourself. Look, here's a little gold whip I got you to go with it."

"You're too good to me," she said sulkily.

"It's for you, not me," he coaxed. "You're opening next week. The Latins like their stars to be exotic. You want your show to be a hit, don't you?"

"I'd also like to be still in it, not all taped up in some hospital," she let him know. "I'm set. What do I need this stuff for now? In the beginning it was different."

"You're never set in your business. Come on, Kick, be game. Look at this, watch me a minute." It was stretched out sidewise, lazily licking one paw. He bent down over it, gently grazed the soft fur of its underside a few times with a hooked forefinger. It promptly rolled over on its back with typical feline coquetry, lolled there four paws folded in air, coyly trying to kick his finger away. "You couldn't ask for anything tamer than that, could you? Come on, just take hold of it. Try it out, see how it feels." He reached for her reluctant hand, passed the looped end of the leash over her fingers.

She still remained up on the table. She was giving in by unnoticeable degrees, however. Her skirts had fallen back to normal level. She was holding the leash by herself now; he'd taken leave of it.

"I'll be right behind you in a taxi the whole way."

On this one point she was adamant, however. "Oh, no, you won't. You'll be riding right in the front seat of the car with me, or I don't leave here at all."

He had saved his most potent argument to the last, the one he knew by experience would persuade her if anything could have; he must have been something of a shrewd psychologist. "You ought to see how it goes with that outfit you've got on. You ought to see what a picture the two of you make together. Come on down a minute, Kick, take a look at yourself in the glass, standing next to it. Zenobia, Cleopatra, weren't in it!" He held his hands up, to help her down.

That seemed to do it. She continued to eye it askance, but she started pointing the tip of one foot warily downward, about to descend to floor level beside it once more.

"Jeezizz," she said at the very last, a touch of her Detroit-era crassness cropping up as it did every now and then, "the things I do for my art!"

Her arrival at the Globo, if it was in the nature of a sensation at all other times, was nothing short of a galvanic shock this time. It was brimming to the very edge of its sidewalk awnings, and beyond, with the usual *apéritif*-hour crowd. Everyone who was anyone went there; it was a gallery worthy of any actress' mettle.

Manning, who was in the front seat of the Packard beside the driver, had retained the leash surreptitiously across the top of it until the very last, at her insistence. He only passed it to her at the moment of arrival, in time for her to make her sortie. The liveried driver jumped down, ran around, and held the door for her. She stood up in the car, held the stance just long enough for everyone to get a look at her, then prepared to step down. There was a momentary, and quickly covered-up, hitch at this point. It was between her and the door and it wouldn't move for a second; she would have had to step over it to get out.

"Push it with your foot," Manning said in an undertone.

She nudged its flank gingerly with the toe of her shoe. Then a second time. It rose reluctantly, wavered for a moment, then sluiced out upon the pavement like a suddenly released coil of black water, giving her arm an awkward jerk that she managed to cover up only with difficulty. She descended in its wake with the smiling grace of a Venus.

It had come into full view of the café crowd for the first time. It had been hidden from sight until now on the floor of the car. One of those deep, somnolent hums rose that are created when dozens of throats all murmur in astonishment at one and the same time. Then a spray of excited comment was dashed up. "*Mira! Mira!* Look what she's got with her!" was repeated on all sides, from chair to chair and from table to table. Those farther back stood up in their places to get a better look at it. Women gave little cries of synthetic fright and dismay. "*Ay, que horror! Que barbaridad!* Is she bringing it right in here?" And they prepared to jump up and get out of the way.

Passers-by along the sidewalk began to bunch up, keeping back at a respectful distance.

"Stay here, don't let him take the car away," she said tautly to Manning, from behind her smiling mask of composure and relaxation.

"He can't stand right here in front of the place, we're not allowed to park. We'll be right down there at the end of the street. Nothing can happen to you, just go over to your table and sit down." Then as the sound of the brakes being taken off seemed to freeze her where she was for a moment, he quickly warned: "Don't stand here like that, Kick. You're onstage. You're on the air. They're all looking at you."

The car glided treacherously out from in back of her, and she was left to her own resources. She touched it lightly with the little toy whip he'd provided her with, and it moved forward docilely enough, perhaps attracted by the odors of food coming from the tables. Those seated nearest at hand edged their chairs cautiously back as it made its way down the narrow center lane left between the tables, its coat all but brushing their legs at times.

The distance she had to cover wasn't far, fortunately. She reached her customary table, which had been held in reserve for her, paused, and managed to get it to halt also by reining in the leash slightly. Then she seated herself with an air of lordly indifference upon the reedy wire-backed chair the waiter had drawn out for her. He prudently took her order from that position, remaining behind her instead of coming out around to the other side of the table.

"A Martini *seco*," she said. She crossed her legs and looked about her with that air of cool indifference fashionable ladies are wont to assume in fashionable places. A renewed tug or two at the leash, meanwhile, had caused it to sink down on the ground at her feet, after an undecided moment or two. The spool-like table, however, remained between the two of them. It remained that way, quiescent, as though overcome by supreme lassitude, only its ears twitching sensitively at each taxi-horn bleat that sounded in the street outside.

There was a concerted if tactful drawing away on the part of those in the immediate vicinity. They moved the adjoining tables wherever possible, or, if not, shifted their chairs around to the other side, so that they were facing it and not sitting with their backs to it. She was left seated in the midst of a small empty circle. Even the waiter, when he brought her order, approached circuitously from the rear and put it down over her shoulder.

She would not, however, have been an actress if she had not enjoyed the inordinate amount of attention she was attracting. People could not take their eyes off her—or rather her appendage, which amounted to the same thing. She took out a gold-tipped cigarette, pointed it up into empty space with her lips in quest of fire. The match came accommodatingly down over her shoulder from somewhere behind her.

The press representatives arranged for by Manning now

materialized from nowhere, converged upon her. "A few words, Señorita Walker?"

"Sí, como no," she said affably.

One of them dipped one knee, sighted a reflector toward her. *"Fotógrafo,* Señorita Walker?"

"Yes, you may."

The flash had a disconcerting effect on the recumbent brute. It cowered, edged cravenly closer under the table.

"What do you call it, *Señorita Walker?"*

"Big Boy. That means *chamaco* in English." This was ad libbing, but she was a performer after all.

"Have you had it long, Señorita Walker?"

"No, I only got it today. It was sent to me by a friend."

A leer creased the corners of the interviewer's eyes. "May we say a special friend, Señorita Walker?"

Kiki dropped her eyes, coyly rotated the toothpick thrust through the olive in her glass. "Yes, you may," she conceded at last.

"What do you feed it, Señorita Walker?"

She was at a loss only for a moment. "Oh, a little bit of this and a little bit of that," her stage presence came to her aid.

It was at this point that it happened. No two versions were alike afterwards as to what the immediate cause was. Some said a Pekingese passing in a car along the street just then had gone into a tantrum of barking, arousing it. Others said somebody at one of the other tables had tossed it a small piece of meat while Kiki was occupied with the interviewers, in a spirit of idle mischief, to see what it would do. Still others were inclined to believe that the intermittent flashes from the photographic apparatus had finally irritated its nervous system beyond endurance.

At any rate, there was no warning. Its furled legs suddenly shot up under it like steel springs, a disembodied snarl winged its way along the underside of the awning without seeming to have any source, the lightweight table went over, and Kiki and chair with it, and the circle of interviewers scattered like chaff.

Panic blazed up among the overcrowded tables like fire spreading through straw. There was a mass stampede to the rear, indoors, where doors could be closed protectively against it, even though they were largely glass. Women screamed, and this time not for effect, men shouted hoarsely, waiters' trays went crashing down flat with tinny reverberations; tables and chairs toppled on all sides, glasses broke, those in the rear stumbled and fell to their hands and knees now and then in their efforts to get through ahead of those before them; finally, even one of the veranda door panes itself shivered and disintegrated in the meelee. No one was quite sure where it was any more, nor what it was doing, and no one stopped to find out.

Kiki, screaming berserkly, couldn't extricate herself for a minute from the position she had fallen into. She was flat on her back, but the chair seat, upended against her, held her legs helplessly in air. She had a horrifying glimpse of an infuriated black head looming upon her, ears flat, jaws balefully open in spite of the inadequate muzzle that still clung to them, to reveal a set of needle-pointed fangs.

There was no time to do anything. A thick, blue-glass, mesh-protected siphon of seltzer had rolled unbroken toward her from somebody's table. She snatched it up, hugged it to her chest, closed her eyes expiringly, and played it madly around her in all directions. Whether that saved her or the fear-maddened beast had had no intention of attacking her anyway and was only seeking its own escape, is one of those moot points that are never satisfactorily decided afterwards.

Moments later, eyes still tightly shuttered to avoid seeing what she could not escape from and the contents of the siphon beginning to ebb dangerously, she felt herself being hoisted upright again by helping hands that had come back belatedly to rescue her now that the acutest point of danger was past.

"Where did it go?" she shuddered, opening her eyes and looking blankly around at the carnage on all sides of her.

Brakes were screaming hectically out in the middle of the road. Somebody pointed. It had managed, almost miraculously, to breast the heavy evening traffic unharmed and get to the other side. She was just in time to see its loping black form, all the way across the Alameda, turn

up into a threadlike little alley, a veritable crack between
the buildings, that opened on that side, and disappear in
the gloom.

"How are you going to get it back, señorita?" somebody
asked fatuously, fanning her with his hat while a restora-
tive was held to her lips.

Kiki flipped her hands violently downward, her face a
mask of wreathed weeping. "I don't *want* it back!" she
screamed hysterically. "I don't care if I never see it again!
Look at the way I look!" She pawed helplessly at her
disarrayed hair tumbling loosely down her shoulder. "Help
me back to my car," she sniffled after a moment or two. "I
want to go home—"

Two of the men assisted her falteringly out to the edge
of the curb between them, and the Packard was brought
up. Manning, fortunately for himself, was no longer in it;
he had jumped out to give chase, along with a few of the
bolder spirits in the crowd.

Kiki flopped limply into the back seat, still weeping
gently, or at least simmering in a resemblance to weeping,
into a handkerchief held just under her mouth. For once
she was not putting on any act; her nervous system had
just received a bad shock, and she felt the way she was
acting.

To complete the catastrophic misadventure, the main
body of the crowd, as it ebbed back amidst the littered
debris of the café terrace, had turned definitely unfriendly
toward her, seeming to hold her personally responsible for
ruining its *apéritif* hour. Hisses and boos could plainly be
heard. And when a Latin crowd hisses you, its like bricks
and rotten eggs up North.

A very disheveled, discredited, and thoroughly unnerved
lady was driven away from the scene of the fiasco.

It had been plainly seen to enter that alley at the Alameda end, by dozens of people. There could be no doubt
on that point. It was a chasm of a lane, winding its way
back through derelict buildings. This was an old section in
here, one of those leftovers that dot all large cities, in spite

of its proximity to the fashionable and ultramodern Alameda.

It should, then, have been simply a matter of following it through to the other side, overtaking it, and holding it at bay—if not physically recapturing it—until the police had a chance to arrive. At least in keeping it in sight, if nothing else.

It wasn't.

It was dusk, but the visibility was still fairish, even if dark-blue-tinted. The distance to be traversed wasn't long. Not only that, but the more venturesome spirits in the crowd that had been around Kiki at the Globo, Manning at their head, were only moments behind it in pursuit.

Yet it had dropped from sight, been swallowed up, disappeared completely somewhere along that short byway, in one of the most built-up, hemmed-in parts of the city! For when the advance posse, Manning still foremost, came surging out into the Plaza de los Mártires, a small, busy, palm-bordered square that the alley gave onto at its other end, a case of mass astigmatism seemed to have resulted. And it was not one brought on by fright and excitement, as sometimes happens, either. The plaza was bustling with people, yet not one person could be found who had seen or heard anything amiss, much less anything so striking as a jet-black jaguar rushing headlong out of an alley mouth into their midst. A shoeshine boy less than a yard past the turn of the alley corner was kneeling industriously to his task over a customer's raised foot. Both were close enough for the wind of its passing to have bowled them over. If it had passed. Nothing had, they both said in surprise. And then, not sure they had heard aright, repeated blankly, "A what?", thinking Manning and the rest crazy.

Farther on, but not much farther on, the usual little knot of hopeful loiterers were scanning the lottery lists. People were getting on and off the noisy trolleys that seemed to fill this plaza at all hours of the day and night, emitting turquoise flashes from their overhead conduit wires as they backed and filled.

It was—the way it always was.

While the rearguard of the pursuit was still streaming in from the Alameda side, clogging up the lane, Manning and the advance guard tried to beat their way back through them, passing the word along as they went that it hadn't come out at the other end.

Three gesticulating, whistle-blowing—and very belated —gendarmes now arrived to take charge, and the chase— or rather problem, for a chase requires something in front of it—now became an official one. Their explanation for their tardiness, and not an unlikely one, was that the report had been utterly disbelieved when it was first made known to them. A holdup, yes. A knifing. But a live jaguar running amuck through the streets? This was Ciudad Real. You better go someplace and sleep it off, or I'll run you in.

Manning, momentarily leaving them to their own devices, buffeted his way straight through to the Alameda side again, to try to find the fellow from whom he had "borrowed" the thing earlier in the day, a ranch foreman named Cardozo, and who was supposed to meet him at a certain inconspicuous corner with one of the ranch produce trucks and take the thing off his hands again as soon as Kiki was through with it.

It took him only a few minutes to get down there, but the news was already there ahead of him, he found when he arrived.

"It's gone," he announced breathlessly. "It broke away from her, and nearly killed her in the bargain! That crowd you see up there right now is where they're looking for it."

"I know, somebody told me," Cardozo said disgruntledly. "Somebody must have done something to it to get it started off like that. I *told* you not to let it get mauled around too much. I thought you said you were going to be right with it, the whole time she had it out with her." He actually seemed peeved at losing the thing, as though he had grown attached to it.

"I wasn't more than two car lengths away," Manning answered heatedly, "and even then I couldn't get over to her in time to stop it! I saw what it did. It took a flying leap over her body; the only thing that saved her was she had a bottle of charged water in her hands and squirted some at it. I thought *you* said it was so tame and harmless, there was nothing to worry about! It would have been a fine thing if it had clawed her up, wouldn't it?"

"It was perfectly docile the whole time we had it out at the *estancia*. The cook's kid used to go right in the pen and play with it by the hour."

"When, two months ago?" Manning said bitterly. "Maybe it was growing up then. It sure came of age to-night!" He cut the discussion short, it being largely a spilt-milk matter by now. "Come on, there's no use standing here wrangling about it. I came down here to get you, because I thought you might be a help in getting it back."

"I've got a riata here in the back of the truck I was going to tie it up with on the trip back," Cardozo assented. "I'll bring it along, it might come in handy."

"It disappeared in there somewhere," Manning told him, as they made their way back to the hubbub on foot. "Where d'you think it lit to?"

"To know that, one would have to be a jaguar," was the ranchman's dry answer.

When they returned, order and organization were rapidly being brought out of the chaos. Order, but not any jaguar. The three gendarmes had already become five, and the five in no time at all became seven. Next a lieutenant of police arrived to take charge of this safari on city streets. Next, even one of the municipal fire trucks showed up; but this solely so that the beam of its high-powered searchlight, the strongest available on any piece of apparatus, could be trained into the alley to show them what they were doing. It lit it up with a strange pale blueness, making the weird affair seem even weirder. Finally—but this last of all and not for long hours yet—the curator of the zoo was sent for, to give technical advice and make suggestions, he presumably being an expert in such matters.

The obvious things were done first. The public at large was cleared out of the alley, with a great flourishing of police batons and repeated warnings of: "Move back, now. Nobody allowed in here, it's dangerous. It may suddenly reappear when least expected and attack." The majority of them needed no second urging. There was a confused milling about for a few moments, and then the alley was clear. Ropes were then stretched across it at both ends, to keep it that way.

The next step was a wholesale ordering out of all inmates who lived along it, for a house-to-house search was impending. Again the order didn't have to be repeated. There was a panicky mass exodus from the disreputable warrens all along it, with bird cages, cooking utensils, and even potted plants.

These people were questioned personally by the police lieutenant as they were filed through. For the most part fruitlessly. There was no single case in which anyone had seen where it *went*. It had flashed through so suddenly that they all arrived at their windows too late; the clamor of the crowd in its wake was what had drawn them to look out, not any sound the beast had made. Two or three were found who admitted they had seen it coming in the distance—although they hadn't known it for what it was, had taken it in the gloom for a large, rabid black dog. But even these were no help, though they had been right out in mid-alley at the time; they all gave the same answer. "Yes, I saw it coming *toward* me up ahead, and knew it was something bad because of all the hollering behind it. Where did it *go*? You think I waited to find out? I dove into the nearest doorway and slammed the door shut behind me. By the time I looked out again, it wasn't there any more."

At last, near the tail end of the procession of refugees, was found a little girl of ten or so who, when her turn came, promised to be of some help. For a moment they thought they had something. She had been at the window *in time* to see it, she insisted proudly, because she had been leaning out of it for a long time before that. "I saw something big and black coming down our street, from way up there."

An alert conclave formed about her for a moment. "Where did it go? Where did it disappear to?"

"I don't know. I ran inside to call my brother to come

and see it, and when we came back it wasn't there any more."

The conclave split open again, like an overripe pod.

It would have to be ferreted out by a house-to-house search, the lieutenant in charge decided. The only tenable assumption left was that it had found some doorway, crevice, gap, somewhere along these moldering walls, had sidled in, and was still lurking somewhere in one of the shadowy interiors, perhaps in a basement, perhaps in some unused flue, perhaps in the cavity under a staircase—there was no electricity anywhere along this cranny, inside or out—breathing latent death.

The search began from the Alameda end—it was nearing eight by then—and it was well on the way toward midnight by the time the posse emerged from the last house of all, flanking the Plaza de los Mártires—empty-handed. The search had failed as completely as the original pursuit had. It had been thorough, even if not successful. They had gone from top to bottom and from bottom to top of every building along the way, flashing lights into corners, tapping walls, poking aside crates and boxes and litter, revolvers and stout clubs ready at hand to deal with it if it should turn up. But it didn't.

The crowd behind the ropes at each end, peering down the hazy blue pathway of the fire-fighting headlight, would hold its collective breath each time while they were inside, the wink of torches through the windows showing their progress tier by tier. Then they would come out again, report, "Not in that one," to their commanding officer, the structure would be given a clean bill of health, and they would go trooping into the next. Finally the dramatic effect began to wear off, after the numerous repetitions. Here and there someone turned away and went about his business; it was getting late. Someone in the thinning ranks of onlookers was heard to suggest half facetiously that maybe it had ensconced itself in the back of some cart or vehicle that had been left standing there with its rear open, been inadvertently shut in by the driver on returning a moment later and all unknowingly transported out of the neighbor-

hood. The only trouble with this theory was that there had
been no such fortuitous conveyance in the alley at the
time; they could be sure of this for the very good reason
that the place wasn't wide enough to admit anything but a
pushcart. Someone also suggested that maybe it had gone
up in a balloon, and drew a big laugh. A spirit of skepti-
cism began to make its appearance among the last ditch
spectators, cheated of the excitement they had expected
and taking it out that way. "Maybe it went into the church
to say its prayers!" someone called down the alley through
cupped hands.

The little church he had referred to sat at the end of a
small cul-de-sac, down toward the Plaza de los Mártires
end. The alley bent sharply in direction several times during its short length. At one of these bends it forked in two,
in appearance though not in actuality. One branch of the
fork was simply a brief dead end, coming up against a
wafer-thin chapel, San Sulpicio, dating from colonial days.
In other words, simply an inset, a niche, lying off the
main course of the alley, only a few meters in extent.

This chapel was, the least likely of all places along there
for it to have found refuge. For one thing, it was no longer
in use, having been abandoned years before at the time of
some damage received during some long-forgotten earth-
quake. Its stout mahogany door, however, was still intact;
it took them the better part of half an hour to force it with
crowbar and chisel. It had been unopened for as long as
the memory of the oldest dweller around there could
stretch. And within, when they had dislodged it finally,
they found simply a desolate litter of rotted pews and
fallen plaster within a roofless shell through which the stars
peered. It could neither have got in here in the first place,
nor, if it once had, have got out again from the four-square
stone cell that was all the place offered.

They came out again, brushing their whitened sleeves,
coughing and sneezing, one man nursing a scorpion bite on
the back of his hand.

Moments later, the Plaza de los Mártires had been
reached; the search was perforce at an end.

The sensation-hungry idlers began to melt away with increasing rapidity. Midnight tolled from a belfry here, a belfry there. The log-maintained fire-equipment spotlight suddenly blanked out, the vehicle drove away. The ropes were taken down. The inhabitants were allowed to return. Oil lamps, kerosene, and candles winked here and there from within the fumigated buildings as they resumed occupancy. They stood for awhile in small clusters outside their doors, talking it over. Then these too disbanded as they went in one by one to their respective abodes to sleep. The alley returned to normal.

The majority of the police were withdrawn. One man was left posted, for the rest of the night, at each end of the alley, though for what purpose, it was hard to conjecture.

The night wore on toward its predestined finish, just as every night before it had in its time.

At any rate, only one thing was certain, so far, out of the whole episode. The jaguar had not been recaptured. The jaguar, therefore, must still be at large somewhere or other.

Morning came, and in its confidence-inspiring light a different view began to be taken of the whole thing. The brilliant, sunny daylight killed fears and vapors. It seemed incredible that such a fantastic thing *could* have happened. Ciudad Real was a town of natural-born skeptics anyway. By the time the morning coffees and *pan dulce* had been swallowed everywhere, a rumor had spread that the whole affair had simply been a publicity hoax perpetrated by Walker and her press agent. Like the usual actress' missing-jewels stunt. That this did not take into account what had actually become of the fleet-footed quadruped did not impair its ready acceptance; it spread from mouth to mouth. Even those who the night before had been the first to lock their doors and peer anxiously under their beds were the first to say: "I knew it all along. *You* didn't believe it, did you?" Whereupon the other fellow scoffed, "Of course not, what do you take me for?" In spite of the fact that there were dozens of eyewitnesses, the rumor very nearly succeeded in downing the reality. The very eyewitnesses themselves felt self-conscious after a while when they tried to insist they'd seen it. They began to wonder privately if they actually had, after all.

The newspapers, those barometers of public opinion, helped to disseminate this point of view. They all carried items about it, but treated it humorously, tongue in cheek. "The great jaguar scare"; "Who has Miss Walker's jaguar? Will somebody please return it?" were some of the headings. People greeted one another facetiously all over town with: "Well, have you seen the jaguar yet?"

The police, keeping their own counsel, may have preferred it so. It at least saved them from the nuisance of dozens of hysterical false alarms all day long. This way, not one came in. They noticeably didn't discontinue the search altogether, a sure sign that there was something to look for, after all. Only it became more diffuse; it was harder for the man in the street to tell just what they were doing, now that there was no longer any one particular locality, such as the alley, for them to concentrate on.

Manning, through all of this, had had a most unpleasant twenty-four hours of it. Not only was he detained in jail all of that first night, charged with violating some ancient city ordinance or other that prohibited the conveying of wild animals through the streets without a permit, haled into court in the morning, severely lectured for his misdemeanor, and fined a nominal sum before he was released; but he was also out of his job with Kiki Walker.

She made this known to him in no uncertain terms over the transom of her locked hotel-suite door when he tried to get in to see her the night after the debacle. Her voice came through ringingly; in fact so ringingly that other doors here and there along the hotel corridor began to open curiously after a moment or two.

"You've got your nerve coming around here again, after what happened! You've made me the laughingstock of the whole town, I want you to know! Beat it! Take your bright ideas somewhere else!"

"Now look, Kick, I didn't arrange to have it happen that way purposely, you know," he tried to reason with her.

"You got my pictures in the paper all right!" her voice

went on wrathfully. "Did you see the one in the *Gráfico?* Flat on my behind with my legs up in the air, and squirting a stream of seltzer water through them! When the curtain goes up at the theater next week, *that's* what everyone'll see—and not the performance that's going on before their eyes! I'll be laughed off the stage!"

"I'll come back when you've cooled off," he said stiffly. "You don't have to make a scene like this, with everyone looking out of their rooms snickering at me."

"And what about me, out in the middle of the Alameda, with the whole town taking it in?"

"All right, I'll see you tomorrow," he said, trying to keep relations between them intact, no matter how brittle they had become. It was his livelihood, after all.

"You'll see me never!" What he didn't realize, and perhaps she didn't herself, was that it wasn't the jaguar episode that was basically the cause of her tempestuous indignation. It was really that first meeting of theirs. He'd seen her when she was broke, down on her luck, unable even to buy herself a cup of coffee. She'd never been able to forgive him for that. "There's your back salary. There's no reason for you to come around any more now. We're quits!"

A handful of large disks, Ciudad Real silver pesos, sprinkled over the open transom and rolled about in all directions over the corridor. One or two of those standing in the doorways helpfully stopped them for him with their feet. A scattering of paper money had fluttered down more slowly in their wake.

He wasn't above picking it all up, every last scrap of it. He'd worked hard for that money, and in a way that basically wasn't suited to his temperament or talents. He needed it. And he didn't know where the next was coming from.

"All right, Kick," he said with injured dignity. "Lots of luck to you, if that's the way you feel about it."

The transom panel snapped shut with a sharp little crack. He turned up his coat collar at the back of his neck, shoved his hands deep into his pockets, and trudged disconsolately away from there.

When a man has lost his job, the first thing he thinks of, usually, is to go out, have a drink, and take the edge off his troubles. Manning did that now too. Only he found he wasn't even to be allowed to forget the damnable affair in peace.

He went into a place a few short blocks from her hotel.

"Well," asked the barman, grinning with what was intended to be social jocularity, "have you seen the jaguar yet?"

Manning put down his drink abruptly, as though it sickened him. He gave the bartender a look in kind, as though he did, too. He snapped down a coin, turned around, and walked out without saying anything and went somewhere else.

Again he ordered. Again the barman, trying to make him feel at home, began cheerily: "What's the latest on the jaguar?"

Again Manning put down his drink short, scowled, and turned on his heel.

At the third place he beat the barman to the punch. "I want two things," he said bitterly. "A whisky and water, and *not* to hear about the jaguar. Will you do that for me, try not to mention it? I came in here to forget it." He drew an imaginary line through the air, lengthwise to his own face. "*Terminado*. Finished. It's over."

But it wasn't.

Night brooded enigmatically over Ciudad Real, seeming to hold its breath. Three quarters of a million people, and somewhere in the midst, shadow slim, with velvet tread, and fangs for those who crossed its ill-omened path—

2. TERESA DELGADO

EVEN THE SEÑORA DELGADO'S trusty broom handle, that persuader of last resource, seemed to have very little effect tonight in getting her oldest girl to do her bidding. She reached threateningly toward it, and that alone was usually sufficient impetus to start her toward the door. Tonight it failed to. Next she picked it up and brandished it. Even that failed. She finally was driven to actually swinging it at the recalcitrant one's calves in order to drive her before her. Even this was a partial failure. The girl simply moved nimbly from side to side, but gave very little ground. Most of the light passes struck emptily against the wall, the girl avoiding being in the way each time.

There was always reluctance, dilatoriness, strife, whenever any question of going out on an errand arose. But tonight there was more than that. There was a deadlock, a form of passive resistance. Such opposition had never before been met with. Something stronger than fear of her mother's light broom whacks seemed to be holding the girl back.

She crouched in implicit unwillingness against the wall, large brilliant black eyes fixed imploringly, yet inscrutably, on her mother the whole time she continued to side-step the broom's corrective promptings. She was fairly tall for her age, and particularly her racial antecedents; already full-grown in height if not yet in girth. She was about eighteen or seventeen. Or perhaps sixteen; they didn't keep very strict count of ages in this household. Her skin was the pale gold of wheat, but would probably darken slightly as she grew older. She had donned a *rebozo**—the ubiquitous head covering of lower-class Latin American girls and women—as a first step toward going out, but beyond that one preliminary she seemed unwilling or incapable of going.

Her mother began to poke the broom forward at her now, its broadside swipes having failed of effect. She was shrilly denunciatory as she did so. "Three times I have asked you already! Will you go?" She lunged. "Has any other woman in town got such trouble with her children? Why do you afflict me like this, Teresa? What is it that has gotten into you tonight? Is it so much to ask you to bring back a little charcoal from the *tienda*, that your poor father may find his food hot when he comes back from working hard? You could have been there and back already, twice over!"

"*Madrecita*," the girl implored dolorously, "why can't Pedro go for a change? I work all day in the laundry and I'm tired."

"Pedro can't be trusted to go, and you know it. He throws the money up in the air all the way there, and then the first thing you know he loses it."

"Why can't you use sticks or papers until tomorrow? Why do I have to go now?"

"Is paper charcoal? How long does it last? It flames and then it's gone!" This reminded her. She desisted momentarily from her broom cudgeling to waddle back to the russet-tiled *brasero* she had quitted some time before. She snatched up a palm-leaf fan, jerked aside an earthenware receptacle, and anxiously fanned the orifice thus exposed until it had begun to glow a dull red again from below.

---

* A shawl, almost invariably blue in color, worn coifed over the head and with one end flung back behind its opposite shoulder.

"See that?" she said accusingly. "It's going down already! If it goes out—"

She rushed back for the broom, this time bent on inflicting the final stage of chastisement, all else having failed: an actual belaboring about the shoulders. In the face of this onset, the girl at last retreated as far as the doorway itself, but then she still hovered there, as though hoping against hope to win some miraculous last-minute reprieve.

A small boy of nine or ten, the aforementioned Pedro, pulled his face out of a bowl it had been buried in until now and remarked jeeringly: "I know what she's afraid of. She's afraid of the jaguar."

The girl flashed him a parenthetic look that was an admission. Then, as though the first reference to it, by coming from someone else, had been enough to free her own powers of expression at long last, she began to importune her mother, in a half-eager, half-bated voice: "They say there's one around somewhere. They say a rich lady had it on a string, and it got away and it hasn't been found yet. I heard the girls talking about it in the laundry today—"

The broom was arrested only momentarily. "A jaguar? What's that, one of those things they have in the mountains?"

"They're big and they jump on you," said the impish Pedro, with a sidelong look at his sister that showed what prompted him to make the remark.

The Señora Delgado wasn't having any of this nonsense. She was too hard-working and careworn to take into account anything not of and within her daily toil and habits. "Did you ever meet one of those things yet when you went to the *tienda* for me?" she bellowed.

The girl swallowed, shook her head mutely.

"Then you won't meet one this time either! Now get out! Do as I told you!" And she gave the broom such a backward swing of final purpose that the girl disengaged the door behind her and slunk out backwards, big liquid black eyes, still futilely pleading, the last to go.

The exasperated Señora Delgado laid her broom aside

and returned to her interrupted duties, grumbling darkly and shaking her head. But a moment later the door had stealthily reopened and the girl was attempting to sidle in again unnoticed behind her back.

She caught her just in time, made a tempestuous start in that direction, but the door had closed a second time before she was able to reach it, and the girl was once more outside.

The Señora Delgado took care of that by driving the midsection bolt home, not without a great deal of difficulty. It was rusted from lack of use. It probably hadn't been driven home into its socket for years past. Their door was never barred; there was nothing in the place that anyone would have cared to make off with. Flakes of scabrous rust fell off the bolt and a little cloud of dust winged up as she finally jammed it all the way in, by main force, and compelled to use both her sculpturesque forearms to master it.

Then she shook her hand at the sightless wooden barrier. "Now you'll stay out there until you've done my bidding! You won't get in again until you've brought that charcoal back with you!"

Outside the girl cowered for a moment in the shelter of the set-in doorway. She gave her *rebozo* a tightening pluck over her mouth. That was to ward off the night air, known to be unhealthful; keep it out of her nostrils and breathing passages. Only strangers, Americans and such, braved it. She peered cautiously up one way and down the other, along the grubby, uptilted little slum lane her house faced. Not straight, but gradually curving. No sidewalks, just a middle of the way. A single wan lamppost gleamed dismally at the far end of it, leaving the rest in shadow. But she had to go down the other way, where there wasn't any. There wasn't a soul to be seen anywhere on it. They were all indoors already at this hour. They worked too hard around here. To stay out at night, that was for the rich. On a night of fiesta, that was different. Or for the head of the house to step down to the cantina for a few hours, that also was a different matter. Even while there they were not out on the street itself, they were indoors.

Well, it wasn't far. She couldn't get in again until she'd fetched it, so the quicker she did, the better. She struck out boldly from the doorway, moved down the middle of the road, arms tightly clasping her sides under the ends of her *rebozo*, eyes watchfully going from side to side in the oval gap it left for her face.

She rounded the sort of blunted corner the alley made in turning in to join the next one below. For a moment she could glimpse the diluted, tawny light shining out from the inside of the *tienda*, down there ahead of her. This new thoroughfare continued the steady downward course her own had maintained. This whole quarter of the city had been built down a slope leading to the dried-up bed of what had once been a river.

But right while she sighted it, as though it had only been waiting long enough for her to identify it, it went out. Old lady Calderón had closed for the night. No system of clock entered into this; she couldn't, as a matter of fact, read one, and didn't have one, any more than any of the rest of them did. She closed up whenever there had been a long-enough lapse after the last customer to suggest that there weren't going to be any more that night. Thus one night she might close at ten, the next at eleven, the next at nine.

The girl gave a warning hail from where she was, to try to hold her at the door until she could get there; she began to run fleetly down toward it. She got there just too late; the padlock was on the inside. This being a depot that dealt in valuables such as sugar, candles, chick-peas, et cetera, it was kept locked during the night, unlike the domiciles around.

She could still make out a faint gleam of candlelight coming from behind a hanging at the rear when she put her face close to the glass display window to one side of the door. Electricity for the front part of the store, candle-light for the living quarters at the back, that was the nat-ural order of things, nothing surprising in that. She pounded her palm on the window hopefully.

The hanging was withdrawn diagonally and old lady Calderón showed herself, already in a partial state of

deshabille, which consisted of being barefooted and of a
braid of platinum hair having been uncoiled from her head
and allowed to dangle down in front of one shoulder.

"I just want a little bag of charcoal for my father's
supper!" Teresa Delgado called through the glass between
her hands.

The *tienda*-keeper shook her head, motioned her away,
while she continued working her way down to the bottom
of the braid. "Mañana."

"It'll just take a second. While you're standing there talking you could measure it out—" She held up the coin for
her to see.

"It means taking off the lock again, putting on the light,
digging down in the sack. It's too much trouble. Once I
close I close." The hanging fell vertical again, blotting her
out.

The girl turned away frustratedly. Now she'd either have
to go home without it or she'd have to go all the way down
to that other store, streets away, over on the other side of
the viaduct. That was the nearest one there was to here.
The viaduct was a parapet of solid masonry supporting a
boulevard that crossed the former river bed at a height
equal to its sides. You had to go through an arched passageway tunneled through its base to get over to the other
side. It had always, even before now (now being that
rumor), given her the creeps to have to pass through there
late like this, when there was no one much around any
more. It was so black while it lasted.

But if she went back without the charcoal, her mother
wouldn't let her in. Or, if she did, would probably disbe-
lieve her about the store being closed and would take the
broom to her some more.

The more embodied fear always overcomes the more
formless one, even when it is the lesser of the two. She
reluctantly resumed her descent toward the causeway
ahead, instead of turning back for home.

When she got down to it and was about to enter, she
took a deep breath, stored up enough air to see her through
to the other side. It was black and impenetrable. The slant
of the ground outside prevented what reflection there was

from street lights in the distance from entering, beyond a slight indentation at its very mouth. You'd think they'd have a light hanging in it at least, or just outside up over the entrance. Well, they'd tried to many times, but the kids who played around here in the daytime had always ended up by busting it in a day or two, so finally they didn't try to keep one going any more.

Her footsteps began to echo hollowly the minute the unseen rounded roof had closed over her, and the stonework all around made it a little damper and mustier. Once, a year or so ago, somebody had been found dead in here. With a knife in him and his pockets— But she didn't want to think of that now. This was no time for it.

She had quickened her gait unconsciously, from the moment of entering. Her eyes, brilliant and large at all times, must have been enormous in the gloom, though they couldn't be seen. *Gracias a Dios*, it wasn't very long, just about the width of the boulevard that ran atop it. She was halfway through to the other side now. Her footfalls went bonk, bonk, bonk, bonk, like the thumping of gourds, the stones above giving the sound back to the stones below.

There—she could see the other opening ahead of her; she was coming out. She began to breathe again, and, only in doing so, realized she hadn't been until now. It wasn't very much lighter out ahead than it was in here; a few motes of dark blue or gray mingled with the smooth-textured black to make it seem threadbare, that was all. But the deep resonance of her tread began to dwindle a little, and the air to become a little less damply oppressive. Those were the chief signals of approaching emergence, rather than vision itself.

And then, as she hurried to meet the open again, she happened to glance over to one side of her. For no reason, or for whatever reason it is that draws the vacant glance when there seems to be no cause yet there is. Her throat swelled with suddenly congested breath. What was that? The stonework must be wet over there, there must be some slight seepage of water trickling down between their seams. For she caught a sort of reflected gleam, an iridescent winking, as though light from outside the tunnel mouth—

But there wasn't any light outside the passage, nothing
that could strike that far in, create such a high light against
the stone tunnel facing. It was not expansive, in a sheet;
nor yet was it continuous, in a perpendicular thread, such
as water might have made. If it was water, it was in the
shape of two drops, side by side. Two elongated, almost
slitted drops; rod-shaped; like bacilli seen through a micro-
scope. Faintly wavering, as if with inner heat carried upward behind them, in a fuming sulphurous yellow green.
Yet not distinct, not clearly etched against the blackness,
nothing like that. Rather a diffuse, a thin-surfaced glistening that, but for the blackness itself, which gave the eye,
her eye, nothing else to rest upon, would have escaped her
notice entirely.

They weren't eyes, were they—other eyes? So steadily
maintaining their twoness, their equidistance, their taut,
stretched-out suggestion of wicked peering— No, of course
not. How could they be? What would eyes be doing in
here, and—whose would they be anyway, and— Just don't
let them be; don't *think* they are; if you think they aren't,
they won't be. Only light glinting from the wetted projection of two small roughnesses, two unevennesses in the
stonework, side by side, that was all.

It had sidled back to the rearward now, as her feet
continued to do their duty, like soldiers who continue to
carry out previously received orders long past the ability of
the commanding officer to issue or even be able to think up
new ones. She didn't dare turn to look back, once the
continuity of her line of vision had been broken; she was
afraid her carefully patched explanation couldn't stand the
confirmation of a second look, might fall to pieces at
it.

A few short steps more, and the night sky had opened
around her again. Look, a star. Another. Oh, the beautiful
openness of night. Space to run in. Even the darkness a
lesser darkness, with color beneath its surface: sooted
white and submerged green and blue. The gourds of her
measured tread became the rattle of her flying feet, one
end of her *rebozo* winging out behind her.

She only stopped again when the silvery pallor of the store, falling in a fan across the ground, lay just ahead, around a turn in the crooked byway. How beautiful it seemed, with its bedraggled fringe of paper strung across the front of it, limp from many rains, and with the colors it once had been dyed transferred to streaks down the stucco wall. How friendly that dissonant jangle of the bell cord attached to the door sounded as she pushed her way in. What a lovely place to be in, with its smell of hemp and cordage and kerosene.

The old Basque who ran it came out of the back, still smacking his lips from his own meal, beret left on his head even while he ate. He knew her by sight. "Ah, Teresita." He shook his head as he weighed out the charcoal. "They shouldn't send you out alone so late, *hijita*."

She was brave, now that she was safe again. She wasn't going to admit how frightened she'd been herself just now. She fluttered her fingers in rotation on the edge of his counter. "What can happen to me? This is Ciudad Real."

"Many things can happen," he said enigmatically.

They exchanged a look of complete mutual understanding. But they didn't say what they meant. It wasn't necessary to. So he'd heard about it too. She knew what he was referring to. And he knew that she knew.

She tried to prolong the trivial little transaction all she could. Because while it lasted it spelled safety, light, another's company. Afterwards would come darkness, fear, solitude again.

"Will it hold that way?"

"Yes, just hold it up straight; hold the two corners together like this."

"Oh, what a pretty cat!"

"You've seen him before. Don't you remember? I've always had him."

"Yes, that's right, too. I guess I have." She gave a brief look at the door behind her, as she put down her money on the counter.

"They didn't give you enough. It's gone up."

"I'll bring it next time. Will you trust me? I live in the Pasaje del Diablo, over on the other side of the viaduct—"

"Never fear. Next time you come in." The poor don't cheat one another, they're all poor together.

"Well—good night, señor." She seemed to have to wrench it out of her throat, it clung so.

"Good night, Teresita. Better get back, don't linger on the way."

The bellpull jangled once more, and she was out in the dark again. What a dismal forlorn sound it had this time, though; a sort of farewell.

The fan of light on the ground behind her slowly closed, wheeled around the other way, as the byway made its turn around. She moved along at a normal gait until the turn had completed itself and she had come in sight of that black arched causeway maw again. Then she began to hurry up, to go faster and faster—*toward* it, it is true, but in order to get through and out again at the other side as quickly as possible. The excuse she tried to give herself was that her father might be home by now, and she would get the broom for taking so long with the charcoal. But she knew that wasn't the reason at all.

She could have gone another way, up and over the boulevard. There was a place where there were stairs built into the side of the structure that carried it. But it would have taken her blocks out of her way, to reach it and then come back again on the opposite side. Oh well, she'd been through here a dozen times before. Just once more couldn't hurt. If she'd passed through it just now without having anything happen to her, then she could surely pass through a second time on her way back and nothing would happen either.

While she was thus engaged in trying to rationalize her fear, the intervening space had petered out and the viaduct had started to climb the night sky mountainously before her, like a sheer cliff wall, blotting out the stars as it rose. High aloft on the top of it there was a faint powdery-blue haze from the arc lights strung out along it, and cars, she knew, were probably whistling by, all unwitting of the little dramatic adventure occurring below them in the shadowed depths of the ravine. That was the city; spiraling planes of existence that had no knowledge of one another.

Here it came now. The stone oval—or rather half oval—swept over her like a black scythe. Again that hollow ringing beat came into her footsteps. She was not going to look, she was going to make sure of *not* seeing anything, when she came near the place where she had imagined seeing those twin phosphorescences the first time; she had made up her mind to this ahead of time. "If I don't look," she said to herself softly, "I won't see it, and it can't frighten me again. There is probably nothing there anyway; I just imagined it." But the real reason was she was afraid it still *would* be there, if she did look.

Since it was, presumably, ahead of her, and it would be difficult therefore to keep it out of the corner of her eye, she advanced holding her face stiffly averted, turned to the other side, as she went by. She could not identify the exact spot at which it had been, in this all-erasing darkness. You couldn't see your hand before your face in it. She had to judge more or less by the distance it had been from the entrance, the one she had just come in by, the first time. It had been very close to it; not more than fifteen or twenty paces in. This was about fifteen or twenty paces in now.

Her neck arched with the rigid curvature she maintained it at. It was hard to walk with your head pointed one way, your body another. It kept trying to pull around of its own accord. She started to say the multiplication table over to herself, to keep her mind off it.

She hadn't stayed at school very long; she'd been working at the laundry since she was twelve or thirteen. But she could write a little, read a little—when the words weren't too long—and she knew a few of the lower tables, the twos and threes, up to about twenty or so. Her breath started to simmer softly with it. "Three times one is three. Three times two is six. Three times three is—"

There, it must be behind her by now. See how easy? See how sensible to do it that way? She let her head swing slowly around to its natural position once more. Nothing ahead of her, nothing at the side; nothing but even, unadulterated black, no greenish glows, no glimmers. Behind her? Well—it was better not to try to find out, to let that alone. Even a little courage came back. A few steps more and she'd be out of the place altogether. She was a big coward to let herself get worked up like that. In a moment more now she'd see the first star out ahead at the other side, and then it would be just a matter of climbing the lower lane, turning up the Pasaje, and she'd be at her own door. The worst was—

Suddenly her heart did something before she could even understand why it had done it, as though it heard better than her very ears. Missed a beat, or got in one too many, or something. Her breath clogged in her throat again, as it had the time before. Only her feet kept on moving, doing the duty for all the rest of her.

That soft, blurred *pat* behind her had been something she hadn't made. No echo or transfer of any sound of hers. Something disparate, isolate, apart, she was sure of it. One's senses can identify one's own aura of sounds at all times. It hadn't been the impact a shod foot makes; more on the order of something padded or bare pressing incautiously on the ground. A cross between a rustle, such as a leaf might make, and the softest of soft slaps. A tiny sound, a ghost of a sound, yet a sound of monstrous swelling terror, expanding balloon-like within her heart and brain.

She nearly dropped the small-sized sack of charcoal and just regained her hold on it as it started to slip from her grasp. She wanted to do two things, diametrically opposed, at one and the same time. Her limbs wanted to stand still, lock there, give her a chance to listen for it again, confirm it, disassociated from the sounds she herself was making. Terror wouldn't permit it. To stand still was to die. She wanted to throw the encumbering charcoal bag from her, break into a headlong run then and there, all the rest of the way from here to the door of her house. Again terror wouldn't let her, held her down to the gait she had been using until now. It was the age-old instinct to avert danger by pretending to ignore its asserting itself in her. Keep walking as you were, and the attack is postponed, if only a moment or two longer. Flee—or try to flee—and you bring it on that much sooner.

She continued to move forward like a rigid automaton,

unaware any longer of what her legs were doing, leaving them to their own devices. Her ears were straining to catch the faintest— It came again, closer behind her this time, and yet, inversely, much fainter. A nothing at all, a whisper of the paving stones. So faint indeed that had she not heard it the first time, she would not have known she was hearing it at all this time.

Something else now assailed her, again from without herself, but of a different sensory plane than hearing this time. A prickly sensation of being watched steadily from behind, of something coming stealthily but continuously after her, spread slowly like a contraction of the pores, first over the back of her neck, then up and down the entire length of her spine. She couldn't shake it off, quell it. She knew eyes were upon her, something was treading with measured intent in her wake.

And at this moment, meaningless now, for terror no longer had bounds, was no longer confined but on the move, the black archway of the tunnel roof fell back a second time and she was in the open once more. But dragging terror out into the open after her.

Her numbed feet, beginning to falter with faulty muscular co-ordination, carried her a few yards onward up the lane. She knew she couldn't manage them any longer; they were slowing, they were stopping, they had stopped. She had fallen still, vibrating all over. A sort of pulsing that came from within, like the ague.

She had to see, she had to know, her fright-distended soul could bear no more. The muscles of her neck started to tug, to pull her head around, to look behind her at the doom-pregnant entrance she had just quitted. And even while they did so, before the motion had been completed, the sack of charcoal started to slowly sidle out from between her nerveless hands, about to topple to the ground at her feet, in catastrophic premonition.

She was trapped there, held fast, as surely as a bird is by a snake, unable to move another step until her head had accomplished that devoted, self-destructive turn to rearward to see what it was that the tunnel mouth was about to spew, rabid, at her heels.

* * *

The slowly mounting anger of Teresa's mother had increased in inverse ratio to the dwindling heat within her
brasero. When fanning would no longer bring the faintest
flush of red to the charcoal ash, then her ire reached its
hottest.

She bent low above it, dexterously manipulated her
breath upon it, trying at one and the same time to skim the
film of incinerated white ash off the top and unearth some
spark of continued heat below. That failed too. Her fire,
the core of her daily existence, had given up the ghost.

She straightened, flung up her arms, let them fall again.
"Out," she said catastrophically. This was the unforgivable
sin, to have one's fire expire like this. Any woman who had
that happen to her—well, she knew what the others about
here would say and think of her.

"Why don't you put some straw on it until she gets
back?" the small boy over in the corner suggested.

"Straw! Is straw charcoal? How long does it last? It
flames and goes, and fills the room with smoke. And there
isn't any anyway." She picked up the broom, shook it
threateningly in the general direction of the door. "It's *her*
fault. Had she gone when I first warned her to— And even
now, is she back yet? Look how she dawdles! How she
lingers on the way! A snail would have been here before
her!"

She gave the earthenware pot sitting on the *brasero* a
slight shift. "He'll come home, and what will he find? A
wife who cannot even keep the food warm for him. A
disgraced creature!"

The boy sat watching her in utter silence, palms to
cheeks, a rapt smirk on his face.

She made some more passes with the broom. "Oh, I'll
give it to her! I'll break this *palo* in two over her back. She
will ache all day tomorrow—"

Something struck against the door suddenly. It was as
though a flurry of footsteps, only audible at the very last,
had suddenly ended with a fling against the door. A scream
winged its way in like a knife slicing through all the seams

at once, above, below, at the sides. And then words, in a smothered paroxysm, as though the mouth uttering them were cupped to the very woodwork itself. "*Mamacita*, let me in! Oh if you love me, let me in!" They were all run together in a sort of spasm of the voice.

The Señora Delgado had waited for this moment, though not knowing that it would take this precise form. She clasped her enfolded arms to her sides, hugging herself and nodding her head in bitter, long-delayed retribution. "*Now* she comes, eh? Running at the last, eh, now that it's too late, now that my fire is gone ánd the damage is done!" She mimicked the suffocating tones outside. " '*Mamacita*, let me in. Oh if you love me, let me in!' Afraid of the dark, eh? Afraid of her own shadow, eh? Well she'll stay out there. We'll see how she likes that. She'll learn next time to make more haste—"

There was the sound of nails clawing helplessly at the wood; the voice was crazed, ungovernable, all but incomprehensible, sputtering a gibberish that had to be guessed at rather than understood. "*Ay, madrecita di mi alma*, it's coming, it's coming closer. I can see it coming by the wall— It's closer, it's closer—!"

The Señora Delgado gave an authoritative bellow that stopped the boy as he was beginning to sidle around the side of the room toward the door. "Pedro! Stay away from it!" Again she mimicked her. "Yes, it's coming nearer, is it? Lies! *Mentiras!* She thinks her lies will save her. You think I believe there is anything out there? There should be, I only wish there were! It would teach you next time to obey your mother better—"

There was a scream of agonized finality, a veritable catharsis of the lungs, that made all the others before it seem like nothing at all. Mingled with it, and blurring it, quelling it at the end, came an impact of such violence that the whole door structure seemed to start with it from top to bottom, curve inward at the middle, then spring back rigid again a moment later. It seemed incredible that anyone could do that with her body without breaking all her bones. A puff of plaster dust welled up around the sides.

A change had come over the urchin's derisive face. *"Carajo, Mama!"* he breathed huskily. "She isn't fooling—"

But the woman, in a reversal of attitude as instantaneous as his own, had already flung herself forward, squat and bulky as she was. "Wait, Teresa," she panted. "I come, I'm here, I open—" She clawed desperately at the bolt. "Only a moment, my beloved, *Mi querida*, only a moment more. Your mother is here, your mother admits you—"

It wouldn't move. It had jammed. It had been too long unused. Its surface had roughened too much with rust, or that last impact had warped it. It was fast in its socket. She continued to pluck despairingly at it. She half turned around in helpless appeal, then turned back again. She struck frustratedly at the wood just above it with one open hand, while she tried to wrench it back with the other.

"Pedro, Pedro, you have smaller fingers—"

The incipient maleness of the boy rose to take the emergency in its stride. That was what men, big and small, were meant for: a sudden crisis like this, a flurry of violence. The rest was for women. "A stone—something to hit it back with— Gimme, I can get it! Get out of the way—"

There was a building brick lying there on the floor across the room, brought in for some forgotten purpose. He snatched it up, ran back with it. A tap, two taps, three; the unruly bar sprang back.

There had been silence for a minute past, ever since the last climactic scream and maniacal lunge, but only now did they have time to realize it. There was a stillness on the other side.

In the fraction of a second's pause that followed, she saw the boy's eyes swollen downward at the floor. A tongue of red was licking out at his bare foot from under the door. Just that in size and shape, the tip of a human tongue. But it was in flux, fluid. Right as their eyes beheld it it was already widening, lengthening, glittering with its own volatility.

He had snatched the door inward upon them before the mother's slowly gathering scream had time to leave her. He jumped agilely back as though something had bitten him.

It was as though clots of red mud had been pelted at the outside of the door, until, adhering, they formed a sort of spattered mound up against it. There were rags mixed in with it, and snarls of hair, and even tiny crumbs of coral, broken off a string.

The mass sidled, disintegrated all over the threshold.

Manning saw her in the Morgue, the *Caja de los Cadáveres* as it was familiarly called by those who had to do with it, the next day, before her people had claimed her. He went there with one of the men from the police department, an inspector named Robles, who felt bound to accommodate him because Manning had once secured him a couple of passes to one of Kiki Walker's shows.

"If you insist on looking, my friend—" this Robles warned him. "I advise you not to, unless you have exceptionally strong nerves. You are liable to see it in your sleep for weeks to come. The authorities should really have her cremated, if her own people can't afford it. Open this one," he said to the attendant. He stood aside, to give the other an unhampered view. "Formidable, isn't it?"

The American looked without flinching. His face whitened a little, that was all. He nodded, spellbound.

"That's enough," Robles said to the attendant. He turned to Manning, evidently with the idea of reading him a little lecture. "So you see what your foolish stunt has led to. It has cost a human life. And this may not be the last, before it is over. *That* thing has not been caught yet."

Manning didn't answer. He was staring down at the cement floor. But in a way that suggested puzzlement of some sort, rather than contrition.

"Juridically, of course, you are not responsible," Robles went on. "That is to say, you did not foresee this, did not mean it to happen, cannot be punished personally for it. But morally you are to blame for it. It is through you alone that this girl lost her life. That is why I so readily acceded to your request and brought you down here with me to let you see her for yourself. It may teach you a lesson."

"It wasn't remorse that made me ask to come here,"

Manning said quietly. "Nor morbid curiosity either. You've got me wrong. It's—well I've had a troubled feeling that I can't seem to shake off ever since I first heard of it."

"You should have," said Robles severely.

"No, you still don't get me." He ran one hand baffledly up through his hair. "Are you sure *that thing*, as you call it, did this?"

Robles looked at him first in astonishment, then almost in scorn. "What are you trying to suggest, it didn't? Well, you've just seen with your own eyes. What else but the claws of such a monster could leave such ravages? She was in ribbons. No, there is no doubt in our minds on that score, how can there be? I could take you over to our laboratory, let you talk to some of the men there. Small bits of fuzz, loosened hairs from its coat, were found upon her body. They are in our possession right now. What more do you ask?"

"Nothing," admitted Manning, looking down. "Nothing more. But then why have I got this dissatisfied feeling—?" He didn't finish it. "Was she—did it make any attempt to—?" he faltered presently.

Robles finished it for him without a qualm, with the matter-of-factness of the professional investigator. "Was she eaten, is that what you are driving at? No. I don't know whether they do or not, I don't know enough about them. I must ask the curator of the zoo. In any case, there is sufficient reason for its having done so this time. It occurred outside her very door, in full hearing of the mother and brother. They came rushing out, and the monster was undoubtedly frightened away before it had time to—accomplish its full purpose. If, as I said, they do that."

"Well, was it *seen?*" Manning persisted discontentedly. "That's what I want to know. If you say this happened right in front of her own door, and there are other houses around there, was there anyone who actually *saw* it? There should have been, if she screamed."

"Oh, unless someone saw it, it doesn't exist, is that it? That's a very risky theory in police work, don't you think? The houses around there are of the poor, you know the kind. One- or two-room hovels, mostly without windows, simply with a single entrance at the front. By the time they began peering timidly forth up and down the lane, it was over. Some claim they *were* just in time to glimpse some black form slinking around the turn at the bottom of the alley. They may have, they may not have. What difference does it make?"

"It isn't that I really doubt the jaguar attacked her," Manning said hesitantly. "I have no theories about this. I'm not a detective at all, just a press agent out of a job. Only—only—I just have that peculiar feeling I spoke of, that there's more to this than meets the eye."

"More? What more could there be?" countered Robles. "What more should there be?"

Manning tugged perplexedly at the skin on the back of his neck. "I don't know myself. I can't explain. But, tell the truth, doesn't it strike you as strange, almost incredible, that a wild thing, a jungle animal the size and conspicuousness of this jaguar, should remain at large, undetected and *absolutely unseen* by the human eye, in a city this large, and for this length of time? This isn't a hill village, with the jungles near by. This is the third largest city of South America. It has not left it and then come back again, obviously. It has been here the whole time. Where? How?"

Robles pursed his lips in conditional agreement, nodded. "It's unprecedented, it's unbelievable, but—it has undeniably happened, hasn't it? The animal has not been recaptured alive, its body has not been found; therefore, it's still at large. That's logical enough, isn't it, Manning my friend?"

"But where does it keep itself, where does it hide in the daytime, where has it found refuge? This place is built all of stone, remember. Asphalt, cobblestones, cement sidewalks, stone houses. There are no trees, except out in the Bosque and in a few small plazas and parks. Where can it go? Thousands of people swarming about it all day long. It was seen to go into the Callejón de las Sombras at six o'clock one evening—with a crowd almost at its heels. Presto! it disappears. Not another glimpse of it from then on. It didn't get out at the other end. The police and fire departments searched every house along that alley from top to bottom. No sign of it. Now this young girl is found torn to pieces all the way over in the Barranca working quarter, half the city away. How did it get over there unseen?"

All Robles could give him on this was, "It's true, it's an amazing thing. Who can say what happened? Perhaps it squeezed itself down into a sewer and traversed one of the big drainpipes that run under the city. The water in most of them would not be deep enough to drown it. And then again there is that so ridiculous suggestion some onlooker was heard to make, that night it disappeared; which may not be so ridiculous as it sounds, after all. That it took refuge in the back of some van or merchandise truck standing in there along the Callejón, was driven unsuspectingly away by the driver, and bolted out again undetected at the next stop the vehicle made."

"Augh!" Manning swung his arm at him impatiently. "Now I'll tell one. Here's something else: what has it lived on during these past days and nights? Where has it gotten its food—and, above all, its water?"

"How do the less ferocious animals, stray dogs and cats, for instance, get theirs? From refuse heaps, from puddles, from the river margin."

"Yes, but they're seen."

"How do we know it *hasn't* been seen, more than once, in the distance or in the dark, and mistaken for some large black dog? There are other ways possible for it to keep itself alive, too, which we need not dwell on. These same homeless dogs and cats, lizards clambering up and down cracked walls, rats from the sewers—"

Manning turned his head away involuntarily for a moment. Then he looked back again, went on: "How is it it wasn't easily tracked down, cornered almost at once, this second time? How is it you lost it again like the first time? Its claws, the pads of its paws, the fur about its belly, must have been soaked after such an attack—"

"It's true, there were numerous traces of blood-dyed paw prints and even drippings found near by. None led very far away, however. The dirt and dust of the pavements must have quickly dried and coated the brute's pads. And then so many people quickly milled about, obliterating everything before we could get there."

"For every objection of mine, you have an answer ready. But still and all, you haven't been able to remove that dissatisfied feeling of mine. What we call in my language a hunch. Something isn't *right*. There's a basic implausibility to this whole thing that I can't accept as easily as you people."

The inspector smiled bleakly, tapped him knowingly on the shoulder. "Tell the truth, Manning. Isn't it your own guilty conscience, about being the indirect cause of this four-legged demon's depredations, that makes you keep trying to raise vague objections, cast shadowy doubts, on what is glaringly self-evident? Of course it is! You would like to believe that it is not the jaguar which did this, for the sake of your own peace of mind. I'm afraid I cannot accommodate you. Our test tubes, our high-powered glasses, our reagents and analyses, have been brought into play; their evidence has been given and found irrefutable. Our report has been made out accordingly, and can be substantiated by the scientific investigation which it is based on. We are not guessing when we say such-and-such and so-and-so. All these things that have occurred to you, they have occurred to us ourselves, and been weighed, never fear, and—discarded. Our findings are: that Teresa Delgado was attacked and clawed to death by a jaguar outside the door of her house in the alley known as Pasaje del Diablo, at 11:15 o'clock Thursday night, May fourteenth. And there is nothing further to be added."

"Except by the jaguar," said Manning grimly.

3. CONCHITA CONTRERAS

THE SEÑORA VIUDA DE Contreras raised her pillowed head alertly. The footfall that had attracted her, in the tiled corridor outside her open room door, had had a hesitant quality about it, as though undecided whether to come down full weight or tiptoe.

"Is that you, my daughter?" she called out.

The Señora Viuda was stretched out on a chaise longue, in a state of infirmity that was becoming more and more frequent of late. She was a handsome stately woman, with unplucked brows as thick and black as charcoal smudges, giving her face the look of habitual serenity that straight, horizontal lines are always apt to produce. Her head of thick black hair, only white as yet in one plume steaking off from her temple, was as glossy as a cockerel's tail feathers and, like them, crisply curling in little bunches. A handkerchief soaked in cologne and placed in a narrowed band across her forehead was the only concession to her affliction. She was not one of your whining hypochondriacs. Pain was a thing between oneself and one's God.

At her interrogation the footfall had made up its mind to come down full force. Or rather the succeeding one did, that one having already been made. A couple more followed, rather reluctantly, and then a young girl appeared in the doorway. It is hard not to be beautiful at eighteen, and for her it would have been a physical impossibility.

Even the dimming devotional mourning that encased her from head to foot, complete even to smoky veil, couldn't obscure that fact. She stood looking in submissively at the benevolent despot on the chaise, who was aware of one's lightest footfall, almost of one's innermost thoughts, it sometimes seemed.

"Did you wake up from your nap, *mamacita?* Do you feel better now?"

The Señora Viuda reached out to the night stand beside her, flicked open a small jet-sticked fan, began to use it. This had nothing to do with room temperature, but was the outward symptom of approaching interrogation. Lengthy, exhaustive interrogation. The deceptive brow line remained ruler straight. "Sit down a minute, Conchita *mia.* Here, by me."

The girl came forward, shifted a chair, sank primly down on the very edge of it.

"There, that's it." The fan continued to move, taking its time. The girl shifted both insteps far in underneath the chair.

"Tell me, *hija.*" There was a pause while the fanning went on. "You were on your way to All Saints Cemetery, to pay your repects at your father's resting place?" The examination was under way.

The girl looked up from the finger she had been wrangling with. "It is his saint's day. It should not be allowed to pass unnoted. And as you were ill, I thought perhaps I'd—"

The Señora Viuda nodded with benevolent approval. "A good daughter doesn't forget her departed father. She keeps the flowers fresh on his grave, doesn't forget to visit it. That's as it should be." The fan whirred blandly on. "When was the last time you were there?"

"Last week, I think—I don't know exactly. Why do you ask me, *mamacita?*"

"I was just wondering, that is all. Why this sudden intense fervor, this devotional passion, this *locura* almost." The fan closed, pointed upward, descended again, reopened, went on fluttering. "I don't like it. Is isn't good at your age. It isn't natural. It is not that your papa passed from us yesterday. It is five years ago, now, may he rest in peace. You were thirteen then. You loved him, you were desolated. *Bueno*. Then it passed, as it should with the young. You were like other girls you age, you enjoyed the *cine* on a Sunday afternoon, having an *helado* in a sweet-shop now and then, those things. Now all at once this frenzy of tragic grief descends on you, excluding every other interest. It is almost feverish, I have seen you brooding by the hour. You cannot go often enough, nor remain long enough, at All Saints Cemetery. You are unable to eat or sleep, unable to think of anything but the departed. It's morbid, it's melancholy."

The fan never stopped a moment. The monologue ran on, with a sort of velvety firmness that didn't raise its voice, threaten, command. That just stated facts. "It is to stop now. No more of these visits to a burial ground. They're not normal. I don't understand them. At your age one shouldn't think of the other world so constantly."

The girl gave her a look of almost tearful supplication. "Just one more time, *madrecita*. Just today, and then I won't go any more—if you say so."

"Very well, one more time. Tomorrow. Tomorrow I will feel better, I will take you myself, if you insist on going."

The girl looked harassed, almost terrified at the alternative. "But today's his saint day! Just this once. Look, I'm all ready to leave. It's after half-past four already. I can be there and back before you know it. Just this once more—"

The Señora Viuda wagged her head darkly, in accompaniment to her fanning. "Always there is one time too many, daughter of my blood. Who knows, this may be it? Don't go; listen to your mother. I had a dream I didn't like when I was napping just now."

The girl showed a momentary interest. "About me? What was it about?"

"Only that I could hear your voice calling to me from some dark place, and I could not reach you."

The girl chuckled indulgently. "Is that all? In school the sisters used to tell us we mustn't believe in anything like that."

The Señora Viuda, who was anything but irreligious,

muttered something that sounded suspiciously like, "Are the sisters mothers?"

She fanned awhile longer, still withholding consent. "Stay here," she urged. "Here, within the walls of your home, where you should be. Read, sew at something, sit by the bars of the window, looking out, dreaming the dreams a young girl does. Or go into the patio at the back, bask there in the late sun, looking at yourself in the water, doing your hair some foolish new way. What is the worst that can happen to you here? Only that time may drag a little. Better that time should pass too slowly than too quick. Tomorrow we will go out, buy you something at one of the stores, have a *refresco,* take in the crowd at the tables around us—"

She sighed. She could see it was no use, even before the answer came. "Go then, if you must," she gave in grudgingly. "But today is the last time." Then as the girl half started up from her chair in unleashed alacrity, a gesture of the fan stopped her short. "And I want one thing understood. You are not to go there accompanied by Rosita any more."

The girl looked stricken. "But I can't go by myself! Who else is—?"

"I don't trust her. She's giddy and only a few months older than yourself, no fit companion! I should have put a stop to it long ago. I don't know what I've been thinking of until now. It will be old Marta who will take you, if you go at all."

A look of unadulterated horror passed over the girl's face at this. Before she could answer, a telephone had pealed distantly, in some remote room.

"Rosita!" the mistress of the house called.

There was a wait that somehow suggested more a stage wait than an actual approach from a distance, and then a comely young girl-of-all-work, with a shawl already coifed around her head, materialized in the doorway, without any preliminary tread along the hall having been audible.

"Sí señora?"

"Was that the telephone just now?"

"The operator must have made a mistake. Nobody answered when I got to it, there wasn't anybody on it."

The Señora Viuda's horizontal brow line arched slightly, then evened out again. "Every now and then that seems to happen in this house. You can take off your shawl, Rosita," she added with an indifferent drawl, "you will not be going out."

The girl put her hands to it, but left it in place, as if hoping the order might yet be countermanded. "But the Señorita Conchita wanted me to accompany her to—" she said with an odd sort of breathlessness.

"Call Doña Marta, she is to go with her instead."

The girl's black-pitted eyes were fixed on her mistress' face with a sort of tremulous fixity that somehow suggested they wanted to direct themselves at somebody else in the room, but were being restrained. She gave a little knee dip, "*Sí, señora*," vanished from the doorway.

The Señora Viuda turned back to her daughter. The latter was sitting almost in the attitude of a penitent by now, her second ankle had retreated far under the chair to join the first, and she was busily engaged with both hands in pleating and smoothing out again a small section of dress over one kneecap. She could feel her mother's gaze on her, looked up through her long lashes to confirm the impression, looked down again when she had.

Señora Contreras said, with an odd sort of kindliness seeping through her mien of authority, "Come here a minute, my child." Conchita got up, moved to the side of the chaise longue, crouched down to the level of her mother's face. The fan had finally stopped, for the balance of the interview; was laid aside. The Señora reached out, tipped up her hand to her daughter's chin, held it under it in a sort of static caress. She looked questioningly into her eyes.

The girl's eyes never wavered, they were crystalline innocence itself.

"I did not come into this world a middle-aged woman, a widowed mother, as you see me now, you know. I was a young girl myself once, and not so many years ago. Always remember, *hijita de mi alma*, anything you think, your mother thought before you. Anything you do, your mother did before you. And her mother before her. There isn't anything new in women. *I* know, *I* know."

"Know what, *madrecita?*" the girl breathed so low it could scarcely be heard.

The Señora Viuda kissed her with classic benevolence on the forehead, then more fondly on the lips. "You are a sweet little thing. You are the morning sunlight in my dreary afternoon sky. It is not that you would do anything so unforgiveable. It is just that there is a way of doing things that is right and a way that is wrong. You are young, and the world is old. When you are a few years older, I don't want you to have to look back on anything lacking in dignity, in which you cut a ridiculous figure. Anyone who may become interested in you should come here to our house, as the established custom is with us; should be introduced to you by myself, or Uncle Felipe, or some other older relative."

"*Mamacita*, I don't know what you mean—"

The Señora gestured leniently. "I haven't said anything. It is just my heart talking to your heart. Now go there if you insist, with Marta, and come right back. The sun will soon be down, so don't linger—"

Without actually springing up, the girl was suddenly all the way across at the open doorway, like something from which a leash has just been detached.

At the threshold she turned for a minute. "What, *madre mia?*"

"Nothing. Run along." What the Señora Viuda had just said, half to herself, with a sigh of resignation, was: "It will do no good. It never has from the beginning, it never will to the end of time. One can't change the world."

In the passageway outside, Conchita crossed paths with Rosita. They brushed by one another like two people unaware of one another's presence, or at least trying to give that impression. The daughter of the house whispered, "She's sending Marta with me, what am I going to do?"

The serving girl reached out backhand and clasped hands with her in passing, as if to lend moral support.

Conchita looked down at something. "What's that?"

"Don't be afraid, it'll just make her drowsy."

"Me? I can't!"

The other fanned both hands at her in a violent affirmative.

"It won't hurt her, will it?" Conchita breathed anxiously.

"It's nothing, just an herb from the mountains. I got it from an Indian down at the market. I've tried it on myself. All it does is— Sh! Here she comes." They resumed their interrupted transits.

An old woman of about sixty, shawled for the street, was coming down the passageway. "Are you ready, my flower? Have you said good-bye to your mother?" And to Rosita, in angry authority, "Go in there and stay with the Señora, useless one! She may need you for something."

Conchita brushed past. "Wait for me at the door. I'm just going back to my room a second."

She stopped before the mirror in there, scanned herself anxiously as though to make sure she was looking her best for the sake of the dead in the cemetery. She threw open a drawer, unearthed a lipstick from some secret hiding place at the back of it, hastily touched it to her lips. Then she lowered the dimming veil over her face, obliterating the improvement she had just made, and hurried demurely back along the passageway to rejoin her companion.

Her chaperon already had a public carriage drawn up at the door and was sitting waiting in it. To go to the cemetery in a gasoline-powered vehicle was somehow improper, she seemed to feel. "To the flower market," she ordered the driver, as the slim veiled figure climbed in next to her.

Ten minutes later, after driving through a number of narrow, elbow-jointed streets, they reached a small plaza fronting a rose-tan church of massive Spanish colonial architecture. What was remarkable about it was the broad expanse of worn stone steps leading up to it, spanning the entire foundation in width. They were invisible as steps save for a narrow lane of clearance left in the middle, running directly up to the entrance. All the rest had disappeared under what seemed to be a multicolored, unbroken flower bed, with patches of shelter over it here and there. It was only on closer inspection that this disintegrated into separate little zones of barter, each presided over by its individual vendor. Some had rigged up little portable stalls, poles supporting awnings, or straw mats to keep the sun off their perishable wares. Others, unable to afford this, simply squatted on the steps in hollow squares, their merchandise ranged around them in open sheaves or clusters thrust into clay water jars. The air was cloying with an indescribable odor of ferns, crushed leaves, bruised and trodden petals and stalks, and, above all else, the peculiar brackishness given off by age-old paving stones saturated repeatedly with water all day long without ever having time to dry off. It was an odor compounded in equal parts of verdant, blooming life and stagnant, mildewed decay. This was the flower market, held on this site for two hundred years past every day from sunrise until dusk.

Conchita's chaperon got out of the carriage at the foot of the steps, turned to ask: "What kind shall I get?"

The girl descended right after her. "I'm coming, too. I want to pick them myself."

Marta started to protest that it wasn't necessary, she would do it for her, but Conchita had already taken the lead, was moving slowly up the main aisle of display, looking about her, assailed from either side by an advancing barrage of shrill, wheedling, poetic, and personally flattering cries that kept pace with her, to die out again forlornly behind her as she passed out of reach into the next vendor's jurisdiction. Hands reached for her, tugged importunately at her clothing. Marta slapped them down again.

"Here, *niña*, roses crying for you!"

"Look, *chiquita*, carnations begging to be bought. Ten centavitos. Five. Any price you say. Only take them, take them!" It was late and the market was about to disband.

Marta halted. "Here are some. Will these do, *niña*?"

Conchita glanced around, but without halting her ascent. "No, up here at the top. I always buy from this one at the end."

The stall she indicated, as a matter of fact, had a less sizable assortment to offer than many of those they had just passed. The vendor was an old woman with a face as finely lined as though mosquito netting had been drawn over it.

"Some of these." Conchita picked up a single white rose and held it to her face outside the veil, causing a small indentation to appear with indrawn breath.

"*Sí*, little angel, *sí!*" the vendor jabbered, bustling to collect them. "White roses, as beautiful, as young, as you are yourself."

"And gardenias." Conchita instructed.

Marta held out her arms for the unbound accumulation. "I'll carry them, they may tear your clothes." She handed the old woman a coin, turned to pick her way down the slippery steps.

The vendor, however, was not yet satisfied. "Look, a little cluster of white violets to go with them. The last one left." She laid one finger craftily alongside her nose for a moment, glanced after the retreating chaperon. "I've been saving them for you all day. Free! I give them to you free!" She pulled twice at the girl's skirt, almost as though it were a bell cord.

The girl took them, moved down the steps in the wake of her companion, holding them close to her face. They were plaited together on a single, large leaf of some sort. She had extracted the thinly folded note twined around their stems even before she re-entered the carriage. She opened it with one hand, read it, holding it down out of sight on the side away from Marta, as they jounced back through the narrow, erratically turning streets on their way to the cemetery.

Just a few words. The oldest message in the world, that said nothing, that said everything. "Sweetness of my life. Will you go there again today? I will be waiting. I have counted the hours all week long, since the last time. Sweetness of my life, have mercy on me."

Somehow she got it inside the lining of her glove, refolded, by thumb motion alone. Then she dipped her face to the violets once more. As the Señora Viuda had said, one couldn't change the world.

They came out of the older part of town with its tortuous, cobbled streets, where respectable, conservative families like hers lived, into one of the new semi-suburban sections, favored by foreigners and the more flashily prosperous who copied their ways—even to letting their daughters run around without an older woman in attendance. They traversed this along a straight, broad asphalted driveway, and beyond emerged into open country for awhile. Then in the distance ahead a symmetrical line of dark-green poplars began to peer over an intervening rise of the ground and, when they had topped it, suddenly seemed to spring forward to join the road, behind a stone wall that ran back as far as the eye could reach.

It turned and followed the roadside for a while. All Saints Cemetery was known as the largest in the city, if not anywhere in the world. It was said of it that it was big enough to accommodate all the world's dead at one time.

On the opposite side of the road, buildings had sprung up once more, called into being to accommodate the living who on Sundays and certain religious holidays came out here in such shoals to pay their repects to the dead. A headstone carver's shop and workyard, littered with ornamental urns, cherubs, mourning angels, and crosses, a refreshment and eating pavilion, and others such. They were intermittent, with large gaps between, and the whole atmosphere was one of abandoned desolation rather than life-quickened activity, somehow.

The carriage drew up at the main entrance, marked by a pair of massive bronze doors set within a stone arch, and they got out. "Come back for us within a half-hour, no more," Marta instructed the driver.

The carriage ambled aimlessly off on some mission best known to its driver—perhaps the nearest cantina at the next crossroads ahead. As it left them, Conchita held back in seeming irresolution a minute.

"Marta, before we go in, can't we go over to that place across the way and sit down for a minute? I'm so thirsty."

Marta objected querulously, flattening the sheaf of flowers so that she could look at her clearly over their tops. "No, *niña*. How can we? Your mother told me to bring

you right back. Look, the sun's already far down. Night
will be upon us before we can get back to the house."

"How long will it take?" the girl coaxed.

"But did we come out here to visit your father's grave or
did we come out here to have *refrescos?*" the old woman
said with peevish stubbornness.

"Just a cup of mint tea. You know how you love your
mint tea. You always take it at this hour at home."

The chaperon wavered, obviously tempted. She cast a
look across the road, as though judging how long it would
detain them to go over and back. "But isn't it better to go
in first and pay our respects, and then have it when we
come out? The place may close."

"I'm faint, Martita. Why do you refuse me?"

Her companion was at once all whimpering solicitude.
"Oh my light, why didn't you tell me sooner? What am I
thinking of, standing here wrangling? Come, my heart,
take me by the arm, we'll go right over."

They inched across the road, held to a painfully reduced
gait more by the stout figure's slowness of limb than by the
slender one's weakness, if the truth had been known. The
devoted Marta even had to caution her charge, "Not so
fast, *linda.* You may get dizzy."

The establishment was bare of customers at this hour. A
waiter with a tray tucked under his arm came attentively to
the door, waiting to see where they would decide to sit
before moving any further. There was a terrace strip of
terra-cotta mosaic tiling laid out in front of the place,
holding a row of reedy, forlorn-looking, wafer-sized iron
tables, each one with more wire-legged chairs wedged
around it than it could accommodate.

"Let's go inside out of the glare," Conchita suggested
demurely.

They continued on into an interior of cavelike dimness,
after the outer brightness, in which a sea of other equally
reedy, equally untenanted iron tables could be made out. A
loosely strung pasteboard sign proclaiming ASK FOR EL SOL
BEER brushed against Marta's head as she passed below it.
She swept it indignantly aside.

They seated themselves opposite one another in a small

booth against the wall, duenna and massed flowers on one side of the table, young mourner on the other. The waiter approached. *"Buenos días."*

"Buenos días," Marta grunted, with the curtness one employee often has for another.

Conchita waited until he had gone away again, then tipped the veil from her face with an air of angelic primness.

The visibility lightened up a little around them as their eyes grew accustomed to the place, though not much beyond the blue-green transparency of a submarine deep from first to last. Then too, the daylight outside was fast toning down, losing its contrasting vividness.

They sat for a moment or two. "We'll be locked out," Marta mourned. "We'll have had the whole trip out for nothing." She shifted her head and shoulders outward along her seat to scan the seemingly lifeless rear of the establishment. She shattered the silence with an explosive double smack of her cupped hands. *"Muchacho!* We're in a hurry!" she called imperatively.

The waiter returned at a trudging walk, his excuse for not hurrying any faster the brimming cup of strongly aromatic tea and glass of lemonade he bore on the tray.

Marta ducked her chin to the cup, smacked her lips expressively as she raised it again. Conchita, who was sitting facing the thoroughfare outside, kept scanning it, more as though she were on the lookout for something to come along and catch her eye than because something had. Suddenly she gave a little sob of suppressed laughter, flexed one finger toward the outer panorama.

"You should have seen that! The funniest-looking man just went by. I wonder what he was."

Marta, who was sitting back to the road, laboriously swiveled herself around and tried to peer out past the edge of the booth partition behind her.

She turned back in a moment, shrugged. "I don't see anyone."

A little ripple was going around in her cup.

"You missed him. He's gone past now."

Marta said, "You do look pale, *niña.*"

Conchita did look pale. She wasn't used to acts of overt treachery against members of her own household. Against anyone, for that matter.

Another minute or two went by. Marta put down her drained cup.

"Come *pequeña*, we must go."

"Just let's sit a minute longer. It's so nice here. I haven't quite finished my lemonade yet."

"The sun is almost all gone. It'll be dark before we know it. We can't go in there in the dark—"

"You look tired, Marta."

As though she had only realized it now that the thought had been suggested to her, Marta admitted: "I am tired. I went to six-o'clock Mass this morning." She sighed self-indulgently. "When one gets to be my age—"

"Put your head back a minute against the leather padding," the girl suggested.

"It wouldn't look right, out in public like this."

"There's no one but us here to see."

The old woman's head went back almost of its own accord, she closed her eyes gratefully, and gave a deep sigh of relaxation. Her head stayed straight for a minute, erect on her shoulders. Then it slanted over until it had found the angle between the two walls of the compartment, remained leaning against it, supported by one of them. Her breathing started to become more gritty. Her lips parted company slightly, just in the middle.

The girl sat quietly on opposite her a moment longer. Then she shifted outward along the seat until the impediment of the table had ended, stood up, never taking her eyes off the deputy guardian's face. The heavy jowls were shaking a little now, with each breath.

She reached cautiously downward for the mass of flowers beside Marta, scooped them up in the crook of one arm, careful to keep them from rustling too flagrantly. She got them all but one, a long-stemmed white rose which escaped her. She let that remain where it was. To have tried to retrieve it might have cost her all the others.

She picked her way through the shoal of spool-topped

tables, moving like a black-garbed wraith against the dying brightness of the day outside. When she had gained the lateral aisle of clearance that led to the front and out, she motioned the waiter toward her before proceeding along it, at the same time cautioning him with fingers to lips.

"Sí, señorita?"

"My *nodriza's* very tired, *pobrecita*. I'm going to leave her here for a few minutes. Don't wake her up, please, until I get back. I'm just going across the street. I'll be back for her in a quarter of an hour."

"Just as the señorita orders it," he murmured respectfully. A refined young girl in mourning from head to foot, an armful of flowers obviously destined for a grave—who could think anything amiss?

She moved decorously enough until she had gained the terrace outside and the street beyond that. Then, because the cemetery entrance was some considerable distance down, not directly opposite, and because the sun was already expiring in a pool of blood in the western sky, and her precious store of stolen minutes was draining away through her fingers like sand, she began to hasten. Unnoticeably at first. In a moment more she was presenting the rather grotesque, not to say scandalous, spectacle of a black-garbed mourner, flowers bobbing up and down in arms, veil ends and skirts streaming out behind her, rushing along full tilt toward a burial-ground entrance, as though the dead couldn't wait, as though she couldn't get in fast enough to offer them her homage. One or two heads turned to look incredulously after her as she whisked by.

She was out of breath as she rounded the ornamental entrance archway, black-silk-encased legs trip-hammering under her so fast they almost blurred. "I don't want you to have anything undignified to have to look back on later." Tell that to love!

Her sense of propriety returned to her just in time; she forced herself to slow to a more sedate though still rather rapid walk, as she passed between the ponderous, bronze gate flaps, outstretched like a pair of wings waiting to receive and fold upon her. The gift of some wealthy private donor, they were expensively worked in bas-relief. On one was inscribed: *That which is so universal as death must be a blessing.* And on the opposite one: *And none may escape its benediction.*

She passed through them without a glance. The living have no time to look at death; they cannot see it even if they try.

A short distance within and beyond them was a little lodge, scarcely more than a stone sentry box, used by the gatekeeper during hours of admission. He was standing in the narrow doorway of it, looking out, as she went by. He was a kindly, commonplace-looking old man, obviously near-sighted as she could tell by the way he squinted at her in peering uncertainty.

She stopped short, moved a step or two over toward him. "Has a young man come in here within the past half-hour or so, have you noticed? Dark-haired and thin and, and by himself?"

"Sort of a good-looking young fellow?" he suggested.

"Oh, handsome!" she agreed fervently, casting a rapturous upward look at the sky.

The old man smiled a little with tolerant understanding. "Yes, *niña*, yes, I have seen someone like that. Three times within the past ten minutes he's been out here to the entrance, looking for someone, getting more restless all the time, asking me if I'd seen—someone very beautiful, in black with jet-black hair, bringing a servant girl with her."

She dropped her eyes, quickly raised them again.

"He's still in there, though? He didn't leave?" she said relievedly.

"He's still in there as far as I know. I don't remember seeing him leave. Unless he left while I was making my last tour of inspection."

"No," she assured him, with a sort of charming inner conviction, "he didn't, he's still in there. Thank you."

She turned and resumed her way down the long broad central avenue that led farther in before it began to unravel into numberless, winding, white-graveled paths, all looking pretty much alike and all already taking on a bluish cast as they filled up with the silt of night shadow.

"Don't stay in too long, señorita," the gatekeeper called

after her in kindly warning. "When you hear my whistle blow that means we're closing. You only have a minute or two left."

She only half heard him. An invisible current that he couldn't see had swept her up, was pulling her irresistibly forward. Whistles and gates and quotas of minutes couldn't weaken or stop it or interfere. This was the time for love, treasured, hoarded, waited for, ever since the time before.

She walked rapidly down the somber avenue, through an eerie landscape fast dimming in the twilight. Eerie because it was neither natural nor human; it was that of the other world. There was a classical severity to it, a cold melancholy, that nature lacks. These cypresses, poplars, weeping willows, artfully disposed here and there, singly and in copses, they were rooted where dead human beings lay. They touched death, they sheltered it, they even lived and were nourished upon it. And scattered all about under them, through every opening in their low-hanging branches, in every space between their trunks, down every vista and at every turn, was a silent, soulless population, gleaming white in the wavering shadows. A population that seemed to be waiting some necromantic signal in the depths of oncoming night to come to swarming, malignant life. A population of angels, phoenixes, griffins. The very marble benches here and there along the paths, they seemed to be put there not for the living to rest upon during the course of their visits, but for the use of unguessed shrouded forms flitting along these thoroughfares and lanes in silent passage late at night.

And over it all hung a violet pall of expiring light, the *crepusculo*, whose very name was a little death in itself. The death of day.

Through this land of the dead, love made its way, nineteen years old, blood warm, eyes bright, breath quick, heart pulsing. She was no longer running. She was in now, that was the main thing. It was just a matter of a minute or two more, and it wouldn't have been respectful in such a place. But she moved along at an eager little walk, with a double step of added impetus every three or four paces, that was not quite a trot but threatened to be one.

She reached a little circular axis that was a landmark to
her. In its center stood an alabaster urn on a slender graceful pediment that she always used to guide herself by. Here
four paths spoked out. The one she had been following
continued on beyond, into reaches of the cemetery that
were unknown to her. Then there was a lateral one that
crossed it at this point, making two more. She knew by
experience you turned left at this place to reach her family's burial plot. Then coming back, of course, you just did
the opposite, turned right, to get back on the main avenue
leading to the entrance gate.

It was just a little further on now. She followed this
lesser, winding, graveled path, with its half-remembered
particulars of surrounding. First it led through a depressed
open treeless patch, a sort of meadow of the dead. The
depths of this were inked in with blue already. Then it
climbed and wound its way through a thick grove of trees,
almost like a tunnel, and just past that was her destination.
She hadn't had a chance to notice these things much on
her previous visits. Going, Rosita was always chattering
away to her. And coming back, more lingeringly, there was
an arm about her waist and a low voice murmuring in her
ear. This was the first time she'd made her way through
here alone.

She arrived finally. She reached the short but head-high
length of box hedge that ran along the path for a few feet,
marking her family's plot. She turned in through a gap in
it, made her way to the newest of the several monuments
and markers it contained, a pylon of bone white, with a
bronze wreath clamped to it circling a simple inscription.

DON RAFAEL CONTRERAS Y GALBO
PRAY FOR HIS SOUL

It was at the far end of the enclosure. The rest were just
great-aunts and people she had never known. *He* wouldn't
be waiting for her in here, of course. That would have been
bad taste. There was a place they had— But first, the
respect due one's dead. She sank down on one knee beside
the mound, firmly put all thoughts of that someone else out

of her mind for the time being, lowered her head, murmuring a short prayer that was a plea for forgiveness. "Father, forgive me for fooling Mother like this. We didn't mean to, but we're both going to be old so long. I'll have him come to the house and meet her this week, I promise."

She rose at last, spent several more minutes arranging the flowers she had brought with her about the base of the pylon, moving from side to side to shift them until the effect suited her. Then she dipped her knees, crossed herself, and left the enclosure, with a lingering backward glance. The dead had received their due, and now for the living.

It wasn't very far away, just a little further over to the left along the same path. It was a little marble pergola, a circular roof supported by slim columns, without any walls. It didn't belong to anyone; that is to say, it was a "public" structure put up by the cemetery itself, like the benches and the landmark urn farther back. That was where they always met. He'd be waiting for her in there right now. She'd probably see the ember of his impatient cigarette moving around restlessly inside it like a red firefly as she came hurrying up. It was a shame; her getting here late like this would give them hardly any time together at all.

It already looked indistinct in the dusk as she sighted it, a misty blue shape peering through the haze, instead of clear white any more. But what did she care what it looked like, it was who was in it that counted. She made a little crowing sound of mischievous delight as she turned and ran in between two of the fluted columns. "Raul," she greeted him. "Did you think I'd never—"

It was empty.

Gone! He'd given her up, left without waiting— No, he couldn't have, the gateman had said he'd just seen him. And if he'd tried to leave after that, the gateman would have told him that she had arrived herself in the meanwhile, and he would have come back looking for her.

She stood there for a moment, uncertainly, in the clear floor space ringed by three semicircular backless benches. He'd be back in a minute. He must have gone just as far as the entrance, to look for her one last time, and the gate-man would surely tell him. They must have missed one another in some way; maybe while she was behind the hedge in her family's plot, he'd passed by unheard outside. Without noticing her in there, all black against the shad-ows. Or taken some short cut to the gate that didn't bring him by there at all. She'd better wait here, where he could find her, or they might miss one another a second time, never get together at all.

Just tonight that had to happen, when the time was so short anyway! She sat down forlornly on one of the three benches. Presently, even in the murky light that filled the place, she made out something on the floor. A half-smoked cigarette lying at her feet. Another. A half dozen, strewn all over. She picked the nearest one up gingerly between two fingers, held it directly under her eyes in the obscurity. Part of the trade name still hadn't been consumed. "Ex-quisito." Those were his, she knew them. She smiled com-passionately. Poor boy, she could see him now, pacing back and forth, fretting at the long delay.

She continued to hold it for a while, looking at it. It was a part of him. It was the most she could have of him for a moment or two, until he got back here himself.

She whispered to it. "Little cigarette, does he love me? Did he miss me, because I wasn't here? Tell me, how did he act? Did he whisper my name when he held you in his mouth? You should know, you were very close to him." She touched it caressingly with the tip of one finger. She was very young yet.

It was taking him long to come back from the gate. He wouldn't fail to come back, though; the gateman would surely tell him he'd seen her. It would be foolish not to wait, now that she was here. This was the only place where they could be unseen, alone together for a moment or two. It was different when she'd brought Rosita. Rosita was one's own age, understood, even aided and abetted one. With Rosita they could have taken a lingering farewell of one another, even out in full sight at the main gate. She would have waited tactfully out of earshot, or walked ahead of them, leaving them to follow to the carriage with arms linked, heads inclined together. But with Marta along! She'd better stay where she was. He'd show up any minute.

How strange it was. You met someone, and suddenly the whole world became different. She remembered the first time they'd met. It wasn't so long ago, just a few Sundays ago, but already she couldn't recall what life had been like before that time, before there'd been a "him." It was on a Sunday afternoon, at the *cine*. Her mother had had one of her spells, and Marta was too strict to go to a *cine* on Sunday, so Rosita had gone with her. You had reserved seats at a *cine* on Sunday afternoons, you rented them by the season and you occupied the same ones every time you went, so he must have known her by sight, watched her each time the lights went up at intermission, for a long time before. Well, she had noticed him herself, but you couldn't stare of course. You could only let eyes meet eyes for a passing instant.

Then when they came out that afternoon, they found that a terrific downpour was drenching the streets. They huddled there helplessly under the sidewalk canopy along with everyone else, unable to move, while the theater doorman blew his whistle up and down the street—that querulous sound just then, chiming in upon her thoughts from somewhere in the distance, reminded her of that day, brought it before her more vividly than ever—calling up carriages and cabs and anything on wheels to the rescue. But everyone else kept getting them, and the two of them, she and Rosita, would have stood there stranded for there was no telling how long, if he suddenly hadn't appeared at their side and forced a passage for them, and arbitrarily commandeered the latest one standing at the curb, to the exclusion of—

Suddenly she was upright, with a sort of shock of delayed timing coursing through her. That had been the gateman's whistle that had blended in so patly with the stream of her thoughts, back there before!

She ran out between the columns, stood poised for an instant on the two low steps that formed the structure's flooring, listening with frightened intensity. It came again;

then, piping, sounding miles and hopeless miles away
across the darkness. Farther away than she could ever hope
to reach in time. The second and the last warning, and after
that—they just locked up without waiting any longer. He
must have missed her in some way, the gateman, just as
she and Raul had missed one another. Because obviously
they would have to do more than just blow a whistle at the
gate, in a place of this size. Perhaps on his last tour of
warning around the grounds he had failed to come near
this pergola, never realizing there was anyone sheltered in
it. And she, in her day dreaming, had failed to note the
distant flicker of his lamp—if he used one—or grasp its
significance. Or perhaps he had mistaken someone else
who had passed him on her way out, garbed in mourning
as she was, for herself, and not bothered to come in looking for her at all. He was nearsighted, after all.

All this in a single, horrified pause on the steps, quicker
even than her fluttering garments could settle about her
into motionlessness. And to add to her dismay, she realized
only now that it had grown completely dark while she was
sitting in there waiting. Even the afterglow of the sun was
gone now. Only a slight greenish blackness, like oxidized
metal, above the trees in the west, showed where it had
been. The rest was dark, dark, dark; night was in possession and had caught her in its trap.

She was running along the winding graveled path now.
She thought she'd never run so fast in her life before. A
spray of gravel flew up, like sea foam, at the tiny prows of
her plunging feet. Through the tunnel of trees. Down into
the declivity of the meadow of the dead. Up again on the
other side. Past the box hedge behind which her father and
the great-aunts lay. A sob of helpless appeal winged back
toward it as she darted by: *"Papacito!"* The whimper of a
frightened thing, tossed over her shoulder as she fled headlong past the place. To someone who once could have
protected her—but couldn't now any more.

The trees were invisible against the black sky. But under
them, and far too visible, the white of the monuments and
the markers made blurred gray ghost shapes here and
there. An angel poised on one toe threatened to spring out

at her from ambush, seize her about the neck with both arms tightly entwined, bring her down. She screamed, and shied aside, and nearly fell, then went floundering on again.

A wind seemed to come sighing up out of the earth around her, damp and moldy with the aroma of long-buried things. It wasn't just static, it seemed to pursue her, threading through the trees, winding down the path after her, moaning, trying to claim her for its own. The pathway under her was just a gray ribbon, an indistinct tape, stretched across the dark. It never seemed to end, it never would end—

This was panic, and she knew it, and she knew it must be conquered or she would never reach the gate alive. Even as she tottered on, chest exploding and collapsing at each in- and exhalation, she fought to regain her self-control. It's all right, Conchita, nothing will happen; it's all right, don't be a fool. In just a moment more you'll reach that landmark of the urn, and then you turn left—remember? —and after that just the one broad central avenue takes you to the gate, nothing to it. Call out now, from here— they'll hear you, they'll wait, they'll hold it open. Call out so they'll know; you should have already, from the moment you first heard the whistle.

She didn't think she'd have breath enough left, but she managed somehow. Shrilly, falteringly, jerky with the vibration of her continued running. "Gateman! Gateman, wait! I'm still in here! Don't close yet! Wait until I get there—"

Then she couldn't any more, there wasn't enough strength of lung left. She was wavering from side to side as it was, no longer able to keep to a straight course. And the treacherous gravel, so easy to tread upon when you were at rest, seemed to roll and sidle under her feet, unbalancing her.

The urn! Oh saints be praised, the urn at last! Rearing there before her, higher than her head, seeming to swim against the darkness without support, until the lesser pallor of its pediment had come into focus under it.

To the left now, she warned herself harassedly; to the left, be careful— She couldn't even tell for a moment which it was. The heart. The heart was always on the left. She put her hand to it, and its pounding was almost a physical hurt, like hammer blows against the hollow of the hand. She let it guide her, swerved around toward that side, and the urn was whisked from sight behind her, like something worked on invisible strings.

The broad, paved alley that led straight to the gate lay before her now, and the worst was over. Its firm surface was easier to run on than the shifting gravel, but she couldn't gain much added advantage, she was already too exhausted. She tottered waveringly on; she daren't falter now. She tried to call out again, and found she couldn't. A muted, strangled sound, that scarcely outdistanced her, was all that she could utter. It seemed to tear at her suffocating throat. "Leave the gates open, wait for me—!"

Straight and broad the avenue stretched before her, its side boundary lines drawing to a shadowy junction in the darkness ahead that kept eluding her, never came any closer. Behind her, that same malignant wind that smelled of the clamminess of tombs and the stench of rotted coffins seemed to have turned at the urn just as she had, seemed to be keeping up its insatiable, humming pursuit, even down this straightaway. It was like running down a track of perpetual motion, whose reverse direction ate up all the gain you made, kept you standing still at a fixed point after all, though limbs and heart and lungs wore themselves out.

A bench went slowly past on one side. Then, after a while, another went slowly past on the other. How she wanted to topple down on one of them and just lie there half senseless—but she daren't. It was so long ago that the whistle blasts had sounded; would they really have heard her cries? Would they still be waiting, keeping them open? Then why didn't they come forward, even a little part of the way; why didn't she see the glimmer of their lanterns down there at the end of this interminable perspective—

There was something wrong. The distance to the gate seemed greater than she remembered it. It *was* greater, there was no mistaking it. This wasn't a distortion of panic, of darkness; it was a question of the length of time she had been running, and the distance she had covered. She should have reached that gate already two or three times over by now. Even at a walk it had never seemed this far, never *been* this far, before.

The thought of what it was, of what had happened, was like ice creeping through her veins, numbing as it wound its way. And then behind it was heat again, ready to claim her in turn; but not the warmth of sanity, of normalcy, any more. The fever heat of burning madness, the temperature of nightmare.

She was scarcely moving forward now. She couldn't any more. She was swaying there, her limbs still trying to carry her forward, only succeeding in making little rotary motions on the ground. And still it stretched endlessly before her, to that immutable vanishing point it had had all along, ever since back there at the urn.

She tried to think. Left. Yes, left. *Izquierda.* That was the word, that was the direction. But left *when?* On coming in, when you wanted to go toward your family's plot? Or on going out, when you wanted to go toward the gate? Left was the word. Rosita had said it that other time, when they had stopped uncertainly for a moment there by it. She could still hear the remark sound in her mind. "No, left, Señorita Conchita." That part was all right. But left *when?* She couldn't remember whether they had been coming in or going out at the time. Her mind had been full of him.

She reeled around and looked behind her. The urn had been lost long ago. All that met her eyes was another of those vanishing points, no different from the one in front of her.

She'd made the wrong turning, come the wrong way. She'd plunged deeper into this fastness of the dead, instead of making her way out. The preliminary sobs of hysteria started to form in her throat, each one rising higher than the one before. She drove both hands distractedly through the ringleted hair that Raul had once admired so, dislodged the coronet of twisted black braid that encircled it and the veiling depending from it. They fell to the ground behind her, and she let them stay there unheeded.

The gates must be closed long ago. They'd never heard

her, never guessed. She was locked in this hideous place for
the night, and no one knew it. They'd gone away and left
her in here, with the dead. She knew that nearsighted old
man didn't sleep here on the grounds. The little kiosk that
sheltered him during visiting hours was dark and locked up
now. Its size had told her that at sight; it was just a daytime niche.

She turned and tried to go back along the way she had
come just now. One faltering step was all she could manage. Her courage failed her. She couldn't do it. She couldn't
go back into that maw of darkness behind her that she had
passed through once already. True, it was as dark ahead of
her, but there was something even worse about darkness
revisited than about darkness already explored. As though
she would be giving latent evil a second chance at her if
she returned. That dolorously crooning wind was coming
from back there. The trees were rustling and hissing, like
living things stalking her, from back there.

She heeled her hands to her eyes, held them tightly
pressed there to try to shut out the terrible sights she had
not seen yet, but was afraid she might have to see at any
minute. Her teeth were chattering with terror, and with the
nervous chill induced by it. She took her hands away from
her eyes at length, and found she had begun to move again,
without knowing it, in the meantime. Slowly now, uncertainly, erratically, without purpose or destination. She was
meandering down the center of the avenue, with the wavering gait of someone about to drop in a heap at any moment. Still in the direction in which she had been going all
along, for she could still go forward if not back. Her jerky,
unpredictable progress was that of something bereft of all
reason. Which, temporarily, she was.

A bench edged up beside her along the perimeter of the
lane, bleached white, cadaverous against the gloom, like
something with an invisible spotlight trained on it. She
turned aside, fell rather than walked over to it, and, as
though its presence and support were some sort of emo-
tional release, flung the upper part of her body prone
against the seat of it, legs trailing out behind her along the
ground, and exploded into a cataclysm of sobbing that was

so violent it couldn't by its very nature have lasted long without rendering her unconscious.

It didn't. She stopped again, from sheer rib stricture and breath stoppage, and remained there quiescent. But not unaware. Fear was creeping back over her again, like a thin glazed coating, even while she huddled there without moving. It touched off reflex action, finally. She scissored her legs suddenly, like a swimmer on dry ground; switched her head around, looked behind her. The instinctive reaction of those in the dark, afraid of the dark. A scream of dismay wrenched through her stiffened lips, and she tried to burrow her head and shoulders into the furthermost inner corner of the bench seat and back with such spasmodic terror that she struck her forehead violently against the cold hard stone and still didn't even feel the blow.

There was something creeping up along one side of the blurred gray pathway upon her. Something black, sinuous, belly-flat, tail snaking. Sometimes the offside gloom effaced it, sometimes the lighter tone of the path outlined its undulation. But on one side only. There was a wink, a tiny flash too dull to be called bright, every now and again from its forepart, as a ray from some star high overhead struck some glistening or liquefied beadlike area receptive to light.

Its advance was irregular, with the irregularity of stealth. It would undulate quickly, covertly, forward; so quickly the ripple it made seemed almost an optical illusion. Then it would stop short, seem lifeless, nothing but a shadow, gathering itself for the next treacherous little creep. Even while she looked, eyes huge with brain-turning horror, she saw its tail, its slender ropelike after appendage, give a little flirt upward, a twitch, then flatten again. It made another little stealthy, squirming run, stopped again with hair-trigger timing.

She was paralyzed. Approaching dissolution robs the body of movement. She was cataleptically silent, after that first scream of discovery, for the same reason. There is a depth of fright beyond screaming that is silent. She had heaved herself upward off the ground without use of her arms, climbing up the joint between bench back and side arm by motion of her shoulders alone, without turning to

look at it. That was the most she could do to try to get
away from it, wedge herself distortedly into the shallow
indentation of a low stone bench, arched backbreakingly at
the waist around its seat. Her face was a frozen grimace of
convulsive anticipation.

It gave no warning. It was as unpredictable as mercury
or lightning. Suddenly it sprang, streaked out at her feet—
and a little beyond, as though it had overreached itself. Its
tail part came lashing, switching after it.

All she did was shudder, in a form of death without
contact. Then she deflated as suddenly as it had leaped, her
waist sank in, rippled down over the edge of the seat, and
she sidled inertly to the ground, retched a couple of times.
There beside her own discarded black coif, with the two jet
ornaments spaced on the front of it, and the long sinuous
length of whipped-around veiling, that bulged like muscular haunches in places, that the wind had been sending
creeping stealthily up on her a little at a time.

Cruel minutes went by, in a gift of renewed life that was
hardly wanted any more, it had been so expensive. She got
to her feet again somehow, presently, the black garment on
her a biased misfit now, too high up on one shoulder, down
off the other one entirely. Smoky ribbons on her white legs
where there had been stockings before. She wasn't a civ-
ilized being any more. She wasn't a young girl of the city.
She wasn't the Viuda de Contreras' daughter. She had no
name, she had no address. She wasn't feminine, and she
wasn't masculine, she'd sunk to a lower genderless plane.
She'd forgotten what love was, and her tears or the action
of her hand had carried a surly red streak of lipstick from
the corner of her mouth down to the bottom of her chin
and under. She was just a blindly instinctive thing, struggling feebly to get from the dark to the light, to get from
fear to safety.

Terror now was only something comparative. There
were accesses of it at times, then at other times there were
diminutions of it; there never at any time was a complete
absence of it. She wavered along, on the move once more,
head lolling downward on her chest, legs splaying stiffly

out behind her, first one then the other, like crutches. There were stars over her, but they were cold and meaningless. They seemed so distant, so aloof; pin-point intelligences without pity, looking down from a great height on something trapped in a black pit, watching it go around and around, trying to find its way out, and knowing that it never would.

Then suddenly a new terror was added to those she was already enduring. A chromatic one, this time. Color began to well up into the cemetery, giving it a new dimension, giving its horrors depth, that the two-dimensional black and gray had lacked until now. It was like a reflection from a distance; she couldn't see where it was coming from at first. It was like the shine of red fire through the trees and between the graves, not rising high, but creeping closely over the ground.

A great, angry eye was opening behind her. The moon. But not the cool, tapered moon of lovers and of wishes. Full-bellied, carnivorous. With animus toward the living, like everything else in here. Fuming, fevered, glaring diseasedly, redolent of evil and of things they had taught you long ago in church not to believe in. Unhallowed things. Ghouls and goblins, grinning cadavers that pushed their way up out of graves, all subcuticle muscular ligaments in crisscross patches, like something on a medical students' dissection table. The moon. The planet that controls madness and psychopathic urge to shed blood.

It doubled, tripled the shadows where it had been black before. And in the places where it had been less than black, it brought a horrifying, threatening simulation of motion, filtering through the restless leaves and branches. It made the forms and figures on the graves seem to waver, to sidle and stir and shift in its rays, to mottle like leprous things and glower and leer, where they had at least been still before. Trees became gnarled shapes bending toward her, reaching down to clutch at her. Monuments became things crouched behind the bushes and the flowers, dropping their heads lower at the moment she skirted by, to rear up again and slink out after her the instant her back was to them.

Even her own shadow turned against her now, treacherously assailed by creeping up on her when she least expected it or flinging itself abruptly at her from one side.

She had no leisure to think of anything but the present
moment, in the midst of all these terrors, but if she had she
would have realized the darkness had already had its vic-
tory. She was already a little dead. Whether she ever got
out of here again or whether she didn't she would never be
the same. Fright had pushed her permanently back into
some atavistic past, lived long ago.

And meantime the bilious planet, like everything else in
the place, seemed bent on pursuing her. It slowly climbed
the sky after her, clearing itself as it went. From angry
orange to a sulphurous yellow, and from that to white,
the bleached white of a skull, eye sockets faintly discernible, inclining downward to look at her from the sky.

A period of trancelike inanition followed for a short
while; she was conscious of still stumbling on, but her
mind was a little hazy. Even terror had become a little
blunted, lost some of its sharp edge, though it was still with
her. She was experiencing a sort of hang-over of the mental
faculties, brought on by shock and overstimulation.

And then suddenly a little sound came to her, roused
her, brought her back to whiplike alertness again. A little
sound of life, the first she'd heard since this horrendous
solitude had begun. The first besides her own screams and
footfalls; the first *objective* one coming from outside her
own travail. The sweetest thing she'd ever heard; sweeter
than the sweetest note of music ever struck, lovelier than
the loveliest birdcall ever trilled. A little discord, a thing
between a squeak and a grunt, faint, far-off, ugly, awkward, gauche, but, oh, how welcome. The distant honk of
a car horn sounded in passage.

The outside world, the world of the living, was someplace near here, closer at hand than she'd suspected. She
stood there straining her ears, forcing them beyond their
powers of attunement, to try to catch it again. It wouldn't
come again. Just once, and then no more. She held her
breath, she even quieted one of the stirring strips of torn
garment hanging from her, so that there wouldn't be the

slightest sound about her that might cause her to lose it. But no, it wouldn't come again.

She didn't know which way to go, for she hadn't been quick enough to catch which way it had seemed to come from. If she moved incautiously she was afraid she might be going farther away instead of nearer to it, end up by losing it altogether. It hadn't came from behind her, that was the one thing she was sure of.

Since her ears couldn't aid her, or were given no second opportunity to, she tried to force her eyes to do service in their stead. But the darkness seemed to lie impartially around her in all the three remaining directions— No, wait; didn't there seem to be an evenness to it, over there, on her right, as though there were a surface backing it instead of it continuing to an unconfined depth? Didn't those motelike flicks of moonlight peering through the leaves over there seem *upright* against something, instead of lying flat upon the ground?

She struck out suddenly, all hopes of recovering the original position at which she'd heard the telltale sound gladly cast away on the single chance of being right about it. Through grass, and over lumpy rises at times that, though they might well have been graves, were robbed of all power to terrify her now, for this was life itself that was beckoning to her through their midst. They could have yawned open under her feet and she would have still leaped across them from lip to lip, the quicker to get where she was going.

And there it was at last, something upright looming there ahead of her, coming closer, gliding toward her with her running, striking at last against the flats of her hands, outstretched to it in appeal, with a roughness of masonry, a scratchy prickiness of mortar, that was more caressing to the touch than velvet or satin could have been. The boundary wall, the limit of death, the line beyond which it did not go.

Pressed against it, motionless at last, arms upright at her sides, she put her lips to it, kissed it in poignant gratitude.

She must have been making her way, all unsuspecting, along parallel to it for some time past, although it was set

out at a considerable distance away from the path she had
been following. It obviously wasn't the front wall, where
the gate was, for she had been moving steadily away from
that the whole time. Unless, of course, she had made a
complete, blind circuit of the place in the dark, and come
back to where she had started from. But more likely it was
either one of the side walls, or the rear one. She had
probably gone entirely through the dread place, to its other
end.

There was a noticeable hum now in the air, coming from
the other side of it. Faint and disembodied, an echoing
murmur from far off, but still able to intrude upon the
stillness that reigned in here. It was the hum, the drone,
that comes from houses, from streets, in the distance, in
the night. It must be built up on the other side of this wall,
or at least to within a short distance of it. A finger of the
city must stretch out toward the cemetery from the rear,
even though the main gate around at the other side gave
onto more or less open country.

And then, in confirmation, the axle of a tramcar wheel
grated as it rounded a turn, off in the distance someplace
but querulously audible.

She began to beat her way along the inside of the wall,
face turned to look up hopefully at the top. It was too
smooth, too high, to be scaled unaided, even if she'd had
the strength left. Why had they had to make it so high?
What had the dead in here to fear from the living?

Some of the trees, she noticed, seemed to grow fairly
close to the wall. The branches of certain ones even
spanned the top of it, occasionally. Perhaps if she could get
up the trunk of one, she could work her way out along one
of those over-reaching branches and transfer from it to the
top of the wall. Even if she couldn't descend from there
unaided, she would at least be in a better position to attract
someone's attention on the outside. She couldn't from
down below here, where she was. Her voice seemed to be
gone, from overuse; she could only make low whimpering
noises now. And there was obviously no ground-level gap
within this solid bulwark, at least not near enough to be of
any use to her.

Most were set too far in; there was a gap up above that would have defeated her even if she had been able to get to the proper height; or else the slenderness of the trunk itself warned that the upper reaches would be even more unsubstantial; she would only have succeeded in killing herself. She found one at last that seemed just right, although it was hard to be sure in the dark. By standing still under it and peering intently for several minutes she thought she could make out a thick, massive bough forking out from it, in a straight line over the wall and beyond. It looked from where she was nearly as broad in girth as the lower trunk itself.

She tried to clasp her arms around its base to gain a fulcrum, and they wouldn't meet around it, it was too large in diameter. She tried to claw her way up it, then, on one side only; to dig her nails into the rough-edged bark and hang her entire weight on them. The bark only peeled off in little segments, her nails broke, and the tips of her fingers grew lacerated. The tips of her prodding, gouging shoes slipped down again each time without being able to gain a hold. Once she was able to get up as high as half her own height again, but then she slid down again, scratching and bruising her own skin. She let herself lie where she'd fallen a minute, to rest.

Oh, if she'd only been twelve again, she knew she would have been able to do it. When she was twelve, and they'd taken her to the country in the summer, she'd climbed many trees for pears and apples and thought nothing of it. And now, the pear, the apple, was safety, life itself—and she couldn't do it!

She cried a little with the bitterness of frustration, pleaded with those who weren't there to hear, with her head lowered toward the ground, there in the darkness at the foot of that pitiless tree. "Raul, Raulcito, why did you go away like that? Mother, mother of my life, let me come back to you. I'll never do it again. Why didn't I listen to you? You always were right. You didn't want me to leave the house—"

The words died to a blurred whimpering, the whimpering muted to disconsolate sobbing breaths.

Then suddenly as she lay there like that, head and shoulders reared off the ground, the rest of her sprawled supinely out upon it, a sound came from over the wall, so matter-of-fact, so casual, so close at hand—she couldn't believe it was real, she couldn't believe she'd actually heard it. It was the hollow, slightly wooden-sounding clap a car door gives when it is carelessly flung closed against the chassis. And then a lesser sound, the snap of a key in a lock.

An empty car must have been parked outside there all along, close up against the cemetery wall, waiting for someone. And that someone had just returned to it and gotten in, and was about to drive off all unknowing!

It was down farther, a few yards below, judging by the direction of the sound. And yet for all practical purposes, its and her own parallel placement could be considered a freak of exactitude; they were as good as diametrically opposite one another, she and this potential savior car. Had she seen it, known it was there all the while, she could scarcely have come to a halt much closer to it than she had. Strange are the geometrical patterns devised by night and the stars.

Oh limbs, lift me, bear me up, just this one time more. Oh voice, call out strongly enough in time to be heard. Quick, quick, a second's inability may be already too late!

She opened her lips spasmodically, and a soundless gush, residue of exhaustion, was all that came the first time. Then a second try and voice followed. She couldn't hear it. A torrent of mechanical noise drowned out her lungs' pitiful effort. He'd started the motor. Six cylinders against one fragile larynx. It was a raucous engine, that must have needed oiling somewhat, that bombarded the night.

She was upright and thrashing, almost spinning, frenziedly along the inside of the wall, and even as she did so it already seemed to begin gliding unnoticeably ahead of her, increasing those few yards of differential there had been to start with, as the wheels began to turn. For a long, unendurable moment there was an equipoise; a hideous contest between her fraying screams and the increasing revolutions of its cylinders. Which could keep it up the longest? She was so tired and the engine was so strong.

Then it began to pull away; not just glide now but accelerate into full career. And in the very act was her salvation. It ebbed a little in volume, the rhythm of a more even vibration set in. Her voice found an opening in that, an echo if it managed to slash through its new regularity of tempo.

There was another ghastly equipoise, a second or two before the effects could show, while it seemed to leap away from her. And she couldn't scream any more, that had been her last one. Then brakes rasped and it slurred to an unwilling, unintended short stop. She could even hear the hiss of reluctant rubber against stone.

Silence.

Then a man's voice, questioning the blank night. "Who is it? Hello? Hello?"

She could visualize his hand starting toward the clutch once more, to continue, thinking he had been mistaken, it had been some flaw in his own car's mechanism.

Her swollen heart leaped up like a salmon, turned over, dropped down again, almost stopped beating with the effort, but she managed to get one suffocating sound out. "No—!" And the rest was just unheard lip vibration.

"Who's that? Where are you?" The car door cracked tentatively open, while he still remained in the seat. Probably one leg out.

"In here, in All Saints, behind this wall." It was all blurred vowel sounds, she couldn't articulate consonants any more, but there were enough vowels to carry the burden of the message, to at least *hold* him there.

A leather sole hit stone. The car door cracked a second time—but in token of egress. Saved!

He said an inane thing. "What are you doing in there?" But oh, the sound of his voice alone, it held the wisdom of the ages in it, it was so welcome to her.

"I'm alone in here. I've been locked in. Oh, for the love of God, take me out—get me out to the other side—"

"Now just a second. Don't be frightened. I'll climb over and get you—"

Shoe leather scorched down stone, futilely, two, three, four times. Each time he landed back on his feet more heavily. Then she could hear him trying to run at it, trying to hoist himself with the help of his own projected momentum. Each time that floundering sound.

"I can't get up it, it's too high." He was breathless now himself. "Wait a minute, I'll get someone. I'll get hold of someone with a ladder, and come back with that—"

The car door spitting again, like a hinge of hell.

Her voice rose to an unendurable scream. "No, don't leave me! Don't leave me, I can't stand it!"

He held back, probably half in, half out, trying to reason with her. "But you're all right now. Someone knows you're in there. I know you're in there. It's just a matter of a moment. *Pequeña, pequeña,* don't you see?"

She screamed again. Just instinct was screaming, there was nothing there any more he could reason with. "You won't come back! Stand there and talk to me, if you can't get me out. At least stand there so I'll know there's someone near me. Señor, señor, whoever you are, have pity on me. Don't leave me all alone again."

"But you *must* be gotten out. There's a paint shop only a few blocks from here. They must have a ladder there. I'll get hold of the proprietor, and in less than five minutes I'll be back here again—"

"You won't come back, you won't come back—"

"Little frightened señorita. I swear to you by all that's holy that I won't leave you in there. Who could do such a thing? I'm a man. This way I'd only stand here all night without doing you any good. Trust me."

She held out a moment longer, instinct against reason. Then she gave in. "All right, señor, I trust you," she said in a watery voice. "But hurry. It's so dark, and there are things moving in the shadows behind me."

"Stand with your back to them. Don't look around. Stand turned toward the wall, until I can get back, and they won't hurt you."

"But that way it's even worse. Then I seem to hear them creeping up behind me, getting ready to pounce, without my seeing them."

His own voice was wrung with pity, whoever he was, at the state she was in. "*Pobrecita.* Just a minute, *muchachita,* just a minute and we'll have you out."

She couldn't resist one final bleat as the car door closed once more. "Don't forget me, señor— You won't forget me, señor—?"

"Just stay where you are, and I'll be back in no time," his voice sounded over the renewal of the engine. "Don't move, now, so that I'll know where to find you."

The engine evened out, drew away, and she heard him go whirring off on his quest. One last wisp of it came drifting back, after the rest was already gone, like a postscript, like an afterthought from the distance. And then no more.

Silence again. Night again, and by herself again.

She stood there for a while in a sort of state of suspended animation, staring blindly toward the black presence of the wall, as though trying to fix and hold the exact spot at which she had last heard his voice, lest if she lose it by so much as a quarter of an inch, if she deflect her eyes, he would not come back, there would be some magic compulsion gone. Frightened children have that fetishism.

"Don't move, he said," she whispered to herself once, in cautioning reminder.

Then suddenly, as though unable to support her upright position any more, as though something had given way under her, she floundered down to her former position on the ground, half-length prone, head and neck and shoulders still upright on one arm. Not senseless, but drained of all strength. Only able to do two things, breathe and wait. Three.

Hope was a white moth, tiny of wing, fluttering around her in the darkness.

Coldness seeped into her legs and the outspread flatness of her own hand from the moss and the damp ground, numbing them. Or was that the ichor of those who lay so thickly scattered about under here being transfused into her by some horrid sort of osmosis? She snatched her hand up and flung it out, as you do when you try to drain something off.

The moth was making wider circles now, not so close around her. How long was it now? Four minutes? Five?

She struggled to her knees, and bunched her hands together, and bent her face to them. "Make him come back. Just this one little thing give me: make him come back."

The moth was going now, the moth was leaving fast, going somewhere else. Its minute wings were glimmering off into nothingness.

She whispered into her hands, as though it were a secret they alone shared with her: "He told me not to move. See, I'm trying not to be frightened. I'm quiet, you can't hear me. That one nearly got out, but I didn't let it, I stifled it. This one isn't going to either—"

And then a bereft scream went winging up overhead and, almost puzzled, she realized it had come from her.

She put her hands to her throat, as if to stop it outwardly, if she couldn't inwardly. They were powerless too. A second one was wrenched from her against her will. "Hurry up! Where are you?" It vibrated in the cemetery stillness like a thrumming knife blade, went winging over the wall into the night beyond.

In the redoubled silence that followed she thought she heard a sound. Nothing definite, like that car door before, or even the chirp of the horn preceding that. Something less easily identifiable, like a—a *pad*. Over somewhere on the other side of the wall, not in here where she was. It must have been simply some leaf, or small cluster of leaves, that had fallen to the ground with a splat. And yet, it hadn't been quite like that either. It had been both firmer and at the same time softer; less scratchy, more resilient. Almost like a velvety tread, the merest silkiest whisper of a tread, except that a tread is continuous, and this was an isolated fragment of one, cast into notice by some uncertainty or flux of the ground being trodden upon. That, at least, was what it could have been taken for, what it bore a resemblance to most. But was it anything at all? The sodden fall of a kernel or heavy burr, or a piece of mortar loosened from the wall surface by his recent gymnastic efforts, could have caused it as well.

Alertness was ebbing again, as nothing followed for a moment or two.

Then a twig snapped. The smallest of small twigs. Little better than a membrane. Still over there on the outside, not in here.

The wind was from behind her, blowing outward across the wall, as it had been all along. Not strong; of an impetus enough only to sway dangling leaves a little, to carry scents from one part to another. To carry the scent of the many dead over the wall and beyond. The many dead, and the one living. But what nostrils could detect such a thing? What senses were keen en——?

There was a huff. The sound of hot body breath being blown against a surface that acted upon it as a sort of sounding board. As if nostrils were being pointed searchingly against the wall. But distended vents of nostrils, tubes of sonorousness.

There was something *living* near her. It was a feeling, a surety, a knowledge, that grew on her without any further audible proof to confirm it. Every nerve in her body, every hair follicle in her head, told her so. And the longer the silence continued, the stronger the impression grew. As though, while she held her breath, listening through, something else was bated near her, listening also. More than just listening with ear. Identifying her with rippling pores of acuteness. Projected waves of awareness, magnetized with some sort of powerful, leashed dynamism, reached her through the bulky stone barrier. Something, someone, was present there, hidden from sight on the other side of it. Stalking her in complete immobility, so to speak.

Her screams, just now, had drawn something to her. It couldn't be a human being, it was too stealthy. A dog, perhaps? But a dog would bark or at least growl its distrust. This thing was still. Deadly still, venomously still.

She couldn't stand the prolonged tension any longer. A tension not alone generated from her, but that was a two-way current, flowing both to and from her. "Is that you?" she quavered. "Why are you so still?"

She knew it couldn't be. He would have come back in

the car. Or if not, there would at least have been the sound
of hurrying footsteps, unconcealed, the drag of a ladder, a
hail to her.

There was a rasping, along the outer side of the wall, in
answer to her voice. A sandpapery friction, directly abreast
of where she cowered. The sound—the sound that a cat
sometimes produces when it tries its claws on something.
Following it an instant later, she could detect a vibration of
the ground, communicated through to where she was. As
though something, some heavy body, had dropped heavily.
Had flung itself up first, and then dropped frustratedly
back again.

"Who is it?" she cried sharply. "Who's there?"

A spring is soundless, until it meets its objective, and yet
somehow she knew that something had sprung. Some disturbance of the air told her. A moment later, in confirmation, somewhere over her there was a creak, as of wood
being strained, a great rustling of leaves. And yet at the
moment there was a lull in the wind, there was nothing to
cause it.

Her eyes flew up to that bough that spanned the wall
almost directly over her. It was thick, well rounded, heavy
enough to bear—many things. Something had happened to
it; it had altered. Dark as it was, she could see that a
change had taken place in it. It had stood out straight until
now, well clear of the top of the wall; it had been horizontal to the trunk. Now it was sloping downward, was far
lower at its outer end, where her eyes couldn't follow it,
than in at the trunk. More than that, it was grazing the
wall. It was emitting sound. It was tapping lightly against
the top edge of the wall in vibration, at point of fulcrum; it
was fluctuating noticeably, it was shivering under pressure.
Something had hold of it—or was on it, clinging in deli-
cate, wary, painful ascent, up and in toward the tree heart.

She couldn't summon up any more voice. "Who is it?"
she whispered hoarsely. She couldn't tear herself away,
turn and run as she wanted to. She was rooted there,
hypnotized as in a nightmare, head straining back, staring
up into the blackness over her, that was like something
gathering itself to a head.

There hadn't been anything to strike light up there before. The tree was shrouded by the other trees around it; the wall and the ground below were shrouded by all alike. The moon was there all along somewhere in the background ready to supply the kindling, but with nothing to receive it.

Now something did. Through the stirring, undulating masses of leaves that garnished the outer end of the bough where it vanished across the wall, something peered through at her, through and downward. Something faintly lucent, palely green, phosphorescent. Like an avid, remorseless eye, become visible by drawing to a head upon itself the unsuspected moon motes swimming invisibly in the darkness, and now aflame, sighted balefully down upon her through the covert of leaves.

Her mouth parted spasmodically, trying to give the last cry that there was already no time for. The death cry that was too late.

Manning arrived on the scene almost immediately afterward, this time. He had been with Robles when the flash reached the central *commandancia*, and came out in the same car with him.

A number of the official departmental cars that had preceded them were strung in a line along the outside of the wall. Three or four ladders, with policemen guarding their bases, were tilted to the wall as the shortest and easiest way of getting in and out. It had happened all the way around from the main entrance.

They tried to keep Manning out, as an unauthorized person, as he tried to clamber up the rungs of one of these at Robles' heels. He grabbed the police inspector by the tail of his coat, hung on tight, refusing to be parted from him.

"He's with me," Robles said briefly.

On the inside of the wall there was a complement to each ladder, to give access to the ground. They turned and went down these backwards.

That whole immediate section of the cemetery had been turned into a grotesque charivari of portable, highpowered, icy-white lights slanted at cross-purposes to one another whose thick beams were edged with violet. Around and about them were the occasional blue flares of photographic flashlights, the yellow bees of pocket lights flitting all over far and near, some of them momentarily playing up the inscription on the headstone as it sidled across it. Red cigarette and cigar embers would glow occasionally from some grave mound, where someone had sat down for a moment to rest or tie a shoelace or compare notes with somebody else. The place was a madhouse of swirling, irreverent activity.

At the foot of one of the ladders a grief-stunned youth in a belted craverette topcoat, hatless and disheveled with shock, was being held up on his feet between a policeman and a man in plain clothes. He kept straining away from them, shoulders and head forward, toward a spot farther along at the base of the wall where the beams of several of the high-powered lights fell interlocked in a pool, terrible in its dazzling clarity. There was sacking spread there. His sobs kept coming, low and pulsing, from his stomach. You could see it go in and out each time one sounded. His face was a white mask that didn't move any more.

"*El novio*," one of the men explained in answer to Robles' inquiry in passing. The sweetheart.

Some martinet near by snapped, "Shut that man up. Take him out of here or else give him something to keep him quiet! He only makes it worse."

Manning, who had lingered behind a moment watching him, hurried to rejoin Robles. Robles was at the sacking, standing there motionless. The American arrived just at the wrong time.

It was awful, even worse than the first one had been. That had been given some semblance of concealment and classic repose at the morgue. This was madness, strewn upon the ground. Manning stepped hastily backward out of the glare and furtively wiped his mouth on his sleeve. Robles stared down, his face impassive but sweating a little at the temples. He did something with his little finger, and it was hidden again.

The pertinent details were being poured into his ear by

one of his men, standing just outside the radius of light. He seemed not to be listening at all. Only one thing about him moved, his eyes. They took in everything, darting about restlessly: over the ground, up the trunk of the death tree, out along the bough, then down again along the wall, boxing in the setting in a complete little square.

He spoke at last. "Eyewitnesses—none, you say. Very well then, secondary witnesses."

A shifty-eyed man in his thirties stepped forward into the light. "Juan Gomez, thirty-six Avenida Betancourt," Robles' second reeled off in the background.

"—luckily he came back with me. He didn't want to trust the ladder out of his sight, I guess. Anyway when we got back here, it was strangely quiet. I called to her, and she didn't answer any more. I put the ladder to the wall and started over, to see what had happened to her. I thought maybe somebody else had gotten her out during my absence. Before I'd even gotten down on the inside, I heard him give a yell out there on his side. He'd already found some bloodstained marks or tracks on the outside of the wall—"

Robles seemed not to have been listening. All he said was, "You'll be required to appear at the inquest. And give us your right name before you leave here tonight, Señor Gomez."

"But I'm a family man—"

"Where you were visiting is none of our business. You were out late in your car, that will be sufficient. Next."

The gateman was shoved forward into the light, spoke his piece, relegated to the outer darkness again.

"—and I thought she'd left already. I'd seen some woman go by, all in black, and, well my eyes aren't so good any more, especially in the twilight. So I gave the warning signal, and locked up. They're supposed to know at what time the grounds close—"

Again Robles acted as though he hadn't heard a word. His head hadn't once turned toward the speaker.

Distant sounds, of men calling to one another from various remote parts of the grounds, attracted his attention. He turned his head away from what lay before him on the ground for the first time, spoke sharply to one of the underlings nearest him. "What are they doing out there? Call them back, the fools. It's not in here any more, they're just wasting their time."

"But the trees are quite thick in places, especially toward the center," remonstrated the subordinate. "And this wall which completely encloses it would act as an effective pen. On the east side it's even lighter than here and spiked with broken bottle glass———"

"Haven't you eyes? You were all here half an hour before I was. Anyone can see that it got out again as it got in."

Manning turned toward him in time to see him crouch down close to the gruesome litter, remove some indeterminate, blood-caked, boat-shaped object adhering to the remains themselves. He straightened again, transferred it to a clean piece of white paper. A tiny stem could now be seen to project from one end of it. Even yet it was hard to tell what it was, without his word of explanation. Its patina disguised it.

"A leaf," he rapped out, in the sudden attentive silence that had fallen. "This was originally a leaf. One of God's green leaves, before it became encrusted with death matter. There are dozens of them, clinging all over her, like feathers to a half-plucked fowl. They don't fall this time of the year. They were not on the ground originally." His eyes flicked to the bough above. "They were shaken down upon her. It dropped down upon her bodily, from up there, in a shower of leaves. Her cries must have attracted it to her as it prowled the outside of the wall. Then, the carnage perpetrated, it sprang up to the bough again, crossed over the top of the wall, and returned whence it had come. Where are your eyes? What were you doing here while you were waiting for me? A glass." It was handed to him and he traced it along the contour of the trunk, at a distance close enough to obtain a clear focus. "Keep your heads out of the light, stand over on the side. Now. Do you see? It is plain enough for you? You detect the livid gashes on the bark from its claws? They are deepest at the top, each one; they are full punctures there, tapering off to a mere shallow scratch at the bottom. That means they were made by the beast *going up*. Its claws dug in to obtain a hold, slipped slightly downward each time with its bodily weight, then were transferred to the next claw hold higher up, until it had reached the bough. Even so, it probably made its ascent almost more quickly than the eye could follow—but the traces of it do not vanish so swiftly, fortunately. Get them on your negatives." And as he handed back the borrowed glass, he added disgustedly: "You should really be provided with alms bowls and sticks and sent to join the other blind on the benches around the Plaza Mayor."

Manning knew he was there only by sufferance, should have kept his mouth shut. But he couldn't resist breaking in scathingly: "And in the face of that, you still think it's a jaguar?"

Robles whirled on him. "What do you mean?"

The American eyed him almost contemptuously. "A jungle animal, once in here, would turn its back on all this greenery, trees and plants and protective shrubbery, all the very things its instinct leads it to seek, and deliberately return of its own choice to the stone and asphalt traps of the streets out there? Ha!"

One of the other operatives rushed to the defense of his superior, probably to regain his esteem, before Robles himself could answer. "There are traces left by bloodied paws on the outside of the wall, where it dropped down *after* the attack had been completed. We have already photographed them."

It was a telling blow; Manning's mouth opened, closed again, without his being able to utter a word.

"And just for *golpe de gracia*, look at that," Robles said crushingly. He borrowed a small pair of forceps, stooped down swiftly over the mangled form a second time, fortunately keeping his back to all of them as he did so. Manning couldn't see what it was he was using the forceps to extract, only the wrench of his elbow joint that accompanied the act.

He stood up again, turned, again bedded it on paper. This time it looked like a small thorn, curved, and thicker at one end than the other.

"And in the face of this, you still think it's *not* a jaguar?" he parodied tartly. "Hold that glass over it a minute, for señor the know-it-all."

Manning peered down at it, magnified. It was enlarged now to a miniature tusk, of hornlike substance, broken off short at the wide end. "What is it, a tooth? A fang?"

"For anyone that knows so much about jaguars, you are not very good; you should study up on your zoology," was Robles' merciless retort. "It is the tip of one of its claws, broken off short. And left imbedded in her throat."

Manning couldn't answer for a minute, but he wouldn't give in, retract. He drew his head away from the derisive proximity with which Robles was holding the nauseating token up to him, muttered disconcertedly: "It's against all the laws of nature for it to turn its back on here and go out there again."

Robles raised his voice overbearingly. "When the laws of nature conflict with indisputable evidence like this, the laws of nature go into the discard. Who is to say what they are anyway—you? I? Are we animals ourselves? Not enough is known about this species, in the first place, to lay down hard-and-fast rules of behavior for them. They can be as unpredictable as human beings, for all we know. Perhaps it is *not* the nature of jaguars to return to built-up streets. *This one* did. Perhaps it has grown accustomed to its lair. Perhaps it is the one exception to the rule. But exception or not, it is still a jaguar!"

The heretic properly and publicly shown the error of his ways, to the obvious satisfaction of all his men, he turned back to the business at hand. "Who is it keeps making that noise?" he inquired irritably.

"*El novio*," someone murmured.

"Have you questioned him yet? Bring him over here."

The grief-crazed youth in the belted topcoat was hurried staggeringly forward between the two men who had been supporting him the whole time.

"Raul Belmonte," read off Robles' assistant. "Fourteen Calle San Vicente. Cashier, Banco de Comercio."

His face was pitiful. A man shouldn't love too deeply,

Manning thought, looking at it; it's better for him not to. He's more defenseless than a woman, when it comes to a thing like this, that he can't fight back against.

"Are you able to talk, Belmonte?" Robles said curtly. "Give us your story."

His voice was dead, listless.

"—I came out to telephone to her home to find out from this little servant girl who was backing us up whether she'd really started out at all. To do so, I must have entered the very establishment she was in at the time with her *compañera*, it's the only place around there one can telephone from. She must have been sitting hidden from me in a booth at the back. My back must have been to her, in the telephone enclosure off to one side, and as she left, we neither of us saw one another! Then, on finding the grounds locked, instead of leaving at once, I returned across the road a second time, to ease my disappointment with a cognac before driving off. And when I finally emerged at last and got into my car, it seemed to me that far off somewhere I heard a faint cry—I remember that now. But I thought it was my imagination, and I was too heavyhearted at not having seen her to care what it was. What had it to do with me?"

He was starting to shiver. Robles made a sign and they led him away. "Lock him up for the time being," the inspector said quietly as soon as he was out of hearing.

"Surely you don't think—?" Manning expostulated.

"Protective arrest," Robles answered. "He is a danger to himself, until he has recovered somewhat. It is written all over him."

Manning turned and moved slowly away from the hideous glare that continued to beat down on the mortal remains of Conchita Contreras. They all glanced after him curiously, noticing the thoughtful way he held his head lowered and kicked at nothing along the ground, to show the personal dissatisfaction and lack of conviction he derived from this.

"He's got an obsession, that man," he heard Robles explaining scornfully to some of his cohorts without troubling to lower his voice much, "that there is some other element than the jaguar involved in this. Don't ask me why!"

"Don't ask me either," Manning turned his head to call back. "But don't ask me to give it up." He put his foot to the lower rung of one of the ladders, to get out of the accursed place.

"It's right here before his very eyes," Robles went on in a loud, carrying voice, provoked by the opposition. "Look, the very ribs are exposed in places! Nothing human could commit such a shambles."

They were dropping slowly below Manning, a rung at a time. "And I say the very opposite," he contradicted over his shoulder, "that *only* something human could be so thorough about it. It's carried too far for even the most vicious brute animal. Their rages don't last that long, the death of the quarry ends them. Their memories are shorter—"

A hard, mirthless laugh went up all around as he straddled the top of the wall with his legs and took his unlamented and somewhat undignified departure.

4. CLO-CLO

CLO-CLO WAS RAPIDLY TIRING of the German merchant-marine officer. She wasn't sure he was German and she wasn't even sure he was a merchant-marine officer. All she knew was he came from one of those countries where the people have butter-colored hair and blue eyes and can't speak Spanish properly, and that he had tarnished brass buttons on his short blue jacket, instead of the bone kind other people wore.

There was nothing personal in this rapid tiring on her part. Just as there was nothing personal in anything she did after six in the evening. Those were her working hours. He hadn't been any too loaded with money even when she first met him—some of his shipmates must have warned him, before he came ashore down on the coast, about bringing his whole pay up to the city with him at one time—and now he had slowed down to about a drink a half-hour. Also, he kept wanting to marry her all the time, and that made for heavy conversation. The main thing wrong with him, though, was he was holding her up, making her behind time on her schedule of nightly rounds. She'd have to skip her ten-o'clock stop and go straight on to the midnight one, from here.

Clo-Clo adhered to a rigid timetable. She lived by the clock. If you didn't you didn't get anywhere. You had to

work fast, you had to keep going. Each night had its fixed
stops, and each stop had its hour and its allotted duration.
The daylight hours up to, say, about seven or eight in the
evening, that was strictly antemeridian, that didn't count.
You didn't expect anything. You didn't get anything. You
stayed home and did your hair. You washed stockings.
You lazed around. If you felt good maybe you even gave
the poor old lady a hand, with that never-ending cooking
and dishing it out to hungry mouths that she was always
doing. Or if you went out, it was just to get something you
needed, a bit of nail polish at the five-and-ten. The grand
sortie didn't come until around eight, eight-thirty. You
looked things over, you got their feel, you warmed yourself
up. Her nine-o'clock stop was the Elite Bar. This was the
Elite Bar now. There wasn't really much doing yet. The
real swells, the real spenders, were all still at home with
their families, lingering over their cigars and after-dinner
drinks. At nine o'clock you got things like this foreign sea
officer, good enough to kill time with, a couple of brandies
over a bar.

Ten to eleven was a notch up the social scale. Places like
the Tivoli and the Miraflor Gardens. The swells were all at
shows around now, they still hadn't appeared yet. You
hung around over a table, with young writers, clerks, busi-
nessmen. Wine now.

Midnight to about two was the zenith. Meridian of her
"day." That was when the shows let out. They let out late
in Ciudad Real. The Casino Bleu, the Madrid out in the
park (she never went out there, though; too far to walk
back in case you didn't connect), the Jockey Club, the
Tabarin, the Select. Those were the places to seek out then.
That was the cream of the night life, swarming with the
sports, the swells, the heavy spenders. Most of them had
cabaret entertainment; if not, tango bands and dancing at
the very least. Benedictine, then. Crème de menthe. Sometimes even champagne.

It tapered off quickly after that. From about three on,
that was the lees of the night. That was the time to watch
out for. That was the time when the laughter died down,
lights started thinning and the shadows came creeping on,

and if you were smart you didn't hang around any more, you went on home. It was a bad time. "The Blue Hour," some of them called it. "The Deathwatch," others. It was a time when things sometimes happened. Things they told you about behind the back of the hand. If they were going to at all, that was when they did.

So it will be seen, Clo-Clo was on the town. The technical designation for her might be a little harder to arrive at. She was acquiring a second nickname, in fact, that threatened to obliterate the first. *"Engañadora,"* the little cheat. Fulfillment withheld for promises implicit in her very presence at the places she went. She honored obligations only when cornered, and even then, in a manner that made it hardly worth while, except for professional wrestlers. She had already had one or two brushes with the police; not because of her supposed activities, but because of their absence. Others in her own immediate bracket would warn her, "Look out, *chica,* you'll be getting a bad reputation. Once you do, they'll steer clear of you like a bad case of smallpox." In other words, in the underworld a bad reputation was directly inverse to what was commonly meant by one in the upperworld.

Nonetheless, Clo-Clo remained stubbornly, you might even say fanatically, virtuous at heart. Her every instinct was that of the good, respectable, industrious middle-class girl who expects to be a wife someday. She had her own future all staked out. By thirty at the latest she was going to be married to some honest, hard-working fellow, and have a raft of kids, and maybe a little produce farm outside of town, just a patch. And if any of them were girls, and so much as *looked* at anybody, she'd knock the left side of their faces loose from the right.

She still had eleven years and six months to go.

This interlude, therefore, was not a question of looseness of character, it was a matter of financial stringency. Her intrinsic morality was not in the least impaired by it. Strangers in bars couldn't reach that. It was simply being bent a little to permit her to achieve financial security.

At home, in the tumbledown shack on Rivera Street, with shoals of kids sleeping all over the place, they knew that Clo-Clo was not exactly a saint, but the money sure came in handy. They didn't inquire too closely into her comings and goings. They had a euphemism for her prolonged and nightly absences, among themselves, among their friends and neighbors, if anyone inquired for her. *"Salió para dar una vuelta."* She went out to take a stroll. Well, she had, in a way. One of these little strolls of hers had once taken her clear across the spine of the continent, as far as Buenos Aires. But she had come back two days later perfectly unharmed, having jumped the train just one station before it got in in order to retain her freedom of movement, and with marvelous tales to tell.

Her fat, slow-moving mother would sigh and shrug as she broomed a few of the younger kids out of the way. She was a good daughter. Here in the home, she was a good daughter. Outside: well, that was outside. After all, who was perfect in this world? Should she, a mother, throw the first stone at her own child? Besides, it was only for now, a great change was coming someday. Didn't she, Clo-Clo, say so herself over and over? "You wait, *mamita,* when I'm thirty I'm going to stop being bad, I'm going to be good after that."

And now here she was, stuck in a nine-o'clock stop with a nine-o'clock patron, and it was rapidly nearing eleven. And one of the sentimental type, the worst kind. The more sentimental they got, the less they seemed to spend. This one, perhaps more perspicacious than she gave him credit for being and sensing something within her beneath the scabby outer shell, wanted her to come back to the ship with him, wanted to marry her and take her to someplace called Copenhague and settle down with her there on a dairy farm that he would buy.

This was sheer nonsense as far as Clo-Clo was concerned. A peso slipped into one's hand at leave-taking, as a little gesture of gratitude for one's time and entertainment efforts, was worth a dozen offers of marriage in Copen, whatever it was.

She was sitting perched there on one of the tall bar stools alongside him, hair a short-cropped black chrysanthemum mop, in a pert bang above the eyes. Her attitude was a clever synchronization of absorption and vacuity; the former assumed, the latter real. She was sitting sidewise, with her face toward him, the point of her elbow to the bar and the back of her head balanced in her outspread hand. She sidled one leg unnoticeably off the rung of the stool, felt for the floor with it, and poised it toe down, having decided to break this off short without wasting any more time about it.

"And you'd like it, I know you would."

"Sure," Clo-Clo said readily. "Where'd you say it was again?"

Clo-Clo was having trouble with this. She knew the names of most of the principal countries, England, France, Spain, like that. You picked them up around town. It was either a country she had never heard of, or it was an utter lie. She decided it was an utter lie, since there couldn't be many more countries than England, France, Spain. It was time to get going. The shows would be out soon. Her second leg shifted down and lined up against the first. There was only one more thing that had to leave the chair now.

He noticed finally that her entire figure was about to leave him, just as her attention had some time before. He thought it was because his hospitality was remiss. He looked a little hurt, stopped offering her his heart and soul. He called the barman over. "Another for the lady." He'd already told her he didn't like to see her drink. He'd already started in trying to change her around.

"No, I've got to go," Clo-Clo said. She was off the stool now, and he couldn't get her back. Every move in these breakaways had to be carried out craftily like that, to accomplish them successfully. Now if he reached for her to hold her, she'd just have to step quickly backwards. "I've got a date."

"But this is one now you're having with me."

"Sure, but I've already had it, it's over now. So long."

"But I want you to marry me."

"Day after tomorrow."

She was two stools away now. The barman cut in sidewise toward her, said in a rebuking undertone. "What's your hurry? He's buying good and steady, what do you want to break it up for?"

"Give me my commission," she said out of the corner of her mouth. "Come on, or I'll tell him you insulted me. And you know what that'll mean; the mirror behind you, all the glasses on the shelves—"

"You little bandit," he said bitterly. Their hands touched briefly across the top of the bar.

"I can go to Robles' just as well, I don't have to come in here. You're not losing money on me."

Her late host tried to reach her with a persuasive sweep of his arm. She knew enough to stay back beyond reach of it. "Come here a minute, Clo-Clo. Little Clo-Clo, don't leave me like this. We were just beginning to get along so well."

"I know, but time's up now."

He wavered toward the entrance after her, both arms out. "I wanted you to marry me. I wanted to take you out of this." He seemed undecided for a minute whether to cry maudlinly or fly into a rage.

She got out over the threshold backwards. "Keep him in there, Manuel."

Manuel just gave her a dirty look, for cutting short what had been a profitable session.

Her recent escort stood there in the lighted entrance, looking out after her. "You're a fine one," he called resentfully.

"You better go back to your ship, mister, and get some sleep. Marry the girl in the next port you come to, instead. After all, we're all alike."

She moved on down the narrow, crooked, poorly lighted street, swinging her bag jauntily at her side, a long-legged dryad in a tight black satin skirt. She glanced back once and he was leaning up against the side of the door, with his face burrowed into the right angle of his upthrust arm, *crying* because he'd lost her, after looking for her half around the world. Probably it was just the alcohol alone. How could you tell when it was real and when it wasn't, anyway, this love stuff?

"Maybe I should've at that," she dismissed him with an

unconcerned shrug. "Who knows, maybe if I could see ahead. I'd be sorry that I didn't."

Around the very next corner a sudden confrontation occurred. He stopped short, came back to her. "Oh, it's you, is it?"

"Have we met before?" Clo-Clo asked with polite uncertainty.

"Have we met before!" he scowled. "You were coming back in five minutes, and I sat up there alone waiting for you all the rest of the night, like a fool! The whole hotel staff was laughing at me behind their hands, when I had to walk out in front of them by myself the next morning!"

Clo-Clo shoveled her hands ingenuously toward him. "I couldn't find the room again, when I tried to get back to you. There were so many halls and turns, I got lost. Was it my fault?"

"You know what you are? You're a cheat. A false alarm."

She touched the underside of his chin lightly with one finger. "Don't be sore. Look at all the fun you'd already had out of me by then, anyway. You told me so yourself. You shouldn't be a hog."

"I wasn't out for fun," he let her know aggrievedly. He reached. "C'mere you. I've got something coming to me." Clo-Clo did the back-step again. "No you haven't," she laughed. "That was then, this is now. No long-term credit extended." She shifted around to the opposite side of an octagonal advertisement kiosk, saw to it that it stayed between them.

"C'mere, or I'll come over there and get you. You're coming with me if I have to drag you by the back of the neck."

She just laughed, flirted her handbag out toward him at the end of its strap.

He saw that threatening wouldn't work, he tried bribery. "C'mere," he coaxed, "I'll buy you a drink."

She made a face at him. "I've just had a drink." Return engagements, she knew by long experience, were no good. Never any good. Not with her, anyway. There was always a redoubled vigilance on the part of the investor, remembering how he had been given the slip the first time, and she found it twice as hard to get away. Fool them once and then stay away from them was the best policy.

He held out both hands toward her, appealingly. "Ah, come on, won't you? I like you. I can't help it, *moma,* there's something about you that's gotten to me. You're so hard to pin down. First you're here, and then you're not here."

"Isn't it the truth, though?" she laughed. "And now take a good look, I'm not here."

She glanced back once, a wholly precautionary measure to make sure that he wouldn't rush after her and try to take her by surprise, and he was still standing there forlornly where she'd left him, in the middle of the sidewalk. Looking after her sort of wistfully, as though hoping she'd change her mind. She really must have made an impression on him, she reflected indifferently. As for her, she already couldn't have told what he'd looked like very precisely, although she'd just left him.

She took a look into the Select from the outside first. It was a little bit slow tonight in there, for some reason, so she decided on the Tabarin instead. It always paid to reconnoiter first. After all, even the best of places had its off-nights, and once you'd sunk your own twenty centavos into a grenadine, you couldn't get it back again.

The Tabarin was brimming over. She retouched herself at a mirror panel in the lobby and went sauntering in.

You couldn't demand a cut in these swell places. You had to be glad if they'd let you in at all.

The barman looked her over, got her immediately. "Take the one on the end," he said, just as she was about to come to rest on one of the coral leather stools. "I want the middle left clear for paying customers."

She shifted acquiescently, at the same time letting him know pertly: "Don't let it worry you, I don't expect to be on it very long."

An unaccompanied, rather insipid-looking youth with a needle-pointed mustache came up the steps out of the dancing room, stood up to the bar, and gulped a quick drink between pieces without taking the time to sit down.

He felt the eye flash and turned to look at her, glass in hand. She smiled, blew a slender wand of smoke at his face. It didn't reach, but there was no mistaking her aim, she'd pointed it with her mouth. He must have had someone waiting for him in there. He turned away again as though he hadn't seen her; just a trifle more priggishly than was necessary. He threw down a coin, went back again, just as the next tango got under way.

The barman cautioned her, as soon as he'd gone, "Now listen, nothing too raw, understand? Leave off this smoke-ring stuff. Watch your manners."

"How much are you charging to give lessons in deportment?" she asked wearily. "Who dolls the place up more, me or that dead-fish face you frighten them away from your bar with?"

"There are worse faces than mine," he grunted.

"You've been looking at people upside down." It wasn't really a wrangle, they understood one another too well. Just idle repartee while they were both killing time.

She would have gone back to the Select after all, only she'd already invested her twenty-five centavos here and she was going to cash in on it.

Somebody else came up the steps from the lower level, presently. This time it was a somewhat portly, dignified-looking gentleman of uncertain years, whose florid mustache was just beginning to whiten at the tips. He carried himself erect enough, and his skin had a healthy coppery tint to it, as though he spent a great deal of time in the open, but just now he wore a harassed expression, as though he had been greatly bored, was wishing he was anyplace but here. He threw away the mangled remnants of a cigar and stepped up to the bar.

"Could you tell me—" Then he became aware of Clo-Clo, muffled the rest of it.

The barman said, "Where that page is standing, señor."

Just before the door closed after him he took another brief look at her. The page turned and entered after him, probably to be on hand in case he required a whisk broom or hairbrush.

He emerged and headed back toward the dancing room,

but not without throwing still one more quick look in her direction.

"Technique a little rusty," Clo-Clo thought with a chuckle. "Probably has had a wife since the last time he tried it."

She put out her cigarette, got up, sauntered over to the page, drink in hand. The barman looked like the kind that would empty it out on you behind your back, if you left it unguarded, to get you out of the place.

"How'd you do just now?" she inquired with ready camaraderie.

The boy's eyes rounded enthusiastically. "A whole solid peso for doing nothing! He just looked at himself in the glass, asked if I knew who you were, and asked me about how old I would take him to be!"

"Ricardo, you're on duty," the barman warned disapprovingly.

"So am I—from now on," Clo-Clo said to herself, drifting back to her original perch again. She'd found out all she wanted to know.

She gambled on it and waited patiently, although if she had turned out to be wrong, the time wastage would have been irretrievable. But she was usually right, and she turned out to be this time too. Two tangos later he had come back again.

He advanced halfway to the bar, took a good hard look at her, then made an abrupt turn and went in the same doorway as previously.

"He didn't come back here to go in there, he came back to see if I was still out here," she told herself knowingly.

She snapped her fingers authoritatively to the barman, to show she was on the warpath, not idling any more. "Put a little more water in this." She wanted to dilute the grenadine dye as much as possible.

He handed it back to her with a lethal scowl. "What're you trying to do, make it last over the week end?" He didn't guess what she was up to, or he would probably have frustrated her intentions by purposely delaying to return the denatured drink to her.

As it was, she got over to the door, glass in hand, just a

bare second before it reopened. She was standing there saying something to the page as her quarry sought to pass in back of her. He would have made it without grazing her, but she moved her elbow back into him as he tried to. The elbow of the hand holding the drink. The glass turned neatly and the grenadine-water went down the side of her dress.

She let him show all the dismay. He showed enough for two. She was good-natured about it. He flung out a handkerchief, dipped one knee, and patted at it all the way down.

"Things like that will happen. I assure you it's nothing, señor. It's my fault, I shouldn't have been in the way."

"You must come over here and at least let me buy you another one."

She shook her head with sad indifference. "It's not much fun drinking alone."

He glanced out toward the dancing room. "I—I'll sit with you for a minute. My family's in there, and I have to get back."

He was taking an awful chance, in Clo-Clo's opinion, but that was his lookout, not her own. She settled herself demurely beside him, on the same stool as before.

"Champagne for the señorita. Pol Roget."

The barman was all smiles for her now. He even scraped, trotted out the two French words he knew, reserved only for champagne buyers. "Monsou. Madamasella."

"To a lucky accident."

"To a delightful accident," Clo-Clo improved on it.

They became acquainted by leaps and bounds. He began to smile more and more often. The smiles became grins. The grins became gusts of hearty laughter. Once or twice he glanced behind him, in remembered caution.

"Don't you think the music is a little too loud out here?" he suggested finally. Since he had just come from where it was actually playing, he seemed to have developed unusual sensitivity all at once. But then maybe in there there hadn't been anybody he considered worth listening to.

Clo-Clo had no fault to find with this point. "Yes it is, it makes it hard to hear what one is saying," she agreed.

"Barman, is there some other place around here where we can get further away from the music, be a little more secluded?"

"There is a little private room, looking out on the rear terrace, if the señor and lady would like to try that. Straight back at the end of the corridor there."

"Send in another bottle, and something to eat." Then, as an afterthought, he came back a step, leaned toward the barman confidentially. "And in case anyone happens to be looking for me, I have gone out to get a breath of air for a minute." He put something in his hand. "*That* way." He pointed in the opposite direction to the one they were about to take.

"Hit me on the back again," he pleaded in a strangled voice. "I can't help it. I laugh until my throat closes up—" The rest of it was lost in an exhausted cough. He continued to shake, wiping the excess water from his eyes.

Clo-Clo jumped up from the table alarmedly, ran around behind him. "You should rest for five minutes." Thump. "You'll kill yourself." Thump. "Isn't there something *sad* we can talk about, just until you get over this?"

He continued to shake. "We tried that," he said weakly. "That was what we were supposed to be doing this time. But even when you try to tell something sad, it comes out funny. Harder than that, there must be a piece of chicken lodged there."

"Wait a minute, I'll pour a little cold champagne down the back of your neck. The shock may dislodge it. Like with hiccups. Do you mind?"

He waved a hand in helpless permission. "Go ahead. I don't care what you do to me. If I die here in this chair, it's been worth it—"

"I'll get up high," the helpful Clo-Clo said. "So it'll give a little splash." She pulled her own chair around to the rear of his, stood up on it, and tilted a champagne bottle with both hands. "Now get ready, here it comes—"

The door was flung open without the preliminary of any knock, and what can best be described as a gasp of virtuous outrage entered and swirled about the room like a current of chill air. Its producer remained posed accusingly at the threshold without coming forward. It was the same priggish young man with the needle-pointed mustaches whom Clo-Clo had glimpsed earlier in the bar alcove.

They were both staring at him by indirection, in a wall mirror opposite that gave them back his reflection, coming from behind them.

Clo-Clo's supper companion murmured ruefully for her private benefit, "That was the shock I needed. It went down by itself."

She regained the floor with a lithe bound, returned the bottle of christening champagne to its bucket.

No one had said anything yet, at least not for general inclusion.

The dinner-jacketed sphinx in the open doorway finally broke the ice. He said a single word: *"Papa!"*

The older man in the chair waved his hand disgustedly, without turning to look at him. "Please close the door. I'll be right out."

"I'll wait for you in the foyer. You came here with *us*, please remember that!"

Clo-Clo's host mumbled something indistinct that sounded like, "Try and forget it!" The door closed.

Clo-Clo gasped, "Not your *son!* Why you hardly look—"

He sighed, shrugged, clapped his sides frustratedly as he rose to his feet. "It is having sons like him that makes one old," he complained half under his breath.

Then his expression changed, he smiled at her, wistfully, almost tenderly. He took her hand between both of his, carried it to his lips. "Never mind, we had some fun, didn't we? I'll have to go now. I don't know whether we'll ever meet again. We live outside of town, and I'll never hear the end of this. But, little Clo-Clo, you're a lovely girl. You've made me feel young again for an hour or two. Like I used to be years ago. You've made me feel happy with your laughter and your little ways. Let me do something for you. You deserve it. That sour-pussed daughter-in-law of mine gets enough of it as it is."

"Not so much, señor!" For probably the first time in her life the protest was genuine, almost alarmed.

He'd given her a hundred and fifty pesos, out of a wallet that must have held close to a thousand.

"Take it, take it," he said. He folded her fingers persuasively back upon it, patted her hand reassuringly. "Anyone that calls you bad, they must be blind," he said with low-voiced sincerity. "To make others happy, what better claim to goodness is there than that?"

She looked down, abashed for a moment. She was used to all sorts of compliments, but not to having her sanctity praised.

He gave a little smile of mischievous approval.

"That's right, put it down where they won't get at it, don't let them take it from you, hang onto it." And then, almost as though some premonition were assailing him, he urged: "Be careful, little Clo-Clo. I know I've got champagne in me, but— Don't let anything happen to you. Your way of life is so dangerous at times. I am a man that would not hurt you. But there are others— Go home, now that I've given you this. Don't stay out any more tonight."

"I won't," she promised fervently, hands pressed tight to her bosom where the money now rested. "Believe me, I won't!"

Something about her must be still getting at him. He even made a move toward removing a large diamond ring on his little finger. Then he changed his mind regretfully. "Those two vultures would miss it the first thing, and only make trouble for you."

The door was flung open again at this point. The younger man was even sorer than before. "Papa! The car is waiting. I've told Elena you've been suffering from an upset stomach. How much longer do you think I can keep her from finding out about this—this situation I've found you in?"

"I'm coming!" Clo-Clo's late host thundered infuriatedly. "I'm coming, you damn kill-joy!"

He turned and went out after him. Even so, his last thought was of Clo-Clo. As he closed the door lingeringly after him, he repeated what he'd said before, in a poignant murmur of farewell. "Don't let anything happen to you, little Clo-Clo. Take care of yourself."

She got up and waltzed around the room, holding skirt aloft at waist level and revealing a sector of abbreviated pink hip trunk. A chair went over at her spinning passage and she let it lie. She snatched up one of their partially filled glasses and drained it on the wing, put it back again the next time she came around. Then the second one. Then she stopped whirling and attended to the bottle remaining in the ice bucket. This was not dipsomania on her part, it was thrift pure and simple. It was a shame to waste good champagne that had already been paid for.

She was standing there with her back to the ceiling-high terrace windows, alternating gulps of champagne and bites of chicken sandwich, when something unaccountably made her turn her head. The drapes had been drawn closed over the window, for privacy, by the waiter when they first came in. There was a gap, however, midway down the long intersection where they had fallen partly open again. A feeling of being looked at through it came over her. It was so strong she even went over toward it and tried to peer through. There wasn't anything or anyone out there. Just the canalized light gleam cast on the terrace flooring by the room lights in here escaping through.

She came out of the room a few minutes later, munching the last of the chicken. The barman, wiping a glass, said jeeringly out of the corner of his mouth as she passed, "Left flat, eh?"

She thumbed her nose at him in a long, lingering farewell insult, that lasted from the third bar stool all the way out to the porte-cochere, turning her head slowly in time with it as she did so.

And now to go home. She was whistling softly under her breath as the pinkish-amber glow of the Tabarin's lights faded out behind her. There were stars overhead, and the night felt cool and good. And the hundred fifty pesos at her bosom felt even better. She snapped her thumbnail at the fluted iron post of a street lamp as she passed it, just for luck. It hummed hollowly for several moments after, like a muted organ note.

She was passing through tortuous, cobbled San Rafael Street a few minutes later, when a church bell somewhere near by tolled the hour. She counted the strokes as they lowered out above her in the night stillness, each one seeming to hang vibrantly suspended until the next had come along to displace it.

Three already. She shivered defensively, quickened her step a little. The Deathwatch was beginning. The Blue Hours. Time to get in, pull walls around you. She quitted the sliver of sidewalk, took the indented middle of the narrow thoroughfare, undeterred by the thread of open sewage coiled along it. A moment later she was glad she'd done so. A columnar blackness standing unsuspected in the niche of a setback doorway found voice as she went by, slurred softly: "Hey, what's your hurry?"

"Shop closed!" she snapped, and quickened to a run, and kept it up until she'd reached the lower end of San Rafael, and it had opened up into one of the subsidiary plazas that dotted the town. This one had palms, a bandstand kiosk, a gleaming white statue of one of the heroes of independence, and faint arc lights gleaming in misty violet around the four sides of it. It was dead to the world.

She cut across it, and on the other side had a choice of two. San Jacinto was the shortest way out to her own place, but it was another of those long, dismal, poorly lighted lanes like the one she'd just left. 15th of May would take her a little out of her way, but it boasted a little better lighting and there was an occasional food or drink shop to be found along it. Other nights when she came along here she never hesitated, she took the quickest way. Tonight, for some reason, she was in a creepy mood, shy of dark and lonely places. She entered the Calle Quince de Mayo. The two diverged like the arms of a narrow V.

She had just gone past a small, dimly-lighted *bodega*, a drinking and eating place patronized by the poor, a few moments later, when someone came out and hailed her.

"Hola! Is that you, Clo-Clo?"

It was one of the others of her own immediate sorority, a girl known as La Bruja (the witch). She had a shawl coifed around her head to ward off the night chill, and might have looked almost nun-like save for the cigarette suspended between her lips without benefit of fingers. She stood there arms akimbo.

Clo-Clo turned and went back to her, glad to find herself in someone else's company, even though it meant a temporary delay in her return home. After all, you didn't have to be afraid of another girl.

"What's the matter, you getting airy?" La Bruja demanded.

"Get out," Clo-Clo chuckled disarmingly.

"Going home already? How are things?"

Clo-Clo hooked two fingers, kissed their tips to denote the indescribable. "What a night! I ran into Croesus himself."

"Who's he, one of these rich *paisanos* in town for a spree?"

"No, it's somebody my mother's always talking about." She described the supper in glowing terms, prudently omitting all reference to the hundred-and-fifty peso bonus. It probably wouldn't have been believed anyway. "You know, I'm almost frightened. When things are so good, they say it's a sign you're in for trouble, to watch out. I hope this night don't end up bad."

They stood for a while like that chatting, two lone figures on the night-bound sidewalk. "Knocking off?" La Bruja asked finally.

"Sure am. I don't want to crowd my luck any."

"I guess I will too. Got a cigarette left on you?"

"I'll do better than that for you. Come on. I'll blow you to a cup of steaming coffee. I keep feeling chilly down the middle of my back."

They went back inside the place La Bruja had just left. There was no one in it but the proprietor, a weary-looking man in rolled shirt sleeves and a floor-length apron. They sat down at one of the battered wooden tables.

The first thing Clo-Clo did was kick off her shoes under it, wiggle her toes. "Some relief, huh?"

La Bruja brooded dully down on the table top, flicked a leftover matchstick away, flapped her hand in disgusted agreement toward her.

"This is the part I like best, when it's all over. Don't have to smile, don't have to listen, don't have to watch what you say next."

"Are you that way? I'm that way, too." Clo-Clo admitted. She siphoned hot, watery coffee noisily into her mouth without lifting the cup from the table at all.

Presently, the warm brew flooding through her, she began to wax philosophical. "I wonder where we'll all be a year from now."

"Tomorrow night, for that matter," said the disgruntled La Bruja, continuing to lower down upon the table.

"Tell my fortune," Clo-Clo urged. "Come on, *chica*."

La Bruja grinned lopsidedly at her. "I know you, you little monkey, that's the reason you offered me the cup of coffee."

Clo-Clo didn't try to deny it. "After all, it's the only relaxation I ever get during the course of an evening."

La Bruja balanced her cigarette on the edge of the table. "All right," she acceded wearily, "pass me your mitt."

"No, try it with the cards. I like it better with the cards, there's more stuff to it." Clo-Clo raised her voice to the shopkeeper in the shadowy background. "Hey, got a deck of cards?"

"Yes, but I'm going to close up." He turned off a light, and doubled the previous dimness.

Clo-Clo looked around at him with a mixture of sudden annoyance and nervousness, totally unlike her usual self. "Couldn't you wait a minute, what's your hurry?" she said sharply.

"I want to get some sleep myself," he grumbled. "Think all I've got to do is stay up all night for two hustlers?"

Clo-Clo gave the table a smack. "You bring us those cards!" She wanted respect for her ten centavos. She was, for once, in the unusual position of being the customer in her own right, and she was going to get everything out of it that was coming to her.

He shuffled grudgingly forward and slapped an unsanitary deck down between them. "Five more minutes, you two," he grunted. On his way back he turned out another light. There was only one left now in the entire place, casting a smoky pool of light down over their immediate table and nothing else. The rest was all shadows.

"Will you be able to see?" Clo-Clo asked anxiously.

"Good enough." La Bruja, cigarette vibrating unsupported between her lips once more, shuffled deftly with a low whirring noise. "Cut," she ordered. She began to pay them out.

Clo-Clo pointed both elbows to the table top, rested her face between her hands, looked on absorbedly. A period of low-voiced intermittent recital ensued, all on La Bruja's part. Then it broke off again suddenly. There was a long pause.

Clo-Clo raised her eyes from the cards to the other girl's face. "What's the matter? Something go wrong?" La Bruja had mangled them all together, was restacking them to start over.

"What're you doing that for?"

"I want to try it over." La Bruja said noncommitally. The low-voiced recital began again. Then it stopped short again, just as before.

Once more she began over. Once more she stopped, as though at a loss.

"What do you keep quitting like that for?" Clo-Clo asked.

La Bruja shook her head slightly, whether at the question itself or at the condition that had caused the question to be asked she left unresolved.

"It's still here," she murmured finally.

Clo-Clo looked them over. "I know, but what is it?"

"It's something, but I can't make out myself what it is. It's nothing good. Wait a minute. I'll see if I can get it for you. It's dark, and that means some kind of trouble. It's a four card. It's the four of spades and it's right over you. Every time I shuffle them it keeps coming out right over you. Whatever it is, it's something that's hanging over you, that's nearing you, that's on its way." She spread her hands helplessly.

Clo-Clo rolled her eyeballs upwards half under her lids in unspoken dismay.

"Wait a minute, I'll try it again." La Bruja's hands reached out, harvested the cards into a bristling heap.

Clo-Clo turned her head stiffly aside, looked off into the shadows. "Call me if—if it comes back again." She cross-barred one index finger over the other, held them that way.

There was a period of bated waiting. She could hear the faint tick the cards made going down on the wood. It was very still in the room. The only thing that moved was a silent thing, the shadow of La Bruja's hand on the floor, rising and falling, rising and falling where Clo-Clo was looking down with averted head.

The hand stopped. The ticks of cardboard stopped. La Bruja spoke.

"It's back again. Fourth time in a row."

Clo-Clo bunched her shoulders. "It's drafty in here," she said. She turned slowly, glanced down as at something coiled to strike her. "But isn't it you that puts them there? Isn't it—isn't it your hand?"

"They come in rotation. What have I to do with that? As soon as you come out, and fall into the center place, all those that follow have their places in order around you. If I meddled with that, the fortune would be worthless."

"You mean it has been in that exact—upper corner of my card, each of the four times?"

"No, but it has been in the row over you each time. It has come out within three or four cards of your own. *It is something on its way to you.*"

Clo-Clo slashed out, caught the other's wrist in frightened appeal. Her voice broke. "Bruja. Brujita. You gotta figure out—you gotta tell me what it is! Try!"

She waited, then seeing that no answer was forthcoming, began to try to coach her in her own metier. "What does the four mean? Is it a date I should beware of? Today's the, let me see—"

"No, it's no date. There are no dates in these cards. It's in the first row over you, so it's *soon*."

"Well, is it a man?"

"No, the picture cards are men, the jacks and kings."

"Well, what could it be then? Something with four legs?

Maybe it means I'm going to be trampled by a black horse."

La Bruja shrugged.

Clo-Clo snapped her fingers. "I've got it. Four. Something with four wheels. I should stay out of a black automobile or I'm going to get smashed up."

"It could be," La Bruja said uncertainly. Whatever it was, it was as disturbing to her as to her client; she wasn't taking it lightly. Perhaps because it was a challenge to her professional skill. She continued to stare downward in stony concentration at it, the brick of still-unused cards retained in her hand, kneading a corner of her lip every now and then between her teeth.

The proprietor had fallen into a doze somewhere in the dusk-laden background. His heavy breathing was the only sound to be heard in the silences between their remarks.

"But they're your cards. Can't you read them?"

"Sure I can read them—as far as they go. The spades suit is always trouble or misfortune. The ace of spades itself is the one to look out for, that's the death card."

Clo-Clo took a deep breath of unutterable relief. "It's not out. So maybe if I just steer clear of a black car—" She lit a cigarette with a hand that was shaking so, the match singed the paper all down one side nearly to her lips. "Go ahead a little further, instead of turning back. Pay more out. Maybe something'll come out after that'll—that'll make it clearer."

La Bruja lidded her eyes acquiescently. Her hand moved. "That's a money card." Her hand moved again. "That's a card that means a trip or journey, a small one."

"I'm to get more money and go on a trip or journey?" suggested Clo-Clo hopefully.

"No, they're in reverse. That means, a trip *back* because of money. Money is going to cause you to take a return trip to somewhere."

This time Clo-Clo didn't comment, she kept her own counsel. She thought: "Sounds like I'm going back to the Tabarin one of these nights and meet that same darling of a *papacito* and be given another—"

"Go ahead," she urged, "put the next one in line down."

La Bruja's free hand moved to the brick she held, stripped the top of it, carried it to the table, reversed it with a deft twist.

There was a sort of impalpable detonation between them; unseen, unheard, but as keenly felt as the flare of flashlight powder.

"Wait a minute, what'd you say just now was the—?"

Clo-Clo, eyes dilated craned her neck toward the layout. Before she could verify it, La Bruja had slapped her hand over it, effacing it.

"Don't look at it." La Bruja suddenly whipped it out of the set-up and left a blank space where it had been.

"The death card," Clo-Clo whispered.

"It wasn't right over you," La Bruja said roughly.

"But it was right over this other one, this four thing. And *that* was touching me. Corner to corner!"

"Now look at your face," La Bruja said accusingly. "You're all white. You shouldn't have asked me—" She swept her hand back and forth across the cards, obliterating their arrangement beyond repair. She jogged her chair back. "Let's get out of here," she said impatiently.

Clo-Clo didn't move for a minute, didn't act as though she'd heard her. Her eyes were still fixed unseeingly on the barren table top, where the cards had been until now, as though she could still see them. Once she backed her hand across the brow fringe of the chrysanthemum hair mop, leaving a little indentation in its evenness of line through which a triangular wedge of forehead peered.

"Come on, don't take it like that," La Bruja tried to cheer her up.

Clo-Clo moved her head at last, but not toward her companion. She turned it slowly, warily, the other way around, toward the half-visible street-level window of the shop, across the room from them, with its shutters already backed together behind it in closure for the night.

She writhed slightly, as if trying to throw something off. "I keep getting a feeling of somebody looking at me, somebody looking at me hard. I already had it once before, tonight, before I even came in here——"

"Maybe somebody just took a squint in, in passing, to

see if Pepito is still open. I was sitting facing that way the whole time, and I didn't see anyone. Pay the guy and let's get out of here," La Bruja said, in reminder that it was her invitation. "You'll feel better outside."

Clo-Clo put on one shoe. Then she felt underneath the shredded inner sole of the other, dredged up a thin ten centavo piece, and put it on the table.

La Bruja had opened the door and gone out ahead. "There's nobody out here," she called back reassuringly. "The street's empty!"

Clo-Clo came out after her. She drew her short elbow jacket closer around her as though she were cold. There wasn't another moving thing in sight but the two of them. Calle Quince de Mayo lay desolate in the gloom around them, a blue-black tunnel running through the night.

"The tailings of the night," La Bruja grimaced. "I always hate it. Well, until next—" She took a preliminary step away from her.

Clo-Clo grabbed her almost spasmodically by the arm. "La Bruja, walk part of the way back with me, will you? You can go my way as well as the other, it's just as near for you."

La Bruja jeered, "What's the matter with you all of a sudden?" She turned nevertheless and fell into step alongside her.

"I dunno, I've got a funny feeling I can't throw off."

"That fortune got you."

"No, I had it even before I met you, but not as strong as now. I was feeling leery already back at the Tabarin."

"I can tell you what's the matter with you," La Bruja told her, with the wisdom born of greater experience. "Don't go in too heavy for this distilled stuff, like brandy or *aguardiente*. It over-stimulates and then depresses you. I used to make that mistake when I was first beginning to go around, too. Don't let them buy you just anything they feel like. Stick to wine and light stuff. These cheap guys are only too glad to daze you, if you give them the chance. Unless you get some system into your drinking, you'll find yourself, at the end of a hard night, with the horrors."

They had reached the lower end of the street by now.

"Well, here's where we split up," La Bruja let her know. "I'm not going out of my way for you, I've done enough tramping around already for one evening. Take it easy."

She turned sharply left, and the tap of her heels, for a moment or two, could be heard receding along the sidewalk. Clo-Clo continued on alone in their original direction. Just before the opposite corner line cut them off from one another for good, she called out, almost despairingly: "See you around tomorrow night."

"Maybe," came echoing back blurredly along the resonant, empty stone chasm of the street.

Clo-Clo went her way. To her surprise, she discovered she felt a little better after leaving the other girl, rather than worse. La Bruja had a sort of dampening personality, she was well known for that; maybe that was it. Or maybe there had been a lack of sympathy there. Not that she didn't hurry, and not that she wasn't still uneasy. Plenty of both. The way home was a long one, and it had never seemed longer than it did tonight. Her feet played chopsticks under her along the sidewalk, and the tubular street, like a megaphone, seemed to carry the sound far in advance of her. They went: tick-chock, tick-chock, tick-chock— And then suddenly they had stopped.

What was that?

It had coursed out swiftly before her, made a wide turn around her out into the middle of the road, before she could identify it. Then it fell motionless out there, poised for further flight, uncertainly looking over at her. It went "Miaow," in slurred remonstrance.

A thrill of horror surged through her. Oh God, no, not tonight, after that card—!

Black, inky black from nose to tail tip; not a white hair in its coat.

She started to draw warily backwards a step at a time, hand out to the wall beside her, trying to get out of the loop it had half drawn around her, before it had a chance to close it entirely. Trying to keep their two paths from crossing at any point.

Just when she had got abreast of it on her rearward way, it took further fright, trickled over the paving stones an additional length away from her. Still in the wrong direction, behind her.

She flattened her back against the wall and tried to edge past it without disturbing it further in its new halting place. Suddenly it sighted sanctuary, closed in again to the same side of the way it had originally emerged from, squeezed through some sidewalk-level vent and vanished, with a delayed withdrawal of its tail a moment or two after the rest of it. *Behind* her.

It had drawn a complete arc around her. She couldn't move now in either direction, backwards or forwards, without crossing its ill-omened orbit at some point.

She called upon her patron saint, sponsor of that given name she so seldom heard any more, except around the shack. "Santa Gabriela, get me out of this!" She touched her shoulders and her forehead and her breast, to ward it off. It was worse, they said, even than breaking a mirror.

But she couldn't stand here all night upon this island of safety. The damage was done now, irretrievable. She gathered herself together, lowered her head defensively as though she were about to charge through a curtain of fire or water; even gathered up her already brief skirt higher still with one hand, to give her limbs more freedom of action. Then she drew a deep breath and went plunging through the cat's esoteric path and brought up short on the other side of it. Free, but tarred by misfortune.

She gave a look behind her, sighed, and continued on her way.

A few minutes later she had hit the straightaway of the Calle de Justicia, a wide diagonal swath cut remorselessly through the maze of crooked older byways, its corners a continuous series of wedges and acute angles due to its biased progression. Now all she had to do was keep on it to its outer reaches and she'd arrive back at the shack.

A street-light pool picked her up momentarily, lost her to the darkness again. A short wait, and then the next one ahead did the same thing. Then the one above that. They were spaced about one to a crossing.

Still as it was, she failed utterly to hear the car until it was almost upon her. It must have been gliding after her with its engine turned down to inaudibility, its lights out, for several moments past. Probably he had sighted her ahead under one of those betraying light pools.

A slithering sound, light as a tape being dragged along the ground, was all the warning she had. She swerved, and it was only a few yards in back of her, pacing her. The lights must have been left off purposely, until the last minute, so that it could get close. They switched on now, drenched her from head to foot, photographed her, so to speak, then dimmed again to a dull glow at the touch of a switch. She faltered there blinded, the back of her hand to her eyes.

But the photographic proof had turned out satisfactory, the car had stopped, and a figure had alighted to the sidewalk beside it. All she could glimpse was a rakishly diagonal hat brim and a figure that was young, almost juvenile, in its symmetry. He must be some rich man's son, out trying to learn about life at first hand. The mere fact that he would alight and stand there waiting by the open door, instead of just sitting tight and calling her over, showed how inexperienced he still must be. They were veritable gold mines. If you were lucky enough to strike one.

"Hey, *chica*, how about a little spin with me?" Yes, she'd been right, the voice was that of a youth, and slightly nervous at its own daring under the man-about-town nonchalance it tried so hard to assume.

She had already taken a step over toward him to parley, both out of long habit and because of the special circumstances involved in this instance, before she realized what she was doing. She jolted to a sudden halt again.

"Wait a minute, what color is that car? It looks to me—"

"It's black," he said proudly. "Some beauty, eh?"

"Get outta here!" she shrieked in sudden unreasoning panic. "Get away from me with that thing! *Ay, dios mio,* don't come near me with it!" She fled full tilt down the street as if pursued by demons.

"It's an Hispano," he called after her in high dudgeon. She looked back to make sure he wasn't coming after her in it. He was standing there by it, looking from her to it, and from it to her, in outraged pride of ownership. He even backed one arm at her in resentment. She had evidently wounded him in a very sensitive spot.

She kept running, to get away even from the very vicinity of the thing. She didn't stop for almost a block, tapering off finally to a bedraggled scamper simply because she was completely out of breath. What a close shave that had been! The thing would have probably telescoped itself into a wall and burned her alive inside of five minutes after she'd gotten in.

Her stockings were loosening from her flight, and she had to bend over and tug them up. Her jacket and the blouse under it were all awry too, and she had to straighten them. Then she continued at a tottering walk, still panting from her efforts.

That got her home finally. That saw her the rest of the way to the shack. It was a one-story, two-room cabin of adobe bricks covered with plaster, and roofed over with broken tiles, out where the buildings were beginning to thin out, the land wasn't worth much, and nobody was exactly sure who owned it. It had a small patch of open ground out in front, with sunflowers struggling up through the discarded gasoline cans and broken water jugs, and usually the old lady's wash strung out. It was home. She liked it. She liked to come back to it. It was what she sat drinking at bars for. It was what she brought home a hundred and fifty pesos—or a peso and fifty centavos—to. She didn't take the money from here elsewhere, she brought it from elsewhere here. That showed where it ranked in her favor. Sure, they'd have a better one someday a little farther out, but the idea, the system, would be the same.

Their mongrel yard dog reared belatedly up from the ground at her passage and gave its usual vociferous, craven bark, while remaining prudently at a distance. "Quiet, Conejo, it's me," she said. Then it went to the other extreme of tail pumping and getting in her way until she had gotten inside and closed the door on it.

She had to pick her way among the pallets on the floor, but she knew where most of them were. The old lady always left a path clear for her from the door over to her cot. Once in a while she stepped on a hand, but that was because the sleeper had carelessly shifted position after the general retirement.

One of the younger kids had pre-empted her cot, she found when she got over to it. She didn't mind if they did that, until she was ready to use it herself. She woke it, remonstrated in an undertone: "Get off, now, *palomita*. I'm back. Go on, get down where you belong." The kid sidled off to the floor, went ahead sleeping. Clo-Clo sat down in its place, took off her shoes.

She stretched luxuriantly, arms high overhead, yawned, sighed blissfully. Gee it was good to be back here, to have the whole thing over with. She sat inertly slumped over there for a moment or two, half asleep already although still upright from the waist, while a jumbled kaleidoscope of the whole night fanned through her dimming mind.

"You'd like it in Copenhague. I'd like to take you out of this . . . First you're here, then you're not here . . . Watch your manners in here, take the one on the end, none of that smoke-ring stuff, understand? . . . Papa, the car is waiting outside, what'll I tell Elena! . . . Five more minutes, I'm closing up . . . Hey, *chica*, how about a spin with me? It's an Hispano. . . ."

One hundred and fifty pesos. If there'd only be a few more nights like this, she could cut it out, chuck the whole thing overboard. She shrugged off her jacket, let it fall down behind her. The cot gave a jolting creak. Suddenly she was erect, awake, appalled. Her hands were pressed flat against the center hollow of her bosom.

Gone!

She gave a choked exclamation that carried through the open doorway into the next room. Her mother stirred in there, called drowsily in: "You back, Gabrielita? What's the matter, have you been hurt?" They didn't call her Clo-Clo here, they didn't even know that was her name.

She found her shoes again. She was too stunned even to cry, to make any further sound. It was a solar-plexus impact. All she could do was breathe heavily, like when she'd finished running a little while ago—

That was it! That run from that car. That was when it

must have happened. That was the only time she'd moved fast all night; fast enough to lose it, anyway. Her stockings had come down, her blouse had shifted around a little. It must have worked its way up over the neckline and fallen out.

She had the outer door open now. No four of spades could have stopped her, no black cat, no black car. Nothing now. Money, security, that was the strongest impulse; that was stronger even than fear of death. Her mother's voice sounded again, just before she got the door closed. "Are you going out again, my daughter? Take care of yourself, it's so late—"

"Just for a minute. Go back to sleep. I'll be right back." she answered inattentively. The breadwinner had no time for fear or explanations; let her dependents do the worrying for her, this was her problem and she had to solve it alone.

She was going back now toward the inner city, fast, all weariness postponed. Walking as though it were three in the afternoon. Her mind was grappling with it. She had a good mind: she would have had, if it had been trained at all. "I didn't lose it when I went spinning around the table there at the Tabarin. I know I didn't, because I felt for it after I left, and it was still in. I didn't lose it sitting with La Bruja; her hands were on the cards, didn't come near me. It was when I ran from that accursed car; then and then only."

She knew, fortunately, just about where that was. He'd come up to her just past Retiro, and she'd run all the rest of the block, up to the next crossing at San Marco. It was somewhere along that stretch, on the right-hand side of Justicia.

Here. It began from here on. She slackened, began a pendulumlike advance along the night-blue shadowed sidewalk, swinging from curbing to building base, from building base to curbing, head rigidly inclined. Every unevenness, every slight flaw in the paving blocks, that cast a deeper shadow than the rest of the surface, she examined by bending still further down over, or even testing with the tips of her fingers.

Minutes went by. The city slept, the night brooded, the broomlike shuffle of her feet, back and forth, and forth and back, was the only sound there was.

The curbing veered in suddenly, thrust a drop under her feet. She looked up with aching, stiff neck. Already? Had she reached the other end already? Yes, here, here was where the car had stopped. and played its lights upon her. Maybe *he'd* found it. But he hadn't come after her. He'd stood there by the car a minute, and then gotten in and driven off. And at this hour hardly anyone was about, hardly anyone was likely to have passed by here since. It must be still someplace around, it *must* be. Until daylight, until the first early risers were on the streets, it would still lie where it had fallen. She wouldn't desist, she wouldn't stop looking until she'd found it.

She'd made one complete round trip to the San Marco corner and back again, when hope finally gave up the ghost. When she finally had to admit that it was useless looking any more, that if it had been there she would already have found it two or three times over. She wavered helplessly about there on the sidewalk awhile, crumbling inside. Then the tears came. Hot bitter tears, of a wrenching intensity that those who lived safely could never know.

She went over to the wall, there close by the corner, and pressed her face against it, under the overhanging splint of her arm, heels out behind her and clear of the ground, and with her other hand she beat the counterpoint to her strangled sobs against the heartless, unyielding, prickling stones.

The whole night for nothing. All those smiles, all that magnetic current, all those kilowatts of personality consumed, with nothing to show for them.

The sobs stopped first. Then the intolerable anguished pounding of her palm slowed to little pats, died away at last. She tried to console herself as best she could. It had been something for nothing. Now she was no worse off, at least, than she had been before she had received it. It wouldn't work. "It was mine," she said smotheredly against the wall. "I had it. Why should it be taken away from me again?"

She flung her shoulder around in defiance, turned at last to face the other way, still propped against the wall. She stared in glowering dullness out at nothing. The night owed her a return. She'd get a little something back, no matter how fractional a part of her loss. She'd stand here until she did. She wouldn't go home empty-handed. The fatal middle-class virtue of thrift. Something to show for it, if it was only a half-peso piece, only a cadged cigarette. She wouldn't leave this spot until she did.

Justicia had been cut ruthlessly through a decrepit, labyrinthine part of the town, on the bias. All the moldering little lanes and alleys that opened out upon it, opened as a result not rectangularly but slantwise. At the corner where she stood, San Marco, running in to join the newer thoroughfare, made an angle so acute it was little better than a fifteen-degree incision. The corner of this wall she lounged against was needle-pointed; San Marco was, not around the corner from her, but directly behind her back, on the other side of the double-flanged well.

Now as she stood there in the blue hour, in the death watch of the night, defiantly determined upon her recompense, the soft crush of a foot upon loose-packed earth, upon imperfectly bedded small stones, reached her from around this projection, from behind her own back. Some-body was coming along there, along the unpaved margin of San Marco, about to turn this razor corner and happen upon her.

Somebody, and no matter who it was, she wanted something of the night, she would not let him by without exacting tribute to repair her loss and assuage her shattered self-esteem. She dried her eyes by stabbing a knuckle into them, in quick succession. She opened her bag and started to redden her mouth with flurried urgency, the smile of gamin friendliness with which she intended to halt him in another moment already turning up its corners as she did so, for the loose top layer of tiny stones and gravel was already shifting in *sight of her*, out there beyond the knife-like corner, like sluggish water riding outwards from an impact still unseen, the cause of it still hidden for a moment more.

In another instant they would be face to face, eye to eye. She could already have reached her hand exploratively backward around the stone screen and touched him as he sidled up.

The lipstick dipped. Her smile was ready now. She turned it up toward the night, eyes half lidded with expectancy.

They had taken her away by the time Manning arrived, at seven that same morning, in a taxi. The flatiron corner of San Marco and Justicia looked dainty in early-morning water colors: peach pink and pastel blue. Pink sunlight in the faces of the men standing around, and light-blue shadows on the ground behind them.

There was one other color, on the wall on the Justicia side: as though somebody had been careless with some kind of overripe fruit.

There weren't many people around. A country Indian on his way to early market with a basket of persimmons on his head seemed to have become permanently rooted to one particular spot on his way past, stood there mouth agape in incomprehension, poised to go on but forgetting to. On the opposite sidewalk a street sweeper also stood looking on, resting on his broom of twigs. Occasionally he would make a couple of passes with it, then stop and look on some more. On a third-floor balcony on that same side a plump woman had come out to watch, but had brought her hairbrush with her and continued stroking her long black glossy hair while she did so. That was about all; the rest were all those whose business it was to be there.

Manning had not only not been informed this time, but could even tell he was somewhat *persona non grata* when he got out of the cab and joined them. Robles glanced up, greeted him uncordially with: "You again? We have work to do here. Please, no more suggestions from the sidelines, if you don't mind!" And then he added, "What are you, a mind reader? How did you know?"

"It's all over town already. The milkman told the *mozo* that brings my morning coffee to me from across the street, and the *mozo* told me. Who was it this time?"

"An habitué of the cafés known as Clo-Clo. A lady of the evening, poor creature. Mendez here knew her. Didn't you, Mendez?"

Mendez dropped his eyelids disclaimingly. "Only in the line of duty."

Manning had caught sight of several small objects awaiting removal, which had been placed, meanwhile, on a sheet of newspaper spread out on top of an opened campstool. "Where does the lipstick come in?" he asked.

"It was lying on the ground close beside her body. It fell out of her handbag, I suppose, in the course of the death struggle."

Manning took a while. Then finally he asked, "What else fell out?"

"Nothing else fell out."

"Was the bag open or closed when it was found?"

Robles was fair enough—and incautious enough—to hold one finger up for the benefit of those around him. "Ah. He has made a good point there, the American. The bag was still closed when we found it. Therefore, it is true that the lipstick could not have fallen out, she must have removed it herself." He waved his hand blandly. "However, it is just a detail, it has no bearing on the matter one way or the other."

"Oh no, no bearing at all," agreed Manning treacherously. "*Except to show that it was a man who waylaid her here on this corner.* She would not have rouged her lips for a quadruped, I believe?"

Robles gave his arms a slight flip at his sides, said in an heroically restrained voice to those immediately around him, but excluding Manning as though he weren't there: "That again. What did I do to deserve this hornet buzzing in my ears? Mendez, Cipriano. Stand one on each side of him. Each of you take an arm. Yes, like that. Now walk him over to that cab over there, put him in it, and see that it takes him back wherever it is he came from."

Robles wasn't kidding. He was a little too white at the corners of the eyes and mouth to have been anything but serious. It might have been, partly, the early hour of the day.

Neither, for that matter, was Manning. "Your theory must be pretty shaky," he said witheringly, "if it can't stand a little honest difference of opinion. What's the matter, afraid it'll fall down flat? Take your hands off me. This is a public street. I'm entitled to stand here as long as I want."

It could very easily have been the starting point of actual ill-feeling, bad blood between them. Fortunately, an interruption occurred just then which took everyone's mind off all lesser matters.

There was a great commotion and fanfare at the curb, and the *jefe de policia* himself stepped down from a breathtaking Bugatti, one of the last to be imported before the war. Everyone fell silent, drew himself up where he stood at stiff attention, as he approached surrounded by a small group of subordinates.

He was a short, wiry, clerical-looking man, with an aggressive manner and a voluminous, resonant voice that must have been ideal for addressing large gatherings. He cast only the briefest of glances at the vestiges remaining on wall and ground, concentrated on the men before him instead. He stood there glittering balefully through his spectacles at them, like an infuriated owl blinking in the sunlight.

"You are in charge here, inspector?" he thundered after a dramatic pause.

"*Si, excelencia,*" Robles quailed in a small voice.

"How many more times is this going to happen? This fiend must be exterminated! I want its carcass shown to me within the next twenty-four hours, is that clear?" He included the others, turning his head to take them in. "Is that clear to all of you? The mayor and the *ayuntamiento* are showing concern, are having a reward posted to the general public, independent of your efforts. It is a reflection on my department. There is already a city-wide panic brewing. The tourist season is about to begin. This can do incalculable harm, people will avoid coming here!"

He strode back to the Bugatti, delivered the postscript from there. "There should be nothing complicated about this matter! If one animal has a better head on it than the

best heads we have on the police force, then it is time there
was a general reorganization, from head to foot!"

Robles sat at his desk dismally scanning a specimen of
one of the municipal council's new posters, fresh from the
printer's. It was so large it curled over the edge of the desk
at both sides. It was a vivid yellow, and dozens like it were
going up on every advertisement kiosk, sign-board, and
vacant wall in town.

At the top, in beetling black letters, it had: Aviso al
Publico. Then numerous lines of fine print. Then at last,
toward the lower right-hand corner, again in heavier type:
$1,000 Reward.

Manning knew, by the very fact that he was being allowed to remain there in the office while Robles struggled
with himself, that the latter intended eventually to give
in.

"I still say I do not agree with you," Robles said, thumping the desk despairingly. "But when my official position,
my job itself, is involved, I am forced to give any possibil-
ity a trial, even though it goes against my own beliefs. I
cannot afford to pass anything by."

"Hold on a minute," Manning said quickly. "I'm not
making an accusation, you understand? I haven't any proof
against the man, none whatever. There's only this one incriminating circumstance involved: I've been inquiring
around, here, there, the next place: privately, on my own
account, you understand; and I find he has been in the
habit of coming in to the city on overnight visits. Every
now and then, every so often, at irregular intervals."

"There is nothing criminal in that. Hundreds of people
come into the city every day and night, just as hundreds go
out again."

"I agree with you," Manning said mildly. "Some have
fixed days for it. Every Saturday night, say. Or every Sunday. Or twice a week, regularly. As the case may be. Then
there are others who come in haphazardly, as he does. Just
whenever the impulse hits them. As you say, there is nothing particularly incriminating in either of those habitudes."

"Well then?"

"Just idly, let me give you the three last haphazard dates on which he repaired to the city. They are authentic, you can rely on them; I obtained them from various disinterested sources: bus drivers on the line that goes out that way, cantina-keepers, and the like. See if they interest you."

Robles looked down at the poster staring him in the face, kept tapping his fingers rotatingly on the edge of it, with a moody sort of thoughtfulness.

Manning took out a scrap envelope, scanned the back of it. "May the fourteenth—"

Robles' eyes went up from the poster before him.

"May the twenty-sixth—"

Robles' head went up, as his neck stiffened.

"June the eighth—"

Robles' whole body went up, to a standing position before his desk chair. Then leaning over, he brought the flat of his hand crashingly down on the desk, left it there for a long moment.

"Teresa Delgado met death on the night of May fourteenth. Conchita Contreras came to her end on the night of May twenty-sixth. The girl nicknamed Clo-Clo was found at daybreak on June the ninth." He glowered at the American. "Once, you would call a coincidence. Twice, you would call suspicious. But three times, what would you call that?"

"I'm not good at naming things," was all Manning said quietly.

Robles thumbed the lever of the voice conveyor on his desk.

"Bring me in Juan Cardozo, foreman of the ranch at Las Cruces. It's about fifty kilometers out, on the overland road. Just follow that and you'll come to it. No charges, just wanted for questioning."

He was burned a deep mahogany from year-around exposure to the sun. He had come in just as they found him: blue cotton work shirt open at the neck, a sort of poncho arrangement slung over one shoulder, corduroy pants, the embossed silver belt of the typical riding man about his middle, and a shapeless felt hat, wavy-brimmed from being continually soaked down and allowed to dry out again, probably right on his head.

He had a small but very stiff-haired black mustache. Occasionally, during the long hours it went on, they let him smoke. As if to let him remember what comfort and ease were like after all this time. The implication being he could have them back again at will if he would only admit the worst about himself. Whenever they did let him smoke, he would take a paper from his pocket and slowly, lovingly roll one for himself. It was almost a pleasure to watch him at it, he was so deft, so artistic about it.

"I found it when I was making my rounds on horseback one day," he was saying when Manning slipped unobtrusively into the room behind all their backs. Strictly speaking, he had no business there. But then, strictly speaking, they had no business holding the man Cardozo there either. Not as yet.

"Its mother had been killed, and it was shivering there by the body. It was just a little mite then, a cub, coal black. I picked it up and took it back with me to the ranch house and kept it there. For a while we kept it right in the house, like a kitten. Then when it got a little bigger, I knocked together a sort of pen for it outside and kept it in that. Then one day señor here happened to come out, and he saw it; he asked me if he could borrow it for twenty-five pesos, he wanted to have a lady show it off in her car with her."

"Who fed it?" Robles wanted to know in a dangerously minor key.

"I did."

"It knew you, then?"

"*Claro*. Any animal knows the one that feeds it."

"You spoke to it when you fed it?"

"Sure. Like you do, you know."

"You had a name for it?"

"*Negrote*."*

"In other words, it knew you, it was familiar with you.

---

* The big black one.

You could approach it more easily than anyone else, isn't that true?"

The ranchman sensed where he was being led. He shifted uneasily. "Anyone could approach it. All of us out there. The señor had no trouble, bringing it in to town—"

"Let us go back to dates, again," Robles said disarmingly. "You have admitted you were in the city all night the night of the fourteenth of May."

"I have already told you where I was. At the Cantina Estrella de Media Noche. Ask all the bunch who goes there; Hipolito, Benito Doinguez, they all saw me—"

"We have already, never fear," Robles said with the placidity of an idol. "There is no clock in the cantina. They saw you, yes; early in the evening. But then after, for instance?"

"After it closed, I was where one always is after a cantina closes: lying with my back propped up against a wall, outside in the street somewhere."

Robles scratched his ear perplexedly, as though at a loss, not knowing what question to ask next. A completely false impression, Manning knew, watching him from the background. "Let us leave the night of the fourteenth, it seems to be getting us nowhere. On the twenty-sixth, you say—"

Cardozo showed his teeth around at them. "I have already told you that too. They will be charging me for three visits, instead of one. Very well, I was at the house run by Doña Sara—"

"Tell me, were you planning to elope with one of the girls there?"

"The *comandante* is joking. One does not elope with—"

"The *comandante* is not joking," Robles assured him icily. "Why then were you seen to have a riata* coiled about your waist the night you visited the house of Doña Sara?"

Cardozo's jaw fluctuated up and down, but all that came from his mouth were two meaningless pronouns. "I—I—"

But Robles hadn't waited. He was asking them faster

---

* A looped rope, a lasso.

now. "Why then did you have pieces of raw meat in a bag with you the night you were at the cantina? Whom were you expecting to feed? Yourself?"

"No, I—I—"

"And what became of that raw meat? You had it no longer when you boarded the morning bus for Las Cruces. And what became of the riata? You had that no longer, either, when you made the return trip."

"The riata—somebody in the house of Doña Sara must have stolen it—they do that in those places, anything of value. The meat—maybe some dog or cat came along while I was sleeping on the sidewalk outside the cantina—"

"And what did you bring those things along for? Was it because you had something staked out, somewhere here in the city, that you wished to lead about with you for a while? Was it? *Contesta!* (Answer!)" His voice exploded. "Was it?"

Manning thought he had never before seen such a look of dawning fear and horror on anyone's face as began to peer out on Cardozo's. "I—I—oh, wait, no, don't think that! I did, I admit it. I did hope to save Negrote alive. I thought perhaps I might come across him just by chance, throw him the meat, sling the riata over him, find some way of getting him back to the *estancia* with me. It was just an idle impulse, a stupid thought that came to me— But not what you mean! Not what you are trying to say!" He looked from face to face, pleadingly. "Señores, what do you want with me? I know, I have known for hours past. I have not said so, you have not said so either. I have been in town other nights, besides the three you mention. Why don't you speak of them?"

"Very well," Robles said accommodatingly, "we shall." He consulted something. "You were in on the twentieth of May, *por ejemplo.*"

"Yes, yes!" Cardozo nodded almost avidly.

"Did you have a riata with you that night? Raw meat that night?"

The lack of answer was the answer.

"You were in on the thirty-first. Did you then, either?"

Cardozo shivered a little, and his head went over, as though he were peering closely at something out before his feet.

"Only on the nights on which *something happened* in this city did you come provided with the rather curious articles we have mentioned. Not on the others."

The man in the middle of all of them leaped to his feet suddenly. Restraining hands were immediately laid on him, but he stood there erect, facing his tormentors. Even though he was shivering spasmodically, there was a sort of innate dignity pulsing from him. Even Manning, the outlander, could feel it. For a moment it made of them, not policemen around a suspect; just men around another man. "I have killed, yes. I spent two years in jail for it, back in my native *tierra*. It was over a woman, any man would have killed. But not this way! One kills in revenge, to right a wrong. How can one be revenged on or wronged by individuals one did not even know existed; one never saw in all his life before? Or one kills to rob. At least some do. What other reason is there to kill?"

Manning had taken a small file out of his pocket, he was shaping a thumbnail with it while he lounged indolently back against the door. "One sometimes kills for the love of it," he remarked unexpectedly.

Their heads all turned to look around at him. He, in turn, had taken his eyes off the file for a moment. Something went wrong. He started violently, seized the fleshy bulge at the bottom of his thumb, bent over it, swearing softly in English. The file dropped with a plink.

He came forward into the light, holding the self-inflicted wound, as if to examine it better. Yet he went on completing the remark he made just before the accident happened. "For the love of it, for its own sake, because they like the sight of blood. Because it does something to them."

He uncapped his protective hand. A skin tear produced by the point of the file was revealed, not very serious, but lavishly blooded, as such things often are. It even dripped down free off his outpoised hand, which he had inadvertently spaded almost under Cardozo's nose, to keep from staining his own cuff with it.

Cardozo blinked twice, as one does in discomfort. Then he sidled his face sidewise, in uncontrollable repugnance at the bleeding wound's almost contact-point proximity.

Nobody said anything; they understood.

Robles let out a faintly discernible sigh after a moment. "Take him outside," he said. "We'll continue later." And to somebody else, as the door closed, "See if you can find some alcohol for the *norteño's* finger—"

"It was worth it," Manning said, blowing on it and wringing it out. "What are you going to do now, turn him loose?"

"Continue to hold him in custody." Robles said vindictively. "Give your theory rope, and rope, and rope—until it strangles itself!"

"I don't get you."

Robles smiled bleakly. "If these barbarities mysteriously cease to occur while he is in our hands, that is one thing. But if one should take place again—"

5. SALLY O'KEEFE

In THE INGLATERRA HOTEL on Corriente Street, Sally O'Keefe had the floor-length windows of their room wide open to a picture night that looked like something on a travel poster.

She was standing there framed against them, arms out in arrested ecstasy. She was short and slight, hair a reddish gold, eyes blue, and rosettes of freckles on each cheek gave her face an elfin piquancy.

"Marj, isn't that incredible? That can't be real. Somebody painted it outside our window for our special benefit."

Through a luminous dust composed of phosphorescent particles of greenish blue and silver, lines of incandescence had been traced, as though someone had drawn a radium-tipped stick through it that left glowing traces. These were the streets and avenues. Around and about was the low black undulation made by the hills against a sky that, where it joined them in the west, was still a glowing turquoise, as though reflecting a hidden row of low-burning gas flames strung out along its base. Up above in the center of its dome it had darkened to night, but the warm rich darkness of semitropic night, so lavishly scattered with stars they were like a blinding shower of permanently up-flung confetti. Or the after-stages of a burst skyrocket.

"Now I can die happy!" the girl at the window rhapsodized.

Marjorie King, her traveling companion, more practical, smiled into the dresser glass before which she sat completing the final touches of her toilette. She was a brunette, with a sort of stateliness to her good looks that the other's pertness lacked. Even seated, she was obviously a good head or two taller than the other girl. The casting director of a stage production could have differentiated them more accurately than the ordinary layman; Marjorie was the show-girl type, Sally the pony chorus girl. Neither of them, as a matter of fact, was of the theater. Sally was the private secretary to a harvesting-machine-company vice-president. Marjorie was branch manager for one of a large chain of candy stores, known as "Handmaid," where everything was done by machinery but the eating. Both were on their first real vacation in years, a long-planned, long-saved-for, many-times-deferred sabbatical that they had practically had to blackmail their respective employers for. It was a freelance trip, they would have nothing to do with conducted tours and large, sardinelike cruise parties rushing about in military formation.

"That's Naples you're thinking of, isn't it?" Marjorie answered the remark. "And anyway, if it's all you say, why spoil it by speaking of dying in the same breath with it?"

"Just a phrase, just a turn of speech," Sally said, turning away at last and coming toward her. "When you feel as I do tonight, it has no meaning at all. I never felt so alive before in my life! This place certainly brings out the dynamism in you. What're we doing tonight?"

Marjorie stood up, ready to go. "This was your night for making the plans, haven't you got anything worked out? That was our arrangement, remember? One night I'm the boss, the next night you are."

Sally essayed analyzing herself, while her friend went around putting out the lights, a habit that they were not accustomed enough to hotels to have broken themselves of yet. "I feel sort of sentimental, romantic. It must be that out there brought it on. None of these jangling, brassy casinos or night clubs for me tonight. I feel sort of pastoral —yes that's how I feel, pastoral."

"Pasteurized?" Marjorie teased, gathering up an outer wrap.

Sally gave her a push at the rear of the waist. "I heard somebody or other mention a place out in a park on the outskirts, where you eat in the open air under the trees," she resumed. "They say it's beautiful, all colored lanterns. Let's take one of these old-fashioned carriages they have around, instead of a taxi for a change, and drive out there and back in the moonlight. The taxis here smell so of gasoline, and they get you there so fast. Yes, that's just what I feel like," she concluded, "a slow, easy-going, old-style carriage ride in the moonlight."

"How far out is this place?" Marjorie asked her. "Isn't there some story going around about a man-eating something or other that got away from some zoo or animal farm and is supposed to pounce on you in lonely places? The maid that does the room was jabbering about it a mile a minute when you were out this morning. I wasn't able to get the story very straight; I only caught about every third word, you know how fast they talk."

"Oh, that. The man at the American Express told me not to listen to it, there's not a word of truth in it. I'm going to get my money's worth out of this vacation, and no hobgoblin story is going to stop me."

She opened the door and stood waiting for her friend to pass through. "Got everything? Don't forget to bring some catnip in case we run into the watchamacallit," she suggested flippantly.

Marjorie laughed as they moved toward the elevator.

Downstairs in the lobby she said, "Let's ask and find out at the desk."

The clerk bowed graciously, lowering his head to the end of his hair part, as they stepped over.

"We understand there's an outdoor restaurant in the big park outside the city. Is it worth taking in? My friend and I were thinking of going there."

His answer was indirect. "Have the señoritas tried the Tabarin or Select? I am sure they would—"

"But those are just night clubs, aren't they?" Marjorie

objected. "We have night clubs up home too. What we're looking for is something a little different, something more atmospheric."

"I know the place you mean." he said somewhat reticently. "The Madrid, out in the Bosque—"

"What's the matter with it?" Sally cut in with characteristic bluntness.

"Oh, nothing, nothing," he hastily retracted. "It is just that it is leetle—how you say?—*lejano*; out of the way, far out. Are the señoritas going unaccompanied? I could perhaps arrange—"

"Oh no, we don't want any hired escorts," Sally grimaced. "I hate that sort of thing."

"The young man seems doubtful, for some reason or other," Marjorie smiled uncertainly at her.

This time he didn't trouble to deny it.

Sally O'Keefe reacted as Sally O'Keefe always reacted. Marjorie had known she would. "Well, people do go there after dark, don't they?" she demanded of the clerk. And at his nodding admission, she plucked her friend by the arm. "Then we are, too! Call us one of these old-fashioned carriages." And they went sailing out to the street to await its arrival.

Outside Marjorie laughed knowingly. "He was doing his best to discourage us, did you get it? But he wouldn't come out with the real reason; afraid we'd cut short our stay, I suppose. You always were that way; let anyone try to talk you out of doing anything, and you're surer than ever to go ahead and do it."

"Steam-roller Sal," grinned the smaller girl beside her. "Here it is now."

They got in, settled themselves on the back seat, left open to the sky with the hood thrown back.

"What'd he say it was called, again?"

Marjorie gave the order to the coachman for her. "The Madrid." He turned and gave them a glance of brief curiosity, then flicked his whip and they started to roll down the street with velvety smoothness. Marjorie had noted the look in passing. It might have been elicited by their festive

attire or their lack of male escort, but she was inclined to
think not; she had an idea it was their destination that had
caused it.

"Was I right?" Sally exulted. "Isn't this nice for a
change?"

The gait of the vehicle was a lot more even and lulling
than a car would have been, there was no denying that,
and it gave them a much better chance to take in the sights
around them. These carriages, although no longer used for
practical purposes during the daylight hours, were far from
being broken-down museum pieces. They were rubber-tired,
their bodies kept in gleaming condition, and they were
anything but an uncommon sight in Ciudad Real, particularly after dark and on Sunday afternoons.

After ten or fifteen minutes of slow coursing through the
vivacious, brightly lighted streets, they came out finally
upon a large *glorieta*, or rounded open space of pavement,
ringed about with multiglobed lampposts. This was the
Puerta Mayor, one of the city "gates," although it had
neither wall nor gate to show for it. Facing them across it
was the main entrance to the Bosque, a vast natural park
in imitation of the Bois de Boulogne in Paris, mute testi-
mony of the days when Paris had set the style in cities as
well as in women's clothes.

The main driveway of the Bosque, when they entered it,
was filled with taxis, roadsters, and sedans. In fact the
stream of traffic was fully as heavy as on some of the city
thoroughfares behind them.

"Now what's wrong with this?" Sally queried delight-
edly. "Do you see anything so lonely or scary about this?
I'd like to give that clerk a piece of my mind!"

"It's lonely like Times Square on Election Night," admitted Marjorie with a chuckle.

"What a night!" Sally exulted. She lowered the bracketed
seat opposite, put both feet up on it, and stared over head
and rearward at a pomegranate of a moon which was
beginning to work its way through the trees into open
sky.

Presently innumerable colored lanterns, like toy balloons staked low above the ground at the end of taut, upright strings, began to peer out at them here and there. The carriage made a turn into a private siding, the trees thinned off, and a whole vast expanse of them, like a flower bed dangling upside down, burgeoned into view. Beneath was a sea of tables in the open air, centering around a pavilion, open at the sides, containing still others. And all alike, inside and out, were filled with a vivaciously chattering, typically Latin outdoor crowd. The nostalgic wail of a tango sounded disembodiedly on the night air, without seeming to have any source, and you could tell that those upright under the pavilion roof in a small compact cluster were dancing, and not just standing there between the tables, only because each two were turned to face one another.

"Now this," said Sally, when they had finally obtained a table far out toward the perimeter, "is what I really call something. You can have your stuffy city night clubs. Look at that." She picked up a leaf that had fallen to the cloth from above, and held it out almost reverently for Marjorie to see.

"Sally, the hard-to-please, the chronic complainer," observed Marjorie, with reverse implication.

Sally was usually good company at all times, pleasant to be out with; that was why they had made the trip together in the first place. Tonight she was in especially fine fettle.

"Are we getting looked at!" she reveled presently, not in the least disconcerted. "Very *déclassée*, I suppose, coming out alone together like this."

"You know it isn't that," Marjorie teased her. "It's probably that carrot thatch of yours, and the funny little phiz that goes with it." She undulated her wrist watch toward her. "You're beautiful, my dear."

Sally squinted at one of the lanterns. "I must owe you money," she said. "Trying to recall if I do or not. It's the only way I can account for it. All right, you're beautiful too, so there. I'm beautiful, you're beautiful, what good does it do us? Two lonely old maids, twenty-four and twenty-five, all by themselves in the middle of the South American night."

"You shouldn't have said that," Marjorie said in a guarded voice, laughing silently down her chin. "Don't look up, but we're about to be accosted."

He was complete even down to white kid gloves. He bowed low between them. "Would one of the señoritas care to do me the honor of dancing?"

The corner of Sally's mouth was twitching in spite of her best efforts to control it. Close as he was, she managed to make herself audible to her friend without appearing to say anything. "Dare me?" she breathed. "Ow! what was that for?" she exclaimed, unabashed, a moment later as the point of her friend's toe found her instep.

Marjorie saw that she would have to answer for the two of them. "No thank you," she said with what gravity she could muster.

"Pardon," the canvasser said stiffly. He gave another bow and left them.

"You hurt the poor man's feelings," Marjorie rebuked, holding her napkin to the side of her own mouth to keep the contagious laughter she was getting from the other girl from being seen.

The two of them had fallen into one of those moods of giddy, causeless hilarity that at times sweep over two women alone; they were laughing at nothing, with one another, at one another, and incited by one another.

"I thought you were feeling so romantic tonight?"

"Yeah," said Sally, shaking her head, "but I don't like 'em with shoeshines on the hair."

This brought on another gale of risibility.

"Have they a union? They'll be picketing this table, the first thing we know."

"Say, wouldn't that look funny?" visualized Marjorie. "Three or four of them carrying signs and doing little dance steps back and forth in front of us—" The mental image she managed to convey sent them into still another spasm.

"Come on, we're going to have wine with these jokes!" Sally said masterfully, beckoning the waiter.

"Old P.J. should see his hard-working secretary now!" Marjorie gloated a few minutes later, tilting a ruddy glass toward her friend.

Sally turned and looked the other way, away from the crowd out into the marginal darkness, for almost the first time since they'd seated themselves. She decided to kid her companion a little. "It may be hiding out there right now, watching us through the trees," she said mischievously. "Do you suppose they pick out whom their next meal is going to be ahead of time and then follow them around? I heard a story once—"

"Brrh! Don't!" pleaded Marjorie. "I was just beginning to forget it. You had to remind me."

"Nobody else here seems to take it seriously, why should we? Look at the mob here tonight. That alone shows it's just some sort of an idle rumor."

Under those gay-colored lanterns strung from the trees, with music playing, glasses clinking, waiters hustling around, shoals of men and women in evening dress on every side of them, Marjorie had to admit to herself it was hard really to believe that there was violent death stalking somewhere about the city at that very moment, on four velvety, relentless paws.

By the time they were ready to leave, an hour later, they had both forgotten all about it once again. They returned in high good humor to where their carriage was waiting for them, still laughing intermittently and for as little reason as ever.

"I liked that place. Aren't you glad we took it in?"

"Wouldn't have missed it for the world," Marjorie agreed.

"Drive us around awhile, slowly," Sally told the coachman as they got in. "It's a shame to go back to the hotel so soon. Isn't it beautiful out here in the moonlight?"

"Don't let's run up too big a bill," Marjorie cautioned.

"Forget it, this is my night. What's a vacation for anyway?" An empty side lane had opened out beside them. "Turn up that way," she ordered the driver. "Take us off this main driveway, it's too full of exhaust fumes from all the traffic."

There wasn't another vehicle in sight on it. It stretched barren into the night, in a ruler-straight line before them.

"There, isn't this much better? We've got it all to ourselves," said the headstrong Sally. "I like to explore new roads, don't you?"

"I can take them or leave them alone," Marjorie had to admit. It was just a little *too* lifeless to appeal to her, but she didn't like to spoil her friend's good time.

It began to curve slowly around to the left presently, and as it did so, a sheet of burnished silver, glistening like a mirror under the moon, came into view through the trees.

"Look at that lake with the swans on it!" Sally enthused. "Did you ever see anything so exquisite?"

The horse was going at a slow walk. Presently the trees between it and them had thinned to extinction, and only a grassy, downward slope lay between the road and it. "Let's get out and walk down to the edge of it," was Sally's next suggestion. "Stretch our legs a little after sitting so long. I love to walk along beside water, don't you?"

"Not at this hour of the night," Marjorie said half-heartedly. "Let's turn around and go back where there are more people. It's getting late, and we're awfully far in—"

"Don't be that way. You're a big girl now. Nothing can happen to us as long as we stay in sight of the coach, don't go roaming too far off. I promise you we won't let it out of our sight." She already had one foot poised out of the carriage.

Marjorie gave in once more, but this time it was the coachman who began to jabber objections to them when he saw them about to descend.

"What's he saying?" asked Marjorie.

"Just about what everyone else has been, I guess. Advising us not to leave the carriage and go walking around on foot, most likely. I think it's a conspiracy on the part of everyone. These high-strung Latins!"

"They live here, after all," Marjorie pointed out.

But the impulsive little redhead hadn't waited, was already picking her way down the gently inclined sward toward the lake below, flashing blindingly in the moonlight.

Marjorie turned to the driver, warned him with one Spanish word and a dozen English ones, her usual ratio: "*Espera*. Don't you dare budge from here, understand? We'll be back in a minute."

He nodded in disapproving acquiescence, but the horse, meanwhile, was pawing the ground uneasily and shifting about between the traces. He had to tighten his grip on the reins to steady it. She saw its ears standing stiffly erect, as though it heard or sensed something that the humans about it were still unaware of.

"Sal," she called down the slope. "I think we'd better get back in again. I don't like the way this horse is acting." But even the attempt to overrule her friend and bring her back again, in itself, was carrying her involuntarily down toward the water's edge herself.

Sally had already reached it, was crouched there on her heels, crumbling some after-dinner wafers she had brought along from the restaurant and holding them out enticingly toward a flotilla of magnificent black swans, who came streaking up from all directions. "Aren't they beauts?" she called obliviously over her shoulder. "C'mon down, what're you afraid of?"

Marjorie made her way down to her, still only to persuade her to come beck. "Come on, Sal," she said reasonably. "Something's making that horse fidget up there. Let's get out of here."

"Oh, it probably just wants to get back to the stable, you know how horses are." She went on paying out crumbs. "Look at them fight one another. That's what you call muscling in!"

Suddenly they all began to reverse, dart out into the middle of the lake again as swiftly as they had drawn shoreward just now.

"What's the matter with them, what're they doing that for?" Sally asked blankly.

"Something's frightened them—and it wasn't ourselves. They were practically snatching those crumbs out of your hand a minute before. I *told* you we'd better get out of here!" She began pulling the other girl insistently by the arm to get her to come away. "This is just the sort of place we were warned to stay away from."

"Oh, all right," Sally said weariedly. She straightened her feet and brushed the front of her dress. "Don't be such a wet blanket."

They turned to face the roadway up above once more, just in time to witness the horse rearing violently upward on its hind legs until it was nearly vertical within its traces. It whinnied with shrill fearfulness. The coachman, nearly overturned, gave an alarmed shout. The animal dropped back again, sparks flashing out from its shoes, and then it plunged forward, bolting off under their very eyes while they stood there rooted helplessly to the spot. In another moment the rapid clatter of its hoof-beats and the driver's excited yells had both alike died away far down the driveway.

They came running up to the edge of it a moment later, stood there aghast, looking down its empty moon-speckled length. A little blue dust, slowly settling in places from the vehicle's headlong flight, was the only trace left of it.

Marjorie's hands struck her sides, rebounded again. "*Now* are you satisfied?" she said pointedly. "You would get out and leave it."

"How did I know that was going to happen? He'll get him under control in a minute or two and come back to get us. That's the only way he can get his money for the whole night's excursion."

Marjorie, however, wasn't taking such a calm view of it. "Well, we're not waiting around *here* until he does!" she let her companion know sharply. "There's something around here that there shouldn't be, and I know what I'm saying. First the swans, and then that horse—"

They started to walk briskly along by the side of the road, following in the same direction the runaway horse had taken. Even though they had no idea where the road led, to keep on along it was their only hope of meeting the carriage again on its return trip.

They were alternately in shadow and moonlight. The macadam surface was hard on their feet after a while, in

the thin-soled evening slippers they were wearing. First
one, then the other, changed over to the turf on the outside
of the roadway, where the walking was easier. This
brought them into single file, however, for trees, tree roots,
and bushes impinged quite closely on the road strip in
places. Marjorie was in the lead.

Their tread fell silently on the soft earth now. It was
when they had been doing this for several minutes that
they first became aware of something. A soft intermittent
rustling sound, a sort of whispering slither, was coming
from the foliage a little behind and off to one side of them.
It seemed to be pacing them. It was very subtle, scarcely
anything at all. It would stop and then go on again.

Marjorie hung back a step, so she could whisper over
her shoulder to the girl behind her without raising her
voice. "Do you hear that?" she breathed. "Something—or
someone—is following us through there. I told you there
was something around here there shouldn't be—"

They'd both stopped short, instinctively, in order to listen the better. But now the sound itself had stopped too, as
if suiting its actions to theirs. There was an interval of
throbbing silence. Then a twig snapped betrayingly, as if
slowly crushed in twain under something's arrested weight.

All Sally's former nonchalance had left her by now.
"Oh, why didn't I listen to you!" she whimpered. She gave
her friend a push forward. "Don't let's stand here waiting
for it, whatever it is! Run, quick! Let's get out of here!"

With one accord they fled swiftly down the side of the
long, heartlessly empty road, again one behind the other.
The moment they did, the rustling resumed again behind
them, quickened in turn now. It was governed by whatever
they did, that was easy to see. It was the pursuer, and they
were its prey. It became a crashing at times, plainly audible
above their slapping footfalls and hot, frightened breaths.
A succession of lopes that cleared the ground and burst
headlong through the impeding foliage at each impetus.

"Scream," Sally panted. "Maybe someone will hear us!"

Marjorie hadn't waited to be told. "Help!" she keened
dismally, "Help!" But she was already too out of breath

from their long run to be able to emit more than a thin, disjointed bleat.

The rustling and crashing were changing direction now, drawing slowly but surely in toward them, coming diagonally at them instead of merely keeping parallel. There were many places where the coverage between was so thin they might have been able to glimpse who or what it was, but that would have meant slowing to turn their heads, and they were both too frightened and too intent on getting away. Or perhaps they realized instinctively that the sight of whatever it was might so add to their terror as to rob them of all further use of their limbs altogether.

Marjorie was the better runner of the two. She was taller and longer-waisted. Twice she caught herself pulling slowly away from the other girl, without meaning to; first by a five-yard lead, then by ten, then by more. Twice she stopped, waited for the gap to close, tried to pull her along with her by the hand. Sally evaded the offered link, perhaps afraid it would hamper both of them alike. "I'm all right," she heaved valorously. "Just keep going—!"

They were both staggering now from exhaustion, wavering, ready to fall. And the road never seemed to end, help never seemed to come, the horror behind them never seemed to tire.

She was aware of Sally beginning to drop behind again. Her shadow, which had been bobbing over Marjorie's own shoulder until now, in the moonlit gaps, fell short somewhere behind her, she couldn't see it any more. The sound of her harried breathing was no longer as distinct behind her either. But she couldn't go on herself any more, Marjorie. There was a knife in her side, and she found herself finally spent. "I can't keep up," she coughed. "I've got to fall down here. You go on—"

She swung around to let her friend go by, stood there swaying and weaving dizzily about in the road, like a drunk, from the long run.

The road was empty behind her, in moonlight and shadow, back as far as the eye could reach. Sally wasn't on it any more. There was only silence, on it and in the thickets that bordered it. Silence and moonlight and shadow.

No, not quite empty either. At the roadside, peering out between the bushes, lay a wisp of something on the ground, back twenty or thirty yards from her. The edge of a dress. A corner of the bottom of a garment, inert on the ground.

Even as she looked, it was slowly withdrawn, this overlooked flounce, slowly dragged in from sight, in a way that showed its wearer's volition was no longer involved. A final whisk, and it had vanished.

Not a sound, not a cry, not a whisper.

She had never fainted before. Her senses were probably overcharged from the run, bringing on vertigo. She knew she wanted to get back there, to help her friend. Instead, somehow, she found herself flat on the ground, without any sensation of having fallen or of striking herself against it. Her eyes seemed to remain open, too. But all she could see was a pattern of spheres or disks of all sizes, big and medium and small, rising slowly before them in straight lines, like the bubbles in champagne.

A quarter of an hour later the coachman, returning belatedly for them with his curbed horse, found her straying dazedly along the roadside, near the place where he had left them. There were flecks of blood on her dress, it was tattered from brambles, her hair was straggling loosely down her shoulders, and she was holding a hand pressed distractedly crosswise to her forehead. She even made to pass him by, as if she didn't recognize the meaning of the carriage when she saw it.

He had to jump down beside her and take her by the arm to stop her. *"Señorita, que le pasó?"* he cried dismayedly.

"Take me to the police," she whispered, in an oddly quiet manner. "My friend's lying in there, torn to pieces."

Robles said on the telephone: "It would be easier if we had someone down here who speaks English. There is a police interpreter somewhere, but I cannot locate him. We have been giving her restoratives in the meantime and treating her for shock—"

Manning was at the *commandancia* within ten minutes.

The girl was sitting there in Robles' office. She was obviously not normal yet, he could tell that at sight. Yet she was not weeping or even noticeably nervous any longer. She seemed, continually, to be lost in thought. A strange icy calm seemed to have descended on her. She had a policeman's uniform coat thrown over her shoulders like a cape, to hide the blood spats and rents on the upper part of her dress. Her unfastened hair, without being recombed, had been pushed back behind her shoulders. It made her seem about sixteen. There was no other woman with her, the municipal police department not yet having any policewomen attached to its staff.

His first thought was anyone's first thought at sight of Marjorie King: what a beautiful person she was. But then he didn't think any further of it after that once—for the present. He hadn't gone there, naturally, to admire feminine beauty.

They weren't introduced. He just asked her a tactful question in English, and that elicited the story. Then he repeated it in his fluent, if somewhat raffish and ungrammatical, Spanish for Robles, and it was taken down stenographically. Even the repetition of it to him, he noticed, seemed unable to alter the numbness of mind that gripped her. It was as though she were speaking by rote, without the words having any meaning to her. It reminded him of cases of shell shock he had heard of, where the effects were delayed from twenty-four to forty-eight hours.

Robles and his camarilla of specialists were now ready to repair to the scene, which had naturally been already under police supervision long ahead of this, awaiting his arrival.

"It will not be necessary—" he started to assure the girl through Manning, but to everyone's surprise she showed a wish to go with them.

"It can't do anything more to me than it has already," she said, looking up at Manning.

He knew that she was addressing him and the rest of them without really seeing their faces, without differentiating among them as individuals at all.

"I don't want to go back to that room and be alone there. Not just yet anyway. I can sit in the car, without getting out."

In the end, because as she had pointed out she was no worse off in one place than in another, they allowed her to accompany them back. She sat in the rear, between Manning and Robles. The man that she had displaced rode outside, clinging to the top of the door frame.

The drive out to the Bosque was a grim and depressing one. They all felt heavy and sick and frustrated, faces broodingly downcast. Robles didn't even have a stomach for doing very much crowing to Manning about the error in the latter's whole thesis that this seemed to confirm once and for all, justified as he would have been in doing so.

"So I was right, you see," was all he said, in a curiously listless undertone across Marjorie's profile. "We've been holding Cardozo, and it's happened again right while he's in custody. I'll have to order his release at once."

"I made no direct accusation against him, if you remember," the American contented himself with remarking. "But the fact that it's not Cardozo doesn't necessarily mean that it's not a m—"

He refrained from finishing it. This was no time to wrangle over points of view, in the presence of this girl's livid grief.

"Are you sure you're all right?" he asked her solicitously, as they swung around the *glorieta* of the Puerta Mayor in a half circle, and then in.

"I wasn't hurt at all myself," she answered simply. "These stains are from twigs and leaves that smirched me when I went in there—where she was."

Robles had caught the sense of the remark by following the gesture of her hands. "You went *in there*, immediately afterwards?" he gasped in amazement. "But didn't you realize it could very well have attacked you, too? It must have been still lurking near by."

She looked at the two of them as though she didn't understand, when Manning had repeated it for her. "But she was my friend," she said. "I forgot about being frightened. You don't go off and leave your friend—even when it's too late."

"Es admirable," Robles commented softly, in an aside.

"Ya lo creo," the American nodded vigorously.

"You saw her?" They exchanged a look of consternation, knowing what it had been like three times before now.

"Enough to know that—it was over," she whispered. "It was dark, and I didn't have to see too much. It hadn't dragged her very far, just off the road into some ferns. I—I could see her foot sticking out through them."

Robles' own troubles came uppermost in his mind again. He bunched a fist against his forehead in despair. "I may as well hand in my resignation tomorrow," he muttered to Manning. "We were all warned, you heard what he said—"

"You've got something more to go by than you've had the times before, at least," Manning tried to encourage him. "For the first time you have a surviving witness to one of these attacks. Miss King may be able to help you in some unforeseen way."

"It isn't that we need to be told anything about it! Robles insisted heatedly. "What is there that we need to be told about it, anyway? This isn't a human murder case that depends on such things as identification, witnesses, alibis, fingerprints. It's that we haven't been able to catch the thing so far, that's all!"

"Stubborn jackass!" rasped Manning short-temperedly, turning his head away.

"Blind fool!" snapped the police inspector.

Somebody came out into the road ahead and flagged them with a pocket light to show that this was the place. The car drew up at the roadside and the men all got out. The girl remained in it, sitting in the middle of the spacious back seat, looking very alone there. She sat staring dry-eyed at nothing, Manning noticed, giving her a last glance as he followed the others down the road and into the thickets.

A tiny constellation of pocket torches, only a short distance in, marked where the advance guard were awaiting their arrival around the inscrutable ferns that formed the bier.

They went over one by one and had their look. It was the same thing over; an attack of ravening ferocity that hadn't stopped with mere death, that had continued, insatiable, long past it.

"This thing must be suffering with the jungle equivalent of rabies," one of the men shuddered. "To shoot it down is not enough, it should be cauterized over a slow fire."

"It should be caught first," Robles seethed.

He and Manning emerged and went back to the car. "Better get the girl out of here before they bring the stronger lights," the American suggested. "She has been through enough already without that."

"Where are you stopping, Miss King?"

"Tell him the Inglaterra Hotel."

"Hold yourself at our disposal for the next few days, that is all. You may go now."

The departmental car turned and drove back with her. The two men retreated into the thickets again.

One of Robles' subordinates shouted out suddenly, "I have found a print! And what a one!" And as they all came converging upon him with a rush, Manning included, he added knowingly: "Maybe this will shut up your American friend, eh *mi comandante*?" He was holding his torch trained steadily downward on it. It was in a soft green bed of moss, not far from the body; the nearly perfect imprint of a gigantic cat's paw—somewhat like a three-leaf clover.

Robles turned on Manning almost savagely, as though taking out his frustration on him. "*Now* tell me that wasn't made by a jaguar, I defy you to!"

"It was made by a jaguar," acquiesced Manning glumly. But then a moment later he continued: "It is too late in the game to ask me to change my viewpoint. I have seen too much that supports it. Now this, for example: these two girls running along one behind the other, the second one nearly at the first one's heels. You heard what she said back at your office. She didn't hear a sound. She didn't even know the girl was missing until she had turned her head. Well? I don't care how swiftly it sprang on her, downed her right behind her friend's back, she would have had time to give her death cry at least, to gasp, to gurgle. The sound of the fall alone would have been heard by the foremost girl. Why wasn't it? Because there *was* no fall. She was *lifted*, not felled. And there is only one way she could have been seized quickly enough to prevent both those things: the fall of her body and the instinctive cry of extinction—and that is by prehensile human hands closing around her windpipe, cutting off sound, *hoisting* her off her feet into the underbrush."

Robles advanced toward him almost with personal menace. "Do you realize that one blow from those terrible paws could crush her skull like an egg, kill her instantly?"

"Not instantly enough to keep a dying gasp, at least, from getting out. Sound is formed in the throat, not the head. It can only be cut off by constriction at the windpipe itself. And then what about the muffling of the fall? One goes down under a blow. She was transported erect, I tell you. She wasn't felled by the leap of an animal, she was snatched bodily off her feet in mid-career—by something upright itself!"

"Do you hear him? He's still looking for a man in this." Robles motioned offensively toward him with a jerk of his thumb. Then he waved him off. "Don't waste my time. I respected you until now, but you get worse as you go along. You're making me lose all regard for your intelligence. We found hairs of the jaguar's pelt on Teresa Delgado. We found the broken tip of its claw imbedded in Conchita Contreras' throat. We have found prints similar to this one on the ground about all of them. The laboratory has even found traces of blood-poison germs in their lacerations, such as these carnivorous animals are known to carry about imbedded in their claws. Do we have to sit the thing upright in your lap to get you to agree to its existence!"

"Man alive!" the American burst out exasperatedly. "There are signs all around you, big as life, and you won't take the trouble to see them, you're so dazzled by that

Crusoe-like footprint of yours! I don't even carry a badge, but I can see them; why can't you? For instance, look at that broken sprig there, bent down at right angles. That says what, to you *gente?*"

Robles curled his lip disdainfully at the naïveté of such a question. "It was swept aside and dislocated by the passage of the jaguar."

"Ah. And what was the jaguar doing, walking upright on its hind legs?" snarled Manning. "One of you stand over there alongside of it. Any one of you, it doesn't matter which. These ferns all around underfoot make the actual ground level hard to establish."

He fairly yelped his satisfaction when the comparison had been effected. "Look at that! It's even better than I thought. There's a depression there under the ferns, a trough in the ground! Your man's a five-and-half-footer and that dangling sprig is at the level of his shoulder. What a two-story jaguar that must be, to have broken it up there at that height!"

If he expected this to hold them, he was sadly mistaken. Robles didn't even pay him the compliment of having to think twice, faltering for an instant before he came back at him. "*Y que?*" he drawled. "*Must* it follow the contour of the ground? Is it a worm or snake? It wasn't crawling flat on its belly. Those two girls were in full flight and it was leaping headlong after them. What does any quadruped do in such a case? It vaulted over this hollow in the ground, its arched back swept that sprig aside, broke it."

Manning flung the undersides of his hands toward him. "You can have your jaguar! You're welcome to it." He took a few steps away, stopped long enough to deliver a parting shot. "Just trace its movements for a second. From the Callejón de las Sombras, where it originally disappeared, around to the Pasaje del Diablo, in the working-class quarter. From there, all the way around again to All Saints Cemetery on the southern outskirts of town. From there all the way across the city to the corner of Justicia and San Marco. And from there, back once more to the Bosque, here on the north side. All without being seen once! Here's another thing. All its victims have been women. Not old, not even middle-aged, but all young girls. That's a very precocious jaguar, *caballeros*. It seems to specialize." He turned his back on them with finality. "But there's no use talking to you. It's just a waste of good breath. I'm going home."

"I'm sure we'll be practically helpless without you," Robles called after him sarcastically.

6. BLACK ALIBI

MANNING AT SIGHT SUSPECTED some of the luggage of being hers when he stepped into the Inglaterra from the street. It was in the center of the tiled patio, and a glimpse of a red "MK" on the corner of one of the pieces confirmed his suspicion. There seemed to be, however, an unusual amount of it, and more was being added to it every time the creaking lift came down.

He went over to the desk. "Is that the *americana*, the one whose friend—?"

"She and everyone else, señor," the clerk said dolefully. "We are being emptied like the—how you say?—epidemic is here. Twenty-three rooms in last two hours—"

Manning was only interested in one of the twenty-three check-outs. "How soon is she leaving, do you know?"

"She take the *Santa Emilia* from Val, on Tuesday." He shrugged pessimistically. "She cannot be blamed, señor, no?"

"No," Manning agreed, lowering his head, "she cannot be blamed. I guess I'd go, too." He took out a cigarette, looking down at it thoughtfully without using it. Then he looked up again. "I wonder if she'll see me."

"I try, señor. Whose name shall I say?"

She probably wouldn't remember his name, from amidst all that horror the other night. She wouldn't have salvaged it. He gave it anyway.

"Mees Keeng, is Mister Manning here to see ju." The clerk nodded. "The twenty-four, señor, on secon' floor."

Manning took the stairs. The lift was still busy disgorging luggage at every down trip. As the clerk had said, there seemed to be a mass exodus on.

In fact, as he passed the open transom of a door on the second-floor corridor, he overheard an unmistakably American voice, feminine, saying to someone: "I don't care, Harvey Williams, business deal or no business deal. I will not spend another night in this city with that thing prowling around loose! You can sign those papers just as well down on the coast while we're waiting for the ship to sail—"

Yes, the panic was on.

Manning knocked on 24. Her voice said, "Come in."

She was in the middle of finishing packing her smaller pieces, the hand luggage. Three or four of them were ranged around her. She was in a white corduroy wrapper, tiny at the waist, spreading on the floor. She looked as though she hadn't slept since that night, and he glimpsed several small bottles of nerve tablets or sedative ranged on the stand beside her bed.

Pallor and the darkness about her eyes only made her more beautiful. You had to be as young as she, he told himself, to suffer and still turn out looking beautiful. When you got to be a few years older, and suffered, it just made you haggard.

The first thought that crossed his mind, before he'd even opened his mouth to her, was: "What made me come here? I had no right to. I should have stayed away and let her alone."

"You don't remember me," he said tactfully. "I'm the fellow—well, I was with them the other night."

"Oh," she said. Even the recollection still made her wince. "I thought it was somebody from the Express, about my reservation and tickets. No," she admitted, "I don't remember you."

"I really had no right to intrude like this," he murmured tactfully.

"No, it's all right. I'm all alone here and—it's nice to

have someone to talk to in your own language." She was not only sincere, she was almost pathetically grateful. "I was in bed all day yesterday. I only got up today because I had to—to complete the necessary arrangements for poor Sally." Her voice shook a little when she pronounced the name. "Sit down, Mr. Manning." She removed a small fitted toilet case from the seat of a chair.

"Won't I be in your way?"

"Most of my heavy packing is finished. I'm taking the night train down; that doesn't leave until ten, I understand. There's plenty of time—as long as I make sure I get out of this place." A look of unspeakable revulsion flitted across her face. "As long as I make sure I get out of this place!" Her intensity made her almost wild-eyed.

"I can understand how you feel," he said sympathetically.

"It's been pretty bad," she went on in a more composed voice, sitting down and crossing her knees, but then robbing the attitude of all repose by plucking incessantly at the fabric of her white robe just over her kneecap. "I had all her things to put away. I could see imaginary rips and tatters on every—" She bit her lip, forbore going ahead.

He was acutely uncomfortable, as men always are in the presence of feminine emotion.

"And the trip up isn't going to be easy either. It's the same ship we came down on together and—well you know how it is."

He supposed not, he said almost inaudibly. He felt as though he had six hands and feet.

"She'd looked forward so to this vacation," she went on after a moment's quiet. "The last few weeks, before we left, she kept coming over to my house nearly every other night, to show me some latest addition she'd made to her wardrobe, to plan some new detail. She was even taking Spanish lessons, at the end. And to have it end like this!"

He thought maybe it was better for her to get it all out of her system instead of keeping it pent up, didn't try to change the subject.

"We've lived next door to each other ever since we were a pair of knock-kneed little brats with braces on our teeth.

Went to school together, went to dances together. Her poor mother's waiting up there now. And I've got to go back and face her. Bring her back in a *box*." She did something to her shapely eyebrows with the fingers of one hand.

"Have you cabled?" he asked gently.

"Yes. I had to, of course. I didn't say what it was. I couldn't bring myself to. Not on teletype strips." She halted, went on thoughtfully: "There's something so unspeakable about what it really was."

If you only knew, he concurred unheard.

"I let them think pneumonia. Now when I do get back, that's another thing I'll have to tell them." Her voice trailed off, and in the silence he got up to go.

He really intended going without a word, without broaching what had been on his mind when he came here. Then unexpectedly, as he was already at the door, she gave him the opening he had no longer been seeking. "They haven't caught it yet, have they?" she asked.

"No, they haven't," he answered, turning and looking square at her. "And they won't."

"Why do you say that?"

"Because, Miss King, it's not a jaguar," he told her quietly.

She stared at him intently for a long moment. He could see her already wan face paling still more, before his very eyes, as his meaning sank in with terrible slowness.

"Oh no," she grimaced sickly at last, drawing the back of her hand across her lips, "I couldn't bear that thought. If anything can make it worse than it was already—that does."

"Shall I go ahead, or would you rather I didn't?"

But the question was superfluous, he could see the damage was done already. She just kept staring at him in a frozen, furrowed horror. If he shut up now, he'd leave her with that anyway.

He lowered his voice. "It's a man. No one else in Ciudad Real believes that but me, but I do. I say it now, and I'll keep on saying it—anytime, anyplace, anywhere. It had already happened three times before the other night. I don't know whether you know that or not; they may have tried to keep it from visitors because of the tourist season. But it's common knowledge among us here."

"I remember now, the clerk downstairs tried to warn us that night. But in a veiled way, without coming out openly with what he meant—"

"Do you think you can stand it if I—?"

"Yes, I think I want you to."

By the time he had finished, he had marshaled every argument for her benefit that he had ever presented to Robles at any time, from beginning to end; every detail, every piece of evidence.

"I'm sure I'm right, I've got to be!" he said, slapping his own thigh fiercely. "But I can't get them to listen to me. They're as sure on their side as I am on mine. And they're the police and I'm just—a loose guy."

She took a deep, shuddering breath. She'd stood it well. Even better than he'd expected her to. Perhaps because it had been presented to her objectively, and not introspectively. There was horror in her eyes, but something else as well; a glint of something steely that hadn't been there before. Call it hatred, call it fury. You don't hate irrational animals.

He couldn't tell whether he'd convinced her or not. She didn't answer for a moment or two. Finally she said in a muffled voice, "To think that a human being, a thing calling itself a man—" And that was the answer, there.

He strode over to the open floor-length windows that Sally had stood looking out of only two nights before at this same time. The city sprang to view below, bejeweled with twinkling lights. Silver talcum seemed to blur the long vistas of the main avenues, and the cathedral reared its graceful twin turrets black against the rising apricot moon coming up over the hills.

"Pretty to look at, isn't it?" he said, turning to her. "But out there on one of those lovely streets you see from here, some young girl is going walking tonight. Or is going to stand waiting for her sweetheart in some secluded, romantic spot. Or maybe is only going to stray away from a lively party for a few minutes, out onto a terrace or down into a garden for a breath of air. And you and I know the rest! A horrid thing on the ground will be all that's left of her. And something that thinks like we do will gloat, safe in his hiding place—while the damn-fool police go around looking for a jaguar behind hedges and under rose bushes! If it isn't tonight, it'll be tomorrow night, or the night after. But it'll happen again. Again and again and again!"

"And—?" she breathed fearfully. He could see she was steeling herself to ask it. "Why do you come here telling me this? I've already lost my own friend that way. I'm leaving here. Why do you tell me what'll happen to the next girl? What is it you want *me* to do?"

He gave it to her curtly. "I want you to be that next girl. Be the bait for him, it, whatever you want to call him."

Her eyes dilated. She drew back a step. "I think you're out of your mind. Do you know what you're saying? I can't get out of this hateful place quick enough, as it is! I can't wait to see the last of it! I can't sleep nights. My baggage has gone down to the ship already. There won't be another for the next thirty days. And you're asking me to stay on here *alone*, by myself, after losing my life-long friend! You, a stranger, have the nerve to walk into my hotel room and suggest, not only that, but that I go out deliberately looking for this—this abomination, seeking him, trying to attract him. All to give you the satisfaction of proving some theory of yours to be right!" Her voice rose. "Will you please leave? Will you kindly get out of here?"

"I'm going, Miss King," he said acquiescently, without taking offense.

"Please do," she urged coldly. "I should think you would have had the consideration to leave me alone. To go to someone else, at least. But to come to *me*, of all people—" Her closing of the door behind him cut the rest of it off.

It was still going on behind that other transom, too, as he repassed it on his way out. "Well, then you'll just stay on here alone, Harvey Williams, I'm warning you now! I'm going to be on that train at ten o'clock tonight and nothing's going to stop me—!"

He didn't blame her, whoever she was. He blamed Marjorie King even less. The one he blamed was himself, for approaching her with such a suggestion in the first place; he should have had sense enough to realize the state of mind she was bound to be in, after such an ordeal.

He strode out through the tiled lobby. The luggage pile in the center of it hadn't diminished any, had augmented if anything. The clerk was nodding his head busily, with one of the spindly, nickel-trimmed Ericsson handsets held to the side of his face. Manning obliviously heard him snap his fingers in mid-conversation, but he had already gone past, thought it was meant for one of the bellhops.

He pushed out through the revolving door, stood for a minute under the glass entrance canopy, adjusting his hat. A dark-skinned bellboy hopped out after him, touched his arm. "Señor, the *dirección*—"

Manning went inside to the desk again. The clerk said, "Mees Keeng, she call down just as you go by. She ask for to have you go up again a minute if you don't mind."

No, Manning's sudden hopeful grin answered for him, he didn't mind. He didn't mind at all. He took the stairs again, but this time by fives, a full leg-spread. The argument behind the ubiquitous open transom seemed finally to have been settled too. "Give me your pajamas, Harvey," the same feminine voice as before was cooing, "there's room enough left in my valise for them."

Marjorie King had opened the door for him before he quite reached it, then turned back into the room again. She began on an oddly aimless note when he stepped over the threshold. "A funny thing happened just now, after you'd left. I thought I'd packed everything of hers away, but I happened to go to the closet and I came across this." She was holding a small woolen vestee or half sweater, with exaggerated puff sleeves, aloft in her hand. "She was never without it. She knitted it herself, I used to watch her doing it. Every morning going down in the bus. The other night, *that* night, before we left, the last thing she said was, 'Think I'll need this?' "

She wasn't being weepy about it any more. There was a flinty decisiveness lurking underneath the quiet poignancy with which she spoke. "You see, Mr. Manning, she was the dearest friend I had in the world. I don't think I'll ever find anyone to quite take her place. What I'm trying to say to you is, if a man did that, and you think by staying I can be of some help in—in settling accounts for her, well, I—I'm ready to be that *next girl*."

"I don't want you going into this blindly," he warned her. "I know it's asking a lot, and I know Robles would put a stop to it fast if he ever caught my trying such a thing. All you've got to do is say no, and I won't blame you." He waited, watching her.

"I've already given you my answer," she said with quiet determination. "If it's a man, I'm staying, I want to. If it's a jaguar, a force of nature, something that doesn't know what it's doing, that can't be called to account, then that's a different matter entirely."

"If it were a jaguar, you wouldn't need to stay, it would have been caught by now, probably within twenty-four hours after it bolted into the Callejón."

"All right, we begin." She moved briskly to the transom, shut it tight. She went over to the phone, said, "Send my baggage back upstairs, I'm staying." And then in answer to something that was asked, she snapped the one word, "Indefinitely," and hung up. On her way back to him again, she caught up her unbound hair and fastened it up the rear curve of her head, somewhat like a ship clearing its decks for action. It made her look a little more sophisticated, none the less beautiful. "Now!" she said. She sat down opposite him, head tilted attentively. The period of futile mourning was past, it was easy to see that. "Help yourself to those," she said parenthetically, "if they help you to think better," and motioned toward a pack of American cigarettes.

There was a moment or two of silence. She was the first one to speak. "To be the bait, he must be drawn to me next. Out of every girl and woman in this city. How are we going to manage that? How can I hope to succeed in attracting his attention?"

"You can't if we just leave it to chance. The law of averages would be too strongly against it. You could walk the streets alone at night, every night for the next ten years, and he might strike all around you, but never come near you again. It must be a setup. Now here's what my idea is. If he reads the papers at all, he's sure to read the rehashes of his own monstrosities, if nothing else. He must have seen there were two of you that night, he must have followed you from the time you both left the restaurant. I'm wondering if there isn't some way I can plant—but very subtly, so that he doesn't scent a trap—in the newspapers, along with the accounts of your previous experience, the idea that you would be foolhardy enough, scatterbrained enough, to go back again to some such place, unaccompanied, even after what happened the last time. And along with an even defter hint that you got a look at him, would be able to identify him. In that way, there'll be two powerful impulses pulling him toward you: his maniacal urge itself, whatever that is, and also his sense of self-preservation."

"But isn't it farfetched? Would even a deranged mind swallow such a probability?"

"It won't be easy to swing it. Let's see if we can hammer something out between us. To begin with, you must realize that they believe an American capable of anything down here, to them we're all half wacky in the first place. That'll help some." He tapped on the ends of his spread fingers one by one. "You have a passion for taking walks in the moonlight, you don't intend to let anything interfere with your habits— No, that's no good."

They both shook their heads in unison. "That wouldn't tell him just where to find you, even if he did fall for it," he added.

He glanced aside at the discarded sweater of Sally O'Keefe, suddenly brightened. "Wait a minute, I've got it—that gave me an idea. Something belonging to one or the other of you. Something of sentimental value, that you cannot bear to part with. You dropped it there that night, by the lake. A locket, say, that was given to you by your mother when you were a child. Or a goodluck charm. Something that you are determined not to leave the city until you have recovered."

"It's better than the first one, but there are still things

against it. Wouldn't I be expected to go back well escorted, even if I did go back to look for it? And why would it have to be at night? Why wouldn't I go during the daylight hours?"

"But he'll be watching for you, and he'll see with his own eyes that you have come back alone, and that you *have* come back at night. What more proof can he want than that? The thing is, his attention will be drawn to that vicinity a second time, and that's the main thing we want. Once he's lurking around, the rest will follow automatically. He'll see that you're alone, and he'll—" He didn't finish it.

"It just may work," she assented.

"It's flimsy, but it just may work; that's the best we can hope for about the whole thing anyway, there's no guarantee it will. Through my press-agenting I have an in at most of the editorial staffs in town, I can get the item in the papers without much trouble. And without letting them catch on, naturally. Just a personal interview with you here at the hotel, submitted to put a little change in my pockets. If it should come to Robles' attention, I can shunt him off by saying there's not a word of truth in it, I just made it up, you're actually scared stiff and taking the next train out of town.

"It must be very delicately done. It mustn't be overemphasized, that would give it away. Just a couple of words thrown in offhand. Just enough to give *his* warped brain the idea, without letting him realize where he got it from himself, if possible. After all, this will be a short cut for him. He'll know ahead of time where to look for another prospective victim, alone and helpless. Before he had to roam around endlessly, waiting for the right combination of circumstances. That wasn't easy to get. I think he'll fall for it. I think his murderous ego must be sufficiently swollen by now for him to disregard minor drawbacks that would have been enough to deter him in the beginning. He must think he can get away with anything by this time. And then there'll be the added little spur that you may have seen him, that he'd better see to it he gets rid of you without further ado, to ensure the continuance of his own immunity."

"What about this police official and his men, aren't they likely to be buzzing around in that park as thick as flies for the next week or so, after what happened the other night? They might frighten him away. Hadn't we better make it some other place?"

He dug his fingers absently through his hair. "I don't know of any other that would serve as well. To shift the locale would do away with your supposed motive for returning, that is, to reclaim something you lost in there the first time. And then its size is an added inducement to him. The others are all pretty small, wouldn't afford enough cover."

"Very well, then, let's make it the Bosque. You probably know best."

"I think we have a beter chance there than almost anywhere else, no matter how farfetched it may strike you at first. For one thing, he probably watched the two of you through the trees at the Madrid, singled you out, even before you got back into the carriage that night. If he has an opportunity to do that again, watch you at his leisure over a period of an hour or two beforehand, make sure that you are entirely alone, I think the temptation will be that much stronger. We will have a chance to get in a sort of buildup of his self-confidence, so to speak. That would be lacking if you were just to roam aimlessly around some small park inside the city. In fact, I think it would look suspicious, more than anything else. For another thing, I think the recklessness, the effrontery, the supreme cheek, of returning to the same place a second time will appeal irresistibly to his egomania, give him an added thrill that he won't be able to pass by." He put out his cigarette. "As far as Robles and his bunch of dimwits are concerned, I think there's an easy-enough way of getting rid of them. I'll phone in a false report to one of the *genedarmerías* of having seen the jaguar, big as life, in an entirely different section of the city. For a few pesos extra I can even get a handful of sidewalk bums here and there to confirm it simultaneously, on other public telephones. That will draw them all away from the Bosque, clear it beautifully for us."

"Yes, but will *he* know that? He may suspect them of still lurking—"

"He can find out for himself whether or not the Bosque is empty, without any added risk, can't he? Remember, they're looking for a beast in all this, not a biped. God knows how many times he has already brushed shoulders with them undetected, maybe even returned to gaze on his own handiwork from the outskirts of those morbid crowds that have gathered at each place. He can go into the Bosque in perfect safety, see for himself whether there are any stray details of police left around, for they are working openly on this jaguar job, not under cover as they would with human quarry, and when he is convinced that there aren't, concentrate on you unhindered."

A cord at the side of her neck stood out briefly, but she gave no other sign. "That's the way we'll do it," he summed up. She was silent for a moment. Finally she asked, with a flicker of a smile that swept by too soon to be able to take a very firm hold on her features, "What night will we pick for this—date with destruction?"

"Night after tomorrow. That'll give us forty-eight full hours to get everything ready. It's too late for me to make the morning papers with my doctored item any more, but I can make tomorrow evening's in plenty of time. I'll arm you, of course, and I'll be close enough by to see that no harm happens to you. But I've got to get another man in on it with me. You've got to be fully protected, I don't want to take any chances on that score, and it may turn out to be something more than I can handle successfully alone."

"Whom will you get?"

He pondered the matter a moment. "I can't go to Robles or any of his outfit, they all think alike about it. It's got to be someone I can count on heart and soul. Wait, I think I know—that young fellow, what was his name again, the Contreras girl's sweetheart, the one she used to meet in the cemetery. He ought to be all for it, if anyone is! That must have turned him inside out."

He stood up, and she accompanied him to the door. He turned there and looked into her face searchingly. "Now look, before we go any further. There's still time for you to back out if you want to. I don't want to frighten you, but it's going to be a grueling experience, as bad or worse than the first time. Worse, in fact, because now you'll know what to look forward to ahead of time. You'll be under a terrific strain, and have to rely completely on your own judgment, for three or four hours at a stretch. We'll be watching every moment, from as near by as we dare, but we can't exactly dog your footsteps or reveal ourselves to you once you're in there, if we hope to succeed; you realize that of course. So here's your last chance to say no, if you want to."

She looked up into his face unwaveringly. Her mouth was just a little taut, that was all. "I'm in it with you, I thought I made that plain from the beginning."

"Swell!" he answered warmly. "Shall we shake on it?" They gripped hands briefly. "I'll make all the arrangements. You get all the sleep you can for the next two nights," he advised her, opening the door. "The night after tomorrow is going to be a tough one on all of us. And try to keep from thinking of it ahead of time, if you can, Miss King."

"Call me Marjorie," she suggested as she started to close the door after him. "You mayn't have the chance for very long."

He got the address from the records of the inquest held over Conchita Contreras. It was a pleasant little one-story house, whitewashed a pastel blue, on the hilly Calle San Vicente. A serving-woman let him into a patio that was a permanent explosion of vivid magenta from the bougainvillaea trailing down its center from the tiled roof overhead. A couple of white butterflies were chasing one another endlessly around in the postage-stamp-sized square of open sunlight, and a dark-eyed little girl peeped shyly out at him from one of the room doorways, then drew back again. It looked like the perfect setting for a very happy home. Manning knew it wasn't, even before he had been shown into the room where the young fellow his own age lay sprawled indolently on one elbow on a cot.

The young fellow's hair was matted, he needed a shave, his shirt was soiled and open at the collar, and he had the red-rimmed eyes that came out of the cantinas at five in the morning. An unlighted cigarette, looped over in the middle like a piece of macaroni, was dangling between his lips.

He saw Manning's eyes go to the photograph that had fallen to the floor beside the cot. He squinted at him with jerky querulousness. "You see a photograph down there, don't you?" he said truculently. "A lovely face, a tender smile, soft beautiful hair. You're lucky, *amigo*. I don't! I'd like to swap eyes with you. How much'll you take? I see a horrid, nameless thing, a smear of blood, clawed rags in a huddle on the ground—"

Manning looked down at the hubs of his own shoes. "I know. I was there too."

"At night, sometimes, I hear a faint cry coming to me in the dark from where that photograph stands. 'Raul, Raul, get me out, I'm locked in!' Just as she must have cried unheard that night. I drink *aguardiente* to kill it. I still hear it anyway. It drives me out to roam the midnight streets—"

Manning put a hand lightly to his shoulder, turned and looked the other way. "Steady, *muchacho*, steady. That's what I came to you about."

Raul reached down, pulled a half-empty bottle of the stinging native brandy out from under the cot. He kicked the cork out with the thumb of the same hand that gripped the bottle's neck. He gave his mouth a preliminary wipe. "I don't know who you are or what you want, but have a drink. That's the best a man can do when his girl is gone for good. More tears for my poor mother, inside there in the other room."

Manning took the bottle, set it back on the floor again. "No, there is something better still that he can do." He sat down on a rickety straw-bottom chair, dislodging a battered hat that had been dangling from one of its uprights. "Look, I know what the trouble is. You are pent up, you are slowly strangling with your own grief, because it was an act of fate. You cannot fight back at it. I am here to tell you you can fight back at it; it was not an act of fate, it was an act of man." He watched the other's face. "That hurts, doesn't it? Like the antiseptic that cleans a festering wound."

It must have. The other man—he was only a boy, really —writhed there on the cot, from one side to the other, protective hands digging into his own face.

"Who are you to know?" he said through them finally.

"Just a guy like you. A guy who uses his eyes. It went *back* over the wall into the stone-built city again, instead of staying in the foliage, the open green place of the cemetery. Does a wild thing do that? Would its nature lead it to?"

The other's hands went down. He looked at Manning. His eyes were dangerous things. Not toward the American, toward the mental image the latter had managed to conjure up before him.

Manning went on speaking, in a low, unhurried voice: telling him about the other cases, telling him all there was to be told. "I may be wrong," he concluded. "I'm no mystic, I haven't second sight. But I don't think I am. There is no way of finding out except by putting it to the test."

"How? How are you thinking of going about it?"

Manning told him that, too.

"We need a girl."

The pronoun didn't escape Manning. "I've already got the girl," he said. "A very brave girl. A girl who has more courage than you or I have any right to expect any girl to have."

Raul gripped his upper arm in a vise of iron that belied his slender frame. "When do we start?" he said tersely.

"Right tonight," the American said. "And we keep it up —every night if necessary—until we find out one way or the other."

"Then what are we waiting for?" He sprang up on the cot with a suddenness that nearly buckled it. *"Mama!"* he

bawled inside to the other room. And the childish epithet
sounded oddly inappropriate coming in his husky, deep-
toned voice. "Black coffee, for the love of God, to get this
porquería out of my system! A clean shirt, and a razor,
and a basin of hot water. You can stop worrying. Your son
is alive again!"

Last paragraphs of an item, in identical language, in *El
Imparcial, La Prensa, Ultimas Noticias*, and all the other
evening papers:

> . . . One left Miss King with a strange feeling that
> perhaps she really meant it, it was not just bravado; that
> she would return some night again soon to the lake in
> the Bosque, seeking this trinket that she seems to place
> such store upon. Perhaps tonight, perhaps tomorrow
> night, who knows? One can only admire such reckless
> disregard for ordinary common sense, even if one does
> not approve of it. The Americans are a strange race.
>
> "We have a saying in our language," she said, as she
> accompanied the interviewer to the door: "Lightning
> never strikes in the same place twice." And then, with a
> smile that the newspaper representative found most
> baffling, she added: "I am not afraid of any jaguar. I
> have good eyes. Very good eyes, even in the dark. It has
> always been said of me that I never forget a face." One
> left with a puzzled feeling that she had not told all she
> knew—even to the police.

It was nearing sundown when they arrived at the Inglaterra. She said, "Come in," in answer to Manning's low,
confidential knock on the door, and they found her standing in the middle of the room. Her arrested posture
indicated they had interrupted her in the act of pacing
agitatedly back and forth, waiting for their arrival.

"At last," she greeted them limply. "I've been dressed
since four, and I was getting more nervous by the minute. I
didn't know whether you'd changed your plans or not, and
there was nowhere I could reach you. You said tonight, so
I went ahead and fixed up for the Madrid anyway, in order
to be ready. Is this all right?" She backed away a step in
order to let them take in a white evening gown sewn with
crystal beads.

"Good. Just the thing!" Manning said approvingly. "It'll glitter in the dark and make it easier for him to pick you out. Are you frightened?"

"I'm getting over it now by degrees," she admitted. "But you should have seen me a half-hour ago. My teeth kept chattering every few minutes."

"Here's something I brought over for you." He took a small-caliber gun out of his pocket, handed it over to her haft first. "Put it in your evening bag. Do you know anything about using them?"

"I can't exactly say that I've been brought up on them, but I'll probably know what to do with it, if I have to, when the time comes."

"Just get rid of this, that's the safety, and tighten your finger, and that's all you have to remember. And, Marjorie, if you should have to, don't just *threaten*. Use it first, and then threaten; you're up against something that—"

"I know," she said, quickly blinking the thought out of her mind.

"Will it go in?"

"I've got a bigger one here, with drawstrings. It'll go in that. It opens faster than this envelope type, too."

Raul had been standing politely by, listening to their unknown talk.

"Excuse me, my manners," Manning apologized. "Miss King, Raul Belmonte. You two will have to communicate by signs."

They bowed to one another, as though it were some sort of social function and not a death party they were about to start out on.

"Have you seen the papers? It worked!" Manning went on. "Oh, I forgot, you don't read much Spanish. Anyway, they've swallowed it hook, line, and sinker. I phoned Robles at his headquarters a little while ago, and he told me there's not a man left in the Bosque. They've all been sent over to the latest danger zone, over by the Hippodrome race track. He got six calls from there inside of twenty minutes, all reporting having seen it in broad daylight, under the race-track stands. Not only that, there's a big shake-up impending, he couldn't dare afford to ignore this sudden flood of notifications. His own sense of duty wouldn't have let him anyway."

"Were those your six calls?"

"I paid for seven, but one guy evidently got cold feet and absconded with the peso gratuity."

"Did you get the other thing in?"

"It's been in since last night. He's read it by now, if he's going to read it at all."

He stopped, ground his hands together a little nervously, like a surgeon about to perform an operation or a dentist about to extract a tooth. "Now, Marjorie—"

"I know; zero hour," she said, with a facial shiver that was only partly a parody.

"You'll have to leave here by yourself. Belmonte and I are clearing out right now, as soon as I run over this with you, so we can get set out there by the lake before dark. We can't start out with you, because there's no way of knowing at just what point freedom from observation stops and surveillance sets in. It may be right downstairs at the door of the hotel. It may be out at the Madrid. It may not be until you reach the lake itself. You leave here about half an hour after dark. Take an open carriage like you did that night. At the Madrid be sure you're given an outside table, at the very edge of the pavilion, so he can ogle his fill at you. Insist on it. Keep your eyes away from the dark, don't try to look for him, you won't be able to see him anyway. Take all the time you want dining and sitting there. Try to avoid giving an impression of tension or restlessness. Above all, don't let anyone tangle with you while you're there. If he sees anyone sit down with you even for a few minutes, it may frighten him off. This is a psychological buildup as much as a visual one."

"And then?"

"The lake and the swans, like with Sally. That's the target range."

"Won't the coachman's presence be an obstacle?"

"Was it the last time? He did something to frighten the horse away. Give him rope, stray away from the horse and carriage, down below by the lake's edge."

She swallowed, held her own throat. "Manning, I'm not

trying to back out, but your mention of that detail makes me wonder. The way those swans and that horse were frightened—they must have *scented* something rather than heard or saw it. Suppose there really is a jaguar in it— what'll I do? It'll be a little harder to save me from that."

"There must be a jaguar in it somewhere," he told her bluntly. "Too much of Robles' evidence points to that. But my contention is, it's a jaguar *and* a man. In other words, a jaguar under control, directed by a human intelligence in some way."

"You mean he—takes it with him, sets it loose upon the victims? But how can you do anything in time to help me, in that case? Those things spring like lightning."

"I don't know what it is or what he does. I only know it's not a random beast. That's what we're trying to find out tonight. I'm asking you to have confidence in me, Marjorie. Belmonte and I will both lay down our lives rather than let any harm come to you. As long as there is a human agency involved, I feel confident we can outmatch it. I realize it's a terrible ordeal to ask you to go through. But we've got to have a girl in it—it doesn't attack men— and there isn't anyone else I know of we can ask to help us."

"There isn't anyone else you have to ask," she told him. "I'm not going to lie to you and pretend I'm not scared; I'm scared sick. But it's been understood since two nights ago that I'm going to do this, and that still goes." Her lips were tight and thin. He touched her clenched hand and found it ice cold. He liked her all the better for that somehow.

"And how long do I stay down by the lake in case nothing happens?"

"Until you've found the missing locket."

"Oh, there really is one there?"

"Yes, I bought one at the five-and-ten and planted it there myself this morning. It's right at the water's edge, under a few loose stones. Smoke a cigarette, for good measure after you've found it, if you want to time yourself. Meander along the lake shore for a short distance, and don't forget what I told you, make sure you stray out of the coachman's sight while you're about it. If, by the time you've finished your cigarette, nothing has happened, you can be sure he's not around, won't show up any more tonight. Simply get back into the carriage and return here to the hotel. We'll follow you back in a few minutes' time ourselves."

"The sun's getting low," Belmonte warned in Spanish, glancing toward the window. "It's hit the cross on the cathedral. We'd better get started ourselves if we want to get there while it's still light enough for us to pick our own hiding places."

He bent gallantly over Marjorie's hand, murmuring, "Homage to a very courageous lady."

Manning took it in turn, shook it encouragingly in American fashion. "Here goes. Now keep cool, and put your faith in us. I looked that gun over for you myself, it's in hair-trigger readiness. Remember what I told you: just flick off the safety and tighten your finger. And if it's a case of real emergency, don't take time to draw it out, fire it through your bag and all."

Raul, unemotional for a South American, perhaps because he was so tense, stood waiting for him in the corridor outside. "Come on, Manning, we'll never get there," he urged in a matter-of-fact voice, as though they were going to the corner for a drink.

She had reseated herself at the glass, was touching a glass perfume rod behind each ear, as he closed the door after him. "See you back here later tonight—I hope," was the last thing she said.

"See you back here later tonight—I know," he answered confidently.

The last glimpse he had of her face it was white as marble, even in the pink sunset glow, with the dread anticipation of what lay ahead of her. She was staring tautly at her own reflection, as at a death's head.

The lake was deepening in the twilight, from ultramarine to indigo to licorice black, as though ink were being poured into it little by little at some unseen source. The Bosque was sinking into darkness all around it as silent and as lifeless as though it were an actual wilderness instead of a great natural park on the outskirts of a big city. All the little harmless things that sounded in it in the daylight hours, the birds and insects, were stilled now. A breathless hush hung over everything, awaiting the arrival of the greatest killer of them all: night; remorselessly tracking down day and slaughtering it, every twenty-four hours, over and over again. The eternal murder, unpunished, unprevented.

Manning squatted low on his haunches at the water's edge, invisible from the higher ground above, tossing small pebbles in while he waited for Belmonte to rejoin him. They had separated to scout the perimeter of the lake, and he was the first one back at their point of departure. A little rounded figure there in the twilight, unimpressive; an ex-beachcomber, a discharged press agent, a do-nothing from the downtown bars, come out of the city to this place to battle the forces of death. No figure of a hero, no figure of a hero at all. Any more than the man who first submitted to the bite of a yellow-fever mosquito.

The swans hung motionless on the water, like dark floating clouds, heads tucked within their wings in sleep, disdainful of his pebble ripples after their first investigation had showed them it wasn't crumbs he was pitching in.

Belmonte returned noiselessly along the water's edge, bent forward so that his form wouldn't show too much from above. He dropped down beside Manning in a similar squat.

"Find one for yourself?" the latter breathed.

"See those reeds there? I've chosen them. They seem to be growing out of the water, but there's actually a flat stone in the middle of them I can squat on. I'll be hidden on all four sides, even the lake side. How about you?"

"I've found a low forked tree, a peach. The trunk splits up into four elbow branches. It's almost cup-shaped in the middle. All I need to do is pull down a few of the outer leaves around me. Made to order."

"Can you get down in a hurry?"

"At a single bound. It's low, it grows out crooked, slant-

ing from the slope toward the lake. See anyone just now?"
"Not a living soul. I went halfway around to the other side."

"No one around my way, either," Manning answered guardedly. "I think we better get in now, without waiting any longer, while we have this in-between darkness before the moon comes."

"Do you still think it's a good idea to separate?" Belmonte whispered. "Once we do, we won't be able to communicate with each other again."

"It's the only sensible way. We can protect her that much more effectively if there's one of us on each side of her. Here—midway between us—is where she will come down to the water's edge. She is bound to. It is the only place where the lake comes within easy reach of the roadway above. The road slowly curves off again from here on. And finally, this is the only strip of the shore that is smooth and grassy and easily accessible. It is where she and the other girl came the last time. He knows that, and it is where he will expect her to come again, if he believes she will come back looking for something she lost. We have her protected on three sides, this way. You up that way, I down this way, and the lake itself all along the third side. The waiting carriage up above seals up the fourth way. To get to her at all, he has to come up from behind one of us and go past. Probably from behind me, because the Madrid's over my way. The thing to do is not jump him at sight; to let him get in *between* the two of us, and then we'll have him coming and going.

"So it's as important for us to be hidden from the back as from the front, where she is. Otherwise he'll be frightened off before he comes within reach, and we're liable to lose him. Now don't leave anything on you or around you that will show. Remember, there's going to be a moon in a little while, and one little glint in the wrong place and at the wrong time will give us away. Fasten your coat lapels up under your chin, to black out the white of your shirt front. Don't leave anything shiny exposed anywhere on you—a collar pin or cuff links or even the clip of a metal pencil fastened to the outside of your breast pocket. Careful of any loose coins jangling in your clothes, too, at the wrong moment."

They each took out a large, square pocket handkerchief and, without opening its folded layers, deposited their accumulated small change on top of it, twisting the ends over and repocketing it that way, in a sort of soundproof cornucopia.

"No smoking," Manning warned. "Can you control yourself?"

"Of course; this isn't a date with a girl. I could wait forever, I could go without food or drink, if I thought it would bring this—"

"Got your gun handy?"

Belmonte parted his coat with a single move and it peered out in his hand.

"Fast enough," commented Manning. He held his wrist nearly to his eye, peering at his watch. "Five to eight. It's going to be a long pull. She's only just about leaving the hotel now. We'll have to give it a good two hours, maybe even three." He unstrapped it and dipped it into his pocket. "The moon may catch the crystal."

Belmonte took his own off, after first setting it back a minute. "I have four to, but I may as well go by yours. One watch, one purpose, one hope between the two of us."

"Well, we'd better break."

"All right, so long," Belmonte said curtly, gripping his hand.

"Take it easy," the American breathed.

They turned their backs on one another, sidled in opposite directions, blended at a yard or two into the impenetrable gloom.

The reeds hissed a little, over one way, stilled again. The leafy branches of a tree rustled a little, over the other way, as Manning hoisted himself up among them, shifted about for a moment or two, settling his weight. Then they too became silent, motionless.

There wasn't a sound about the shadowy lake. The Bosque all around it was as silent and as lifeless as though it were an actual wilderness, instead of a great

natural park on the outskirts of a big city. A breathless
hush hung over everything, awaiting the arrival of the
greatest killer of them all—

It was the going-out hour, when Ciudad Real answered
the call of night life heart and soul. She stepped out of the
hotel entrance, looking so glittering, so frivolous, in her
crystal-beaded white gown, a silver poppy in her hair, a
looped silver evening pouch dangling from her wrist, pulled
a little out of shape by something heavy resting in it—
perhaps opera glasses—that it was obvious there could be
nothing more serious on her mind than dancing and champagne. People passing on the sidewalk turned and smiled a
little in sympathy as they saw her emerge, she looked so
festive and so carefree. They may have even envied her,
some of them.

Lights were flashing everywhere, and she was one with
them, and with the mood they conjured up. A fiery monkey high against the night sky kept disappearing and returning again, once with its eyes covered, the next time
with its ears, the next with its mouth, proclaiming, "Anis del
Mono." A rooster with green tail feathers, more steady,
urged without interruption: "Cinzano Vermouth." The
sidewalks were like noon under this flashing, blinding, man-
made constellation. Every table at every café was taken,
and taxis swarmed through the streets with a furious twit-
tering of their horns.

The going-out hour; now let's relax, now let's have fun,
now let's forget there's such a thing as work and care.

She stood there, the tiny silver wedges of her slippers
poised at the brink of the curb, and stopped the hotel doorman as he was raising the looped whistle about his neck.
"No, not a taxi. Carriage with a horse. *Caballo*, understand?"

He ran down to the next corner to get her one personally, came back poised on the step of it, one leg swinging
free.

She got in. "To the Madrid."

The coachman and the doorman exchanged a glance.
Indistinct Spanish phrases passed between them.

"You tell her."

"No, you tell her."

The doorman leaned solicitously into the carriage. "Excuse me, is the señorita going there alone? No disrespect intended, but—" He smiled placatingly, as if not knowing how to go ahead. "It's—it's that it's a little far out for these nights."

She knew what he meant by "these nights." He was evidently unaware that she was the identical girl who had been out there with a companion only a few nights ago, and whom it had last happened to.

She put a small coin into his hand, to show that she had taken no offense. "To the Madrid," she repeated firmly.

The grizzled coachman touched his cap. "Sí, señorita."

"And drive slowly, I want to enjoy the air before I dine." She said it over in her mind. Dine? Die? They sounded so much alike; in English, anyway.

She saw them look at one another again and shrug helplessly, as if to say, "What can you do with these Americans?"

The hotel starter closed the carriage door for her. He glanced curiously at her face, as though it struck him she had on too much powder. It probably did look chalky white, she realized, but not from powder.

She sank back on the upholstered seat: the hotel and the safety it offered glided slowly backwards, like a lighthouse on a receding shore, and the ride began.

It came to her that, somewhere else in the city, at about this same time, perhaps at this very minute, somebody else might be starting out too. Somebody whose path, evil, horror-laden, would slowly, surely draw nearer to hers through the hours, until at last the two would cross—and after that there would only be one, hers would have ended.

Strange rendezvous! Yes, somewhere, in some noisome alley, from some hidden unguessed lair, a cloaked form, faceless to the night, was emerging, to keep an appointment with her: lady in a white and crystal dress, silver-shod, raven-haired, wafting scented traces of a perfume whose trade name was, ominously enough, "Je Serai Seule à Minuit," on the soft evening air about her, as her carriage took her from her lighted hotel. And no one's heart, going to any other rendezvous, had ever beat any harder than hers was now, as she lolled there in the back of the carriage, so gracefully at ease. Silver-tipped feet crossed before her on the floor, the curve of one arm negligently resting on the curve of the seat around her; the hand of the other—down out of sight—clenched into a tormented little lump close at her side that no instrument could have pried open, it had frozen so solid.

Slowly the peaceful, resonant clop-clop of the horse drew her toward the Puerta Mayor, the main outlet into the Bosque. And, as they went along, it was like leaving the stratified reflections of a vast central bonfire, with the street shine dimming progressively the farther away they got. First the holocaust of the downtown night-life district, bleaching everything with noonday brilliance, then the soberer luster of the intermediate sectors, with just their shops and occasional small electrified signs, finally the gloomy austerity of the outlying residential districts, streets lighted solely with the cool white of their own lampposts and the occasional yellow square of a window.

And then the Puerta Mayor, and darkness closed in, complete, triumphant, on both sides. Everywhere but overhead, where a long line of lonely center lights marked the double-laned main driveway that led back into the depths of the Bosque, toward the Madrid.

The long talcumed vistas of the city's periphery avenues fell behind them, finally blotted out. The air became damper, cooler with a penetrating quality. An odor of ferns and foliage and dank wood crept up, worsting the gossamer perfume that still clung about her.

The main driveway was anything but empty, however. A constant procession of cars, some closed and lighted, others topless and open, went past her, going the other way. It was only being used in one direction tonight. "These nights," as the hotel doorman had expressed it. Everyone was coming out, leaving. In to town—and safety. No one was going the opposite way. No one but she. Her coachman had his lane all to himself.

They had very little to fear, these others, seated in their

lighted limousines in twos and threes and fours. But their
machines didn't loiter along the way, just the same. They
all went by fast, maintaining a general level of accelerated
speed that was not lost on her. As though, now that they
had proved their courage to themselves and all their friends
by dining early at the Madrid, they couldn't wait until they
got out of here, to continue their revels somewhere else
with greater peace of mind. Even though it was general
knowledge by now that it was no longer in here, had last
been seen all the way across town by the Hippodrome race
track.

So she went slowly by, counter to the stream, in lonely
grandeur. A sheet of coruscating white flame licked over
her form each time the carriage passed beneath an overhanging arc light, then dwindled again until the next one
came along.

At last, through the darkness ahead, the lanterns of the
Madrid began to show, like a bed of luminous, multicolored confetti lying scattered about under the trees. The
ghostly echoes of accordion and violin notes seemed to
drop down on them from those same trees like a fine, impalpable rain, as he turned in the short looped spur that led
in toward the entrance and then out and around again.

An attendant helped her down and she stepped through
the low box hedge that bordered the outside dining place.

"You'll wait, of course," she ordered the coachman.
There was a depleted line of cars still standing there along
one side of the drive-in.

"But not too late, señorita," he pleaded cravenly, "it's
not advisable these days."

"You'll wait until I'm ready," she said severely. "See that
he does," she instructed the attendant.

A headwaiter had come forward to greet her. They were
all inside the main building, an octagonal pavilion raised
several steps above ground level. There were still people
here, but in vastly diminished numbers. Last-standers, either trying to show how daring they were, or having had
too much wine and too good a time to care very much any
longer one way or the other. Even so, the few there were
banded together in large table groups, as if for mutual

protection. So much the better, she thought; he can pick me out more easily this way than if the place were crowded. One or two couples were moving about on the black glass dance floor in the slow languor of the tango, each with its complementary pair reflected upside down, so that there seemed to be twice as many as there were.

"Is the señorita expecting anyone?"

She concealed the shiver this succeeded in eliciting. The señorita was, but not anyone to look forward to.

"No, dinner for one." Then, as he started to precede her toward the entrance steps of the building, "I want a table outside here. All the way over, by the hedge."

He gave her a look. "Are you sure you want to sit that far out?"

"I'm sure," she cut him short. "I don't like crowds."

There was no one out here at all, in all this sea of tables, as she took her seat. The hedge that ran beside her was low; even seated she was visible almost from the waist up, for the tables were set on a platform in order to assure an evenness that the natural ground lacked. The trees, and the impenetrable darkness below them, looked uncomfortably close, close enough for someone to reach out through them and snatch her bodily away, in an unguarded moment when everyone's back was turned. Suppose—suppose something happened right here, where he and Belmonte weren't expecting it to, couldn't help her?

She turned her eyes away, remembering what Manning had warned her: not to show strain or awareness: studied the bill of fare. A bill of fare that vibrated slightly in her hand, so that the printed words on it all showed double, as if seen through the beveled edge of a thick slab of glass.

"You recommend?" she said in a smothered voice.

"The purée of mango."

"Very well, the purée of mango." How could she get anything down her throat, the way it felt now? To swallow, something inside the throat had to open, didn't it?

"And at the end, an ice and coffee."

She had been in many restaurants. She had never yet been anything but slightly relieved to have the ordering done with and the headwaiter take himself off, viewing it as a minor annoyance at best. Now she found herself regretting having reached the end of it so soon, reluctant to see him go in and leave her there alone. She even deliberately held him there a moment or two longer beside her, repeating a redundant instruction or two.

Her eyes followed him all the way in when he finally left. She felt so alone, so cut off out here. True, there was a chasseur over there by the break in the hedge, to open car doors for arrivals, but he looked awfully far away, and these trees immediately about her were awfully close. She opened the little bag on her lap, pretended to fumble for a handkerchief, and touched the butt of the gun Manning had given her. She felt a little better after that.

Just as she finished her soup, a vermilion lantern directly over her, *hers* in view of the table she occupied, went out without any warning, and a pall of gray shadow was cast over her in its place. She closed her eyes dismayedly. Was that some kind of omen?

As soon as it had been noticed, two of them came hurrying out with a short stepladder, one of them climbed up on it behind her chair, fitted a new bulb into place, and in a moment it went on again brighter than before, so that was all right.

It was hard to eat. And when not eating, it was even harder still. She kept her eyes away from the direction of the trees by sheer will power. Sometimes she was sure she could feel other, malign eyes boring steadily into her from the shadows beyond the hedge. Sometimes she was sure it was just her imagination.

Once a small animal, perhaps a squirrel or a chipmunk, scurried along the ground on the outside of the hedge. Luckily her napkin happened to be in her hand at the moment. She got it up to and partly into her mouth before the scream had a chance to come. She dug the nails of her other hand into its palm, nearly piercing the flesh, until she had conquered the spasm. The next time the waiter approached after that, she said a little breathlessly: "Ask them to play a little louder. I can't hear them very well out here."

"Certainly, señorita. Any favorite selection?"

She felt like saying, "Nearer My God to Thee," but it would have been in earnest, not in jest, the way she felt, so she didn't.

"And bring me some champagne," she added. "It's dull here."

If she was being watched—and she was almost certain by now that she was—that would create a desirable impression. Of nonchalance and celebration. What she really wanted it for was to keep from fainting here in her seat.

They brought it and the cork popped and it foamed out in cheery beaded strings. She raised her brimming glass high up over hedge level, so it couldn't fail to be seen. She felt like turning toward the trees and holding it out in an ironical toast—"Here's to you and me"—but it would have been too ghastly.

She touched it to her lips, set it down again. A mouthful or two was enough, to warm the lining of her throat. She didn't want to dull her senses, they were the only armor she had tonight. After a while she surreptitiously emptied it out on the floor, on the inner side of the table, where she couldn't be seen doing it, and conspicuously refilled her glass.

Her request for champagne and louder music must have misled the management into thinking it had been remiss in attentiveness. A tall young fellow with a telltale white carnation in his jacket came down the steps and over to her place of exile. He bowed ingratiatingly. "May I have this tango?"

"Thank you, I'm not dancing."

He wasn't easily discouraged. "Then does the lovely señorita mind if I sit down and keep her company?" He had already drawn out the chair opposite hers.

Manning's warning came back to her: *Don't tangle with anyone, you may frighten him off.* "No, don't!" she cried, so alarmedly that he drew back a step. "Please! Please don't stand here, please leave this table—"

He was persistent. Business must have been rotten these nights, with everyone staying away. "Just one small dance the señorita refuses?" he coaxed.

She gave in finally, as the quickest and easiest way of

getting rid of him. After all, of the two evils, it would look less suspicious—to *out there*—to be seen dancing with him than to have him stand parleying beside her table for any length of time.

She got up and he led her back inside on his arm like some kind of a living trophy. There were three others of his kind sitting disconsolately around the dance floor, one to a table. Probably they worked on a percentage basis.

She'd never tangoed before. She didn't have to now. He tangoed for both of them. He was good at it, as one should be at one's livelihood. Even the scissors step she found herself doing without realizing it. Over his shoulder she could still see the trees out there. Whichever way she turned, they were waiting, on three sides of her, out beyond the hedge, as if to say: "We'll get you. You're coming. We'll get you."

Even a gigolo, a gigolo to cling to, was better than being alone with the darkness lying in wait all around.

After they'd gone once around the black glass, she said: "What's the name of that, they're playing?"

He had to hum the words over to himself first in Spanish, to marshal them for translation.

> *Adios muchachos, compañeros de mi vida,*
> *Se acabaron para mi todas las jarras—*

"I do not speak the English very well. It is of someone whose life is soon to finish. It say, 'Goodby, boys, my life companions, For me is ending—' "

Even the music. "Please don't go ahead," she said in a sick voice. "Will you excuse me now? I'd like to go back to my table."

"I have displeased the señorita?"

"Not at all. I have a headache. Would you mind telling me how much I owe you?" They were back at the table by now.

He wasn't in the least dismayed. "The señorita is too generous. She did not complete her dance—"

"Take this anyway," she said, to get rid of him, and touched his hand briefly.

Then she was alone again, a motionless, doomed figure

sitting passively under a blood-red lantern. She sat on for half an hour after she'd finished her coffee. That sense of being watched kept growing stronger all the time. Her very *skin* felt it, kept trying to crawl away from it. She had to keep fighting, not to turn her head and look. Once she almost had an impression of something luminous, phosphorescent, glowing out at her through the bushes. She had to throw down a spoon and then stoop for it, the impulse to turn and see was so strong. When she had straightened up in her chair again, she could resist better. By then it was gone anyway, whatever it had been; the corners of her eyes no longer felt it.

It seemed so silly, somehow, expecting to meet violence, perhaps even death itself, face to face within a short while; expecting to have to claw and rake at it with your bare hands, in defense of your life perhaps; and yet to be sitting here now dipping those same fingers into a bowl of tepid water with a gardenia floating around in it. If she lived, she knew, she'd never be able to look at finger bowls again without thinking of this night, living it over again, if only for a moment or two. At some gay dinner party years from now, in the midst of the wine and the chatter, her face would suddenly pale and her laughter freeze as the dark memory came back, and people would wonder why and ask her. *If she lived.*

The last thing she did before leaving was to crumble up a roll, gather the pieces in a napkin. "For the swans," she smiled at the waiter as she paid her check.

"At this hour?" The terrified, unspoken warning on his face was plain to read.

"I like animals," she said. ("But not jaguars," she added to herself.) She stood up, turned, walked slowly out toward the break in the hedge. The carriage glided up. She put her silver shoe to the step. "Here I go," she thought sickly.

Then she was in, and the lanterns were withdrawing through the trees. One last one, a green one, lingered on longer than all the others, seen through a break in the trees. Then that snuffed out too, and the Madrid was gone into the night.

He started to whip up his horse, anxious to get out of the accursed Bosque as fast as he could.

"Drive slowly," she ordered sharply. "It's too nice a night to rush." Then when they came to the side road, "Turn down this way."

"Ah, no señorita," the old fellow almost whimpered. "Not down there. That is exactly where it happened the last time."

I ought to know if anybody does, she thought dismally. Aloud she said, "Don't you read the papers? It's on the other side of town now. It's not in here any more!" This in English; then in her capsule Spanish, and with gestures to complete the thought: "No here. *Otra parte.*"

He understood, language not being the barrier between human beings that is commonly supposed. "They may be mistaken," he whined.

"In, in!" she insisted.

He headed his horse around and reluctantly turned in where she had told him to. It was a long leafy tunnel in the moonlight, tree meeting tree above. A greenish black tube, freckled with silver. Infinitely beautiful, infinitely dangerous. The horse's hoofs resounded along its empty length like a knell.

It was lifeless. The public was giving the Bosque a wide berth these nights, all but the one main driveway that led straight out. It stretched on for a while, straight as a ramrod. Then it started making that leisurely turn at last that told the lake was coming near.

The moon wasn't as bright as the other night, was waning now, but the lake still flashed out beside her like a sheet of hammered silver when at last they had reached that place where the road drew nearest to it and it could be seen. That unforgettable place. The screen of trees drew back, like a curtain parting for the last act of a tragedy, and there was just a grassy slope left between her and it.

She could hardly breathe any more, she was choking with rigidly suppressed yet steadily mounting terror. "Stop here," she managed to articulate.

He either didn't hear her or pretended not to, as an

excuse for going on past with the least possible delay. She had to strike him lightly and repeatedly on the back, as if she were knocking on a door. "*Para, entiende?* I said stop here. Wait for me. I want to feed those birds a minute."

"Ah no, senorita, *válgame dios!*" he wailed almost in falsetto. "That is the very way in which it happened to that other—"

"Did you hear what I said?" she snapped. "You won't get a centavo that's coming to you if you don't do as you're told!"

The carriage fell motionless. She rose up in it, stepped down to the ground. The stillness was unearthly now that the horse had stopped. It was malign in itself, it was so unnatural. One foot forward, the next forward, the first forward again. The roadway changed to turf, but the ground remained level the first few steps. Then it started downward, in a gentle, grassy decline. It wasn't hard to manage even in high-heeled silver slippers, it wasn't steep enough for that, but it was all she could do to keep walking in a straight line, she felt like reeling unsteadily from side to side. She was almost drunk with terror. "I must keep my head clear; if I don't, I'm a goner," she warned herself.

The carriage was slowly going up over her head, behind her, as the roadway rose. She could never be so frightened again for the rest of her life. She had to keep talking to herself inwardly. "Manning's somewhere around you, you know it, even if you can't see him. Look for the locket first. Then stray out of sight of the coachman. Smoke a cigarette. Shoot through your bag, without pulling it out, if you have to— Is it that bush there, over to the left, coming up toward you? No, that's just a bush."

The carriage had gone up as high as it could now. It was starting to sink from sight behind the top of the rampart.

The gleaming water was coming slowly up toward her. The swans, already detecting that she had something in her hand for them, were starting to course gracefully in to meet her along its moon-burnished surface.

For over three hours now those same swans, floating asleep, had been the only signs of life around Manning, inert as they were. The rest was just a piebald still life of moonlight and shadow. Not a stir came from the reeds where Belmonte crouched concealed, and if he hadn't told him where he was going to be, Manning wouldn't have known anyone was in them.

The circulation had long ago begun to leave his own extremities. He pinched and kneaded them from time to time, in preference to shifting his position to ease them, but it was a losing battle. He could scarcely feel the pinches themselves after a while.

The moon was waning now from the full that had witnessed Sally O'Keefe's death, but it was still large enough to cast an aluminum sheen where it was unobstructed. He looked down along his own curved length carefully, to make sure none of the coinlike disks of it that splattered through the leaves struck him in any place that might be revealing from the ground: the white of his hands, the dull sheen of his silk socks, the glossy toecaps of his shoes. The slightest thing like that might have been sufficient to indicate, to a wary antagonist, something that didn't belong up in a tree.

The strain had become almost unendurable. He wondered whether Belmonte was feeling it as much as he. Worse, probably; he had nothing to rest his back against. He didn't bother looking at his watch. That was a fool's stunt, which always made time seem to stretch out longer than it was. When she came, that would be the right time. Until she came, they'd wait—even if it meant staying up here in this tree until he fell out of it from numbness. They weren't in this for fun.

The slow clop-clop of a horse sounded far off in the distance somewhere, and sound had come back into the world. It was like something carried through a hollow tube or bore, it had that sort of blurred resonance to it. It died out again, then came back once more, clearer, nearer, than before. Was that she, now? It must be, who else could it be? A carriage alone on the Bosque at this hour, and coming this way. Nothing else had traversed that road up there since he had taken up his position. Pleasure drives were a thing of the past in the Bosque these nights.

The hoofbeats were clear and ringing now, belltoned almost, for there was nothing in the vast stillness around to compete with them, and approaching more closely every moment. Manning caught himself taking deeper breaths than he had a minute ago; that was his body instinctively trying to store up oxygen for possible approaching action. On they came, jewel clear, so calm, so unhurried—in the evenness of rhythm that is nature's gift to the horse, clop-clop, cloppety-clop. In other circumstances there would have been something almost soothing in their cadence. At last he could even make out the slight creak of the axles, the whisper of the rubber-tired wheels along the roadbed.

A woman's voice said something. The hoofbeat faltered to a stop. There was a slight protest from the carriage step, weighted down, released again. He could hear her next remark plainly, for she had raised her voice slightly: "You won't get a centavo if you don't do as you're told!"

He couldn't see the vehicle itself, for there was too much overhanging foliage in the way obscuring it, but a moment later the white of her gown came into full view, coruscating in the moonlight, up there on top of the rampart, and she started to walk slowly down the open grassy slope under his very eyes.

If she felt fear—and she must have—she gave no sign. Her bearing was matchless. Her grace, the fluid dignity of her carriage. To him, at any rate, there was nothing strained or rigid in the way she moved. Just the precautionary hesitancy of a woman dressed in her best, picking her way delicately in order not to soil her shoes or gown.

He narrowed his eyes in admiration of her poised self-control. It took a woman to put on a show like that, a man never could have, never in the wide world.

She came abreast of the tree that hid him, passed on down without a glance over at it. She couldn't, of course, know exactly where he was. All she had to rely on was his assurance that he and Belmonte would be watching from somewhere close by.

The swans were gliding in to meet her, each leaving a spreading fan of ripples in its wake. They'd already spotted the little white ball the napkin of crumbs made in her hand.

She reached the water's edge at last. Manning was now roughly midway between her and the carriage. He was watching the terrain around him on all sides, now, more than he was her. Nothing could get at her from in front, across the water, and to reach her from the rear it would have to pass his tree first. Belmonte's position protected her on the right, and his tree, again, did as much for her on the left.

He saw her looking for the locket. With her free hand she had lifted the hem of her skirt a little to avoid wetting it and was picking her way along the water's edge, head attentively bent. The hungry birds, meanwhile, were banked nearly solidly around her on the water side, jostling and nudging one another aside, and the whole body of them moving first up the shore, then down it, in company with her own slow coursing.

Behind her heroically oblivious back, nothing stirred, nothing moved. There wasn't a rustle from the dark feathery masses of bush and underbrush all about. Not the snap of a twig.

She'd found it at last. He saw her dip suddenly, draw something from the outermost inch or two of water that winked in the moonlight as she straightened with it, holding it semi-aloft. She hovered with proprietary delight over it for a moment or two, in clever pantomime. Drying it, turning it this way and that. Then she put it in the bag on her wrist. Now she began her feeding of the swans. Her arm went out toward them, in toward the napkin; held back a moment, then out toward them, in toward the napkin, while she slowly strolled along, a bountiful lady on the banks of the Styx.

Manning's position had changed slightly when she had first come into view. The one alteration was: his forearm was up now, holding his gun motionless at belt-buckle level, butt against his body. His head kept swiveling slowly from side to side, covering every inch of ground within a 180-degree arc.

Suddenly he heard the horse, unseen up there on the driveway and motionless until now, whinny uneasily. Its hoofs shifted about a little within the confines of the traces.

His head was instantly pulled tautly around the other way—toward her. The swans were streaking out away from her like so many black rays across the silvery lake surface. In a moment more she was standing there alone at the water's edge, hand extended uselessly with offered crumbs.

Manning drew the gun up higher, to the level of his bottom rib, froze it there.

She was standing still, facing the receding swans. A shimmering line of brightness coursed down her motionless back. Was she trembling at the imminence of danger, or was it just the moonlight rippling on the beads sewn to her dress? He couldn't tell.

The horse's forelegs struck the ground sharply, as though its full weight were behind the impact, and the carriage joints groaned and strained protestingly. It must have reared and then dropped down again, Manning realized. It neighed rebelliously. He started his own leg downward out of the tree socket, let it dangle to within a foot of the ground in readiness, on the water side, where the trunk hid it.

And still the space between, from up there where the carriage was to down below where she was, remained blankly inscrutable.

She didn't look around, although she must have heard the telltale sounds from the driveway as plainly as he had. She was bending slightly forward above the waist now, pretending to try to coax the recalcitrant swans back within range. They refused to come. Finally, with a studied gesture of impatience, she flung the napkin holding the remainder of the rejected crumbs away from her, as if disappointed at their lack of interest.

She fumbled in the small bag looped to her wrist, he heard the crackle of wax paper, and a match flare glowed before her face as she lit the test cigarette he had told her to. All without turning her head.

It was the height of courage; he had never seen anything

like it before. For, for all she knew, something might be creeping up behind her at that very moment. He was in a position to see that nothing was, but she wasn't.

The horse took an abortive two or three rapid steps forward, as if about to break into a headlong run, then was quickly reined in, backed up again, with further creaking protests of the carriage joints and a jiggling of the wheel rims.

A halo of cigarette haze about her head in the moonlight, she was following his instructions to the letter. She began to saunter aimlessly still further along the lake margin, well out of sight of carriage and driver—but fortunately over toward the side on which the reeds lay, although she could not have known that there was a safeguard in their midst. She stopped about halfway to them, well out of sight of the carriage, and stood there as if idly contemplating the lake, arms folded tight across her chest. The red mote of her cigarette made an occasional spiral out from them and up to her mouth and down again. Manning could barely see her any more at this distance, she was just a white blur in the gloom over there, for she had stepped out of open moonlight into the shadow of some trees. It was up to Belmonte now to guard her, over on the side where he was.

There wasn't a sound, except for an occasional pawing or clump from the horse up above, whose restlessness had become chronic by now but apparently was being kept under strict control by the driver. The animal's whole demeanor showed there was some unseen danger close at hand in the shadows of the Bosque, but it stubbornly remained concealed, failed to materialize. The tableau of palpitant tension protracted itself almost unbearably; the two hidden men and the visible girl, the magnet midway between them, smoking down by the water's edge as if lost in thought.

At last she finished it. Its red dot described an arc and went out in the water. She turned and began to make her way back. Once she stumbled slightly, and he knew it was in sheer terror, but to someone else it might only have seemed as if her toe had caught in a root.

She came out into the open moonlight again and started up the slope. She passed the tree where Manning was, as unseeing as the first time, and went on up the rest of the way, over the lip of the declivity, onto the level where the roadway was, and out of his direct line of vision.

He let his tentatively suspended leg reach down the remaining foot or two to solid ground, and let the other one trail down after it. The blood came rushing back into them in excruciating repossession.

Her voice carried clearly to him as she reached the carriage once more. "All right, now you can take me back." The footrest creaked as she mounted it. The coachman didn't even have to click his tongue or use the whip to start the horse, Manning could tell. At the first slackening of the reins he had been pulling in so tightly until now, the terrified horse instantly broke into a rapid trot that soon became a headlong gallop. So anxious was it to get away from the threatening spot.

Manning sidled noiselessly out from under the tree and stood waiting for his companion-in-hiding to break cover and join him. The reeds failed to part at his whistle. When he had repeated it a second time and still no sign of Belmonte, he made his way over to them himself, a strange sort of foreboding beginning to chill him.

"Raul!" he whispered urgently, picking his way into their midst across the waterlogged stones. The reeds were empty. He could see some of them bent flat, around where his companion had been crouched, but there was no one in them any more.

He emerged, went back, and started up the slope alone.

The road was empty in the moonlight when he reached it. He had hardly taken a preliminary step or two along it than he became aware of some sort of disturbance, off-side to him. On the side away from the lake, that is. He stood rigid, listening. It came again, a muffled scuffling or threshing sound, as of a large animal caught in a trap or incapacitated in some way and trying to free itself.

He veered toward it, moving warily. It came a third time, unmistakable now: a violent, frantic agitation against leaves or plants, an attempt at extrication. He drew his

gun, plunged in off the road toward it, warding off branches
and briars as he went.

The thrashing accelerated, as though driven to a frenzy
of haste by his very approach.

A moment later he went down flat and his gun crashed
deafeningly, set off by the fall itself. Something or somebody lying tied up in his path had tripped him.

He groveled around rearward, wiping a smarting powder
smudge off his cheek, found his light, and thumbed it on. It
revealed a huddled human form lying face down, hands
bound behind it with a knitted necktie evidently taken
from its own attire.

Manning turned him over and it was a grizzled man of
fifty, with bedraggled walrus mustaches. A mass of rum-
pled linen had been compressed into his mouth to gag him.
Manning pulled it out, and it seemed to keep coming endlessly. It turned pinkish toward the end. He'd been badly
bludgeoned about the head; thin but numerous streams of
blood were crisscrossed all down his face.

He was only barely conscious, the whites of his eyes
roled expiringly as Manning propped him up. He shook
him urgently.

"Who are you? What happened? Who did this to you?"

"I don't know," the dying man said faintly. "Somebody
—from behind—down off the box—" He went limp, with
a sort of convulsive spasm.

Manning let go of him, jumped to his feet with a hoarse
cry of horror that went crackling through the trees. This
must be Marjorie's coachman, who had brought her here.
And if he had been struck down, left trussed up here like
this, it could only mean one thing—!

The very Thing he was out to trap had hold of her at
this moment, had driven off with her to finish her at his
leisure!

He burst out through the underbrush, sprinted down the
road, pocketing his gun as he went. He veered off-side into
the small tree-surrounded clearing in which Belmonte had
left his car, hoping against hope, almost praying—he
found what he'd dreaded to find all along; the place was
empty, the car was gone. And no one could have taken it

but its owner; Manning himself had seen him pocket the keys when they both got out.

He emerged again, went staggering down the long desolate tube of silver and black that was the road, forced to go on afoot now. The odds were hopeless this way, he could never hope to overtake her in time.

Just before the desolate road turned in to unite with the main driveway once more, something came sidling toward him along its surface. Something that glinted as he approached. He recognized it as he stooped to pick it up. It was the revolver that he himself had handed her at the Inglaterra only a few hours earlier. He put it to his face. Odorless. She'd never had a chance to use it. His chin was puckered into a weazened expression as he went trotting on.

Didn't this road ever end? And while he asked himself that, it did. The main driveway was empty under its lights. No one was leaving the Bosque now any more; they all had, long ago. He padded on. Ahead a wan glow began to brighten, fan out. The Puerta Mayor, the entrance to the city.

Suddenly lights gushed up like illuminated oil seeping out of the ground, and the periphery of the city lay spread before him. He stopped with sudden hopelessness; partly because of his pounding lungs, mostly because he didn't know where to go any more from here on. He was confronted by six radiating avenues that branched out from the Puerta Mayor like spokes on a half wheel. To follow one through to the end was to slight the other five. She was lost for good now, buried alive somewhere in that wilderness of stones and buildings that stretched before him as far as the eye could reach.

The expression on his face was that of someone trying to retch. The third largest city of South America. Three quarters of a million people. Minutes to find her.

Finally, still breathing heavily, he cut across the *glorieta*. Sweat was running down his forehead. He was still unable to make up his mind which street to choose. The odds were too heavy, the stake was too high. Six to one, a girl's life. He felt as helpless as when he had first come here, in the days when he didn't know his way around town yet. When it was just a blur of strange streets with strange names, all leading in strange directions.

He passed one of those direction finders that he used to have to rely on. He hadn't paid any attention to them in years. City maps with an adjustable indicator, that you found at some of the busier corners. Copied from Europe, they weren't known up in the States. He remembered they used to straighten him out each time he got balled up. You set the indicator for where you wanted to go, and also for where you were, and it would show the straightest line between the two points.

Suddenly he flung around, went back to the one he had just passed, as a thought struck him. It was set at chest level for the convenience of passers-by. He reared one leg up and rammed into it. The glass protecting the map trickled off. He wanted it to be able to take pencil marks for what he had in mind; the indicator wasn't enough.

He poised his pencil over the denuded chart, began marking off the locations of the attacks, mumbling to himself as he did so.

"One, Teresa Delgado—Pasaje del Diablo." He ground out a black sworl of penciling to mark it clearly. "Two, Conchita Contreras—All Saints. Three, Clo-Clo—at the corner of San Marco and the Calle de Justicia." He moistened the pencil tip. "Four, Sally O'Keefe—beside the lagoon in the Bosque." Tonight's didn't count, it was simply a repetition at the same spot as the one before.

He had four black marks on the map now. He drew a line from each cross to its opposite. They made a slightly irregular X, one arm a little longer than the other.

He peered closely at the finely printed diagram, to see where the two axes crossed, to determine where the focus was. He drew an arbitrary circle around it, to identify it still more plainly. It encompassed the Alameda district; roughly the section between there and the Plaza de los Mártires. And dead center through this ran an almost indistinguishable thread, marked minutely on the map— Callejón de las Sombras.

In other words, the place where it had originally disappeared was still the one locale in the city equidistant from all four of the attacks. Somewhere around in there was the base of operations. Somewhere around in there was the lair.

True, that alley had been thoroughly searched once already. True, there was no guarantee that he necessarily covered an equal distance away from his starting point each time. But it was all Manning had, it was the best he could do. And it was still a whole lot better and quicker than having the whole sprawling city to comb over. At least he knew which one of those six radiating avenues to take from here, now. The stake was still as high as ever, but the odds had come down a lot.

He sighted a cab in the distance and bayed to it at the top of his lungs. Five minutes later he had alighted at the mouth of the Callejón. The cab drove off, left him there alone. It was black as the mouth of hell; not a light showed along its entire tortuous length, from where he was through to the other end.

He plunged in, to begin a one-man search from doorway to doorway.

Half an hour later he had dead-ended in the roofless chapel. His torch moved up and down the walls in a series of scallops as he clambered up and down the varying mounds of debris. His face looked gray in the pallid reflection of its small glow, and there was the shine of sweat, the sweat of failure, in the pinched indentations at the corners of his eyes and mouth. After his third time around, he turned and moved back toward the entrance.

There was a small click, and his light went out, just as his hopes had long before this. He let the door flap idly to and fro behind him on the slight current of his egress, sat soddenly down on the worn steps outside, his spine a bow of dejection. There was no place else to go from here.

Minutes went by. He looked up once, at the patch of black over him. It was still night. How long a night lasted —sometimes. But not when you are dying.

He rose to his feet at last, began hobbling painfully

along toward where the inset rejoined the main part of the alley. A piece of gravel had got into one of his shoes, climbing around inside there, and was half killing him. He had to stop finally, brace his foot against the wall, and strip off the offending shoe. He shook it out, felt along the sole of his sock to make sure the irritant was not imbedded in that. It was, and it rolled into the hollow of his hand.

The dangling shoe dropped with a clump, and he flickered on his light, turned it into his palm. Something winked there in its creases. A diminutive oblong, tiny but bright. A microscopic tube. A bead. One of those things from her dress.

It had only been hurting him since he'd come out of there.

He shoveled his foot back into the shoe, ran up the short steps and inside once more.

He only found it at last because he knew there was something there to be found now and he wouldn't quit looking until he had. It was a lead trap set into the floor and indistinguishable in size or color from the massive paving blocks set around it. He'd missed it because he'd been chiefly occupied with the walls until now, not the littered flooring underfoot, which had seemed solid. His quest had been for a gap, an orifice, not anything of this sort.

He was squatting down by it now, getting excited. It had a flattened ring nose through it. He pried that up and pulled, and the whole thing tilted up quite easily, on a sort of chain-brace arrangement on the underside.

He shot his light down into it, to reveal a narrow oblong pit, with breakneck stone steps leading down, but from the side, not lengthwise. On the lowest step of all there was another of those tiny winking points of light, like the one that had rested in his palm awhile ago, outside.

"This is for me," he told himself with grim conviction.

What it was, where it went to, he didn't know; only that she'd come this way, so he was going to come this way, too. A cold long-buried air arose in his face, like something from another world, as he disappeared down into it by

sections, like someone being swallowed in a quicksand:
first his legs, then his thighs, then his middle. Finally it
closed over his head.

There was a tunnel stretching before him, almost to
infinity, it seemed. It was shored at the sides and top by
age-blackened beams, like a mine shaft. As he moved along
it eating up distance, he almost received the impression of
standing still. There was always still more empty blackness
out there ahead of the furthermost limits of the beam of
his light. Once his light swam over the droppings of some
animal, weeks old and half dust.

So it had been down in here—at one time.

A few paces farther on he shied suddenly, gave an instinctive quirk to the gun he was holding in readiness, as
something white gleamed out at him unexpectedly. It was a
bodiless skull, nestled there in the angle of one of the
shoring beams, grinning teeth to ground as if biting it. It
was ivory smooth with centuries of fleshlessness.

Then just when he thought this passage was never going
to reach anywhere, never end, his light head suddenly fore-
shortened, deflected upwards by steps before him again.

Up over them was the same type of chained trap that
had admitted him just now at the other end. He put his
foot to the lowest step, and then stopped for a moment.
Something made him put his light out and sheathe it in the
waistband of his trousers, before he reached upward to
open the enclosure. The gun he retained. He knew he was
getting near the end of the trail now.

It lifted without any more recalcitrance than its complement at the other end, showing, if nothing else, that
both had seen frequent use lately. It was not, though, nor
could it be expected to be, completely noiseless. It whined
as it went upward, and the chains jangled as they stayed
it.

As he came up into the dark, he was uncannily aware of
some other presence near him. Some bated presence that
had detected him first, and was holding itself craftily motionless. He could feel the skin across the back of his neck
tighten, and he began fanning his gun warily against the

sightless gloom that faced him. He took a cautious step away from the topmost step. Then another.

A current of air set in flux by some unseen movement near him reached him too late.

The bore of a gun ground into his backbone with electrifying lack of preliminary and, as though it were the nozzle of a powerful vacuum cleaner, seemed to draw him from behind into paralyzed motionlessness.

A hand, as cold with tension and deadly purpose as his own, suddenly came to rest on his, took away the gun. A surly voice breathed close to his ear, *"Quieto!"* Before he could identify it further, there was a snap and a light flashed on full in his face, blinding him.

Belmonte's voice suddenly sounded, full-tone. "My God, it's you, *hombre!* I nearly—"

"What did you run out on me like that for?" the American railed angrily.

"Sh, keep your voice down!" the other cautioned. He handed him his gun back. "My instinct told me to follow that carriage. I had no time to warn you. Even so, he nearly gave me the slip. When I finally caught up with it, three blocks away from the alley, it was already empty—"

"How long have you been in here?"

"Only a few minutes ahead of you. I was only beginning to look around when I heard you coming up through the trap—"

"What is it? What is this place anyway?"

"It's the old underground dungeons of the Inquisition. That must have been a secret passage they built in the old days. There's dozens and dozens of little cells, it's honeycombed with them. Come on, I'll show you how far I'd gotten when you interrupted me. Don't make any noise, he's somewhere down around here."

Although they had been anything but noiseless, there was no indication that anything around them in the dark had heard—or was there to hear. A cautious spurt or two of Manning's torch showed him what Belmonte had presumably already discovered for himself before his arrival: that they were in a crumbling vaulted corridor, squat stone pillars every few yards supporting the succession of arches that roofed it. Between each two were grim-looking iron doors.

"You take this side, I'll take the other," Belmonte breathed.

They separated, were immediately lost to one another in the gloom. From then on a brief flicker of torchlight every few moments, quickly doused again, alternating from side to side, marked their progress. Occasionally there was a querulous whimper of hinges, but many of the iron plaques were already askew from age, didn't need to be moved at all. One or two were gone entirely. Behind them in every case, were mortar and packed-earth cubicles, most of them little bigger than the delayed-action coffins they had eventually proved to be for their inmates.

The endless succession of niches holding these vents unexpectedly right-angled, cut across to meet Belmonte's side. Meaning this catacomb had ended here. In its lateral face there was but a single iron door. Manning reached it first, having outdistanced his companion in the forward search. The cartwheel of his light lapped over it momentarily, then quickly dissolved again.

He shot it briefly downward at the floor, in a signal to Belmonte. The latter came up beside him in the dark. Manning's voice was less than a whisper. It had to be guessed at. "Don't make any noise. Put your hand to this one."

"Warm."

"Warmer than the rest, anyway; they're all stone-cold. Something going on behind it—"

He started feeling along it tenderly with splayed fingers for the old-fashioned staple grip his light had shown him before. Before he could complete the gesture, Belmonte had elbowed him aside, his own hand was on it instead. There was a dangerous sort of quietness about the South American all at once, as though he'd been waiting a long time for this approaching moment.

The thing swung out past them on its appointed arc, and a flash of unreality, of fantasy, exploded into view.

It was that their minds, conditioned to the realistic,

couldn't assimilate what their eyes were trying to show them. This must have been the torture chamber of this whole cruel place of correction and exorcism. Against the wall were strange outlines that the modern mind had no names for: things well forgotten, left behind, as the race progressed away from its childish delight in pulling wings off flies. Chains hanging like fungi, and iron girdles riveted into the wall, and a thing like a hand printing press, to cripple the straight bones nature had formed.

They seemed to have been carried back four hundred years. Beyond that, even, into the never-never land of demonology and medieval allegory. The place was in use again.

Again, as in the long ago, the lurid red of fire glowed within the stone kiln at the end of the enclosure, with its open flue above; once used for turning iron bars red-hot or melting dipperfuls of lead. And again, as in the long ago, the subject lay senseless atop the thick, curved-top block, somewhat similar to a butcher's chopping block. A subject, this time, in a twentieth-century beaded evening gown, or the tatters that were left of it. Legs dangling down over the end of it, one silver slipper fallen off and lying on the floor. Her head fell back the other way, neck arched, hair streaming free and seeming to move in the moving firelight.

Between her and it was poised a grotesque silhouette. Something that belonged on a feudal coat of arms. An upright animal. The lion, or leopard, rampant. The outline of the cat head could be seen, two small triangular ears thrusting up.

The two feline claws were poised over her in striking position, about to descend, to stroke, softly, gently at first, just tearing the remnants of clothing, just scratching the smooth white skin below. Then faster, faster, deeper, deeper, as the frenzy mounted—and the life-tide welled forth.

Manning could feel his senses trying to darken out, in some form of vertigo or dizziness, because this thing wasn't there, wasn't real; so that when his faculties cleared again it would be gone. Just the empty unlit chamber would be there, the way it probably was. He also wanted to get sick for a minute, because animals don't stand upright, and men—who do—don't have short pointed ears and spade-shaped feline heads, as this apparition did.

A voice screamed something unintelligible, but not from over there, from somewhere close beside him. A revolver shot cracked, and he thought it was the cleanest, loveliest sound he'd ever heard. The *thing*, whatever it was, reared up even higher than before, claws threshing the air, then started to go over backwards.

The revolver exploded a second time. The thing in the background went down faster, rolled over with an air of finality, lay there inert; jaguar, or man, or jaguarman.

Manning could feel himself stumbling forward; he lurched to his knees beside the trestle, picked her limp form up in his arms, held her protectively clasped to him, but more in a state of bewilderment than active helpfulness. Presently he became aware of a heart beating somewhere close to his own, and he knew she wasn't dead.

The revolver kept crashing out, meanwhile, and a sort of chant of vengeance accompanied it. "That's for Conchita." *Bam*. "And that's for Conchita." *Bam*. "And that's for all the others." *Bam*. "But this, this one is for Conchita all over again!"

Brief flashes kept flickering over Belmonte's face, lighting it momentarily from below each time.

"Belmonte, quit," Manning remonstrated at last. "Pull yourself together. The thing's dead ten times over."

But the revolver kept on clicking emptily, over and over again.

After a while, he took the empty gun away from Belmonte, and said, "Take care of the girl." Belmonte took the girl from him and carried her out of the place. Manning went over closer to the huddled form lying on the ground, and stood looking down at it. It had fallen face downward. He turned it over with his foot. He bent down for a moment, just once, then straightened up again.

When Belmonte came back presently, Manning was standing beside the kiln, thrusting a small deep-curved shovel down into it. Before Belmonte knew what he was about, he had tipped it up again, overturned it. A freshet of live coals spilled down over the exposed face on the floor, forming a glowing puddle, blanketing it. They only darkened momentarily, then almost immediately they had brightened again as fiercely as ever. Dank steam struggled up between the livid nuggets, like thin snakes.

Manning threw down the shovel and they both came away fast.

They sat sipping small stinging brandies in the morning sunlight, at a little café on the Alameda. A shoeshine boy was crouched at Belmonte's feet. All around them life was going on as usual. It was hard to believe that just a few hours ago, not a stone's throw from here—

"If you hadn't lost your head the way you did—" Manning began.

Belmonte tossed the bootblack a coin to get rid of him. "I lost my head?" he smiled. "On the contrary, I kept my head very well. There is no capital punishment down here. The most they could have given him, by statute, is twenty years to life." He shrugged. "Do you see what I mean?"

"I see what you mean," Manning assented.

"One thing I don't understand," Belmonte mused. "How did it get into the chapel in the first place? The entrance was locked tight; the police had to take crowbars to it themselves when they were looking for it that first night, you remember?"

"The chapel is roofless, just four walls and open sky. My conjecture is it ran into the doorway of the house immediately adjoining, came out on the roof, or some projecting ledge, of that, and seeing its escape cut off, jumped from there down into the opening offered by the ruined chapel, unseen by anyone against the surrounding blackness. A leap from such a height wouldn't be prohibitive for an animal of its type, particularly spurred on by fear.

"He got hold of it in some way, anyway, we know that much. Your revolver, last night, deprived us of ever finding out the exact details. Probably stunned it with a big rock and dragged it back through that tunnel, that he'd already been using for some time past."

He waited until the waiter had put down their new jiggers, gone away again. "He was ripe for murder, anyway. The tinder was there, waiting. The jaguar was the spark. The spark came along and bang! all over the place. Every large city has dozens of his kind. Fortunately, most of them never blow a fuse. One in a hundred gets started off, and then you have it! Jack the Ripper in London. Blue-beard in France. That ax killer—what was his name? —in Germany.

"He got hold of it, anyway, and kept it for a while. They found its grave last night, in the earthen floor of one of those cells, before we came away, remember? And you heard what they told us they found after they dug it up." He made a slicing motion. "The forepaws had been am-putated, and the head skinned—"

Belmonte quickly hoisted his brandy and cleaned it out.

"But I don't think he did that right away, that curing and fashioning of the gauntlets and the mask. I think the first time he found some way of transporting it, under his control and still alive, to the vicinity in which the attack on Teresa Delgado occurred. In some car, or in some hamper, who knows how? Held it there by him in that pitch-dark tunnel under the viaduct, waiting for the first likely passer-by to come along, and when she did—unleashed it to see what it would do. Probably he had starved it into a state of ferocity by then."

"Then why didn't it turn on him and not the girl?" asked Belmonte.

"He probably had something along to cow it with. He must have, to be able to recapture it immediately after its foray."

"Que barbaridad, hombre!" Belmonte inhaled shiver-ingly.

"But that wasn't enough for him. It was too brief, too vicarious. He couldn't approach close enough, nor linger to gloat. It was too complicated. So he didn't repeat that. But his blood was up now. *He* would be the jaguar instead. So he killed it, and from then on he was. With gauntlets that retained the death-dealing claws. He found some way of manipulating them, making them emerge and recede just as in nature—by tiny springs or wires, who knows just how?"

Belmonte passed his hand quickly across his eyes as if to shut out some too-insistent sight. He went on hastily, as if to get away from that particular phase of the subject, "How could he go around rigged up like that, though?"

"He didn't, of course. You noticed that loose, enfolding overcoat with big pockets we found there last night. He probably muffled himself in that, took out the paraphernalia at the last minute."

"How is it he didn't leave footprints?"

"Rags wrapped around his shoes would take care of that. But this is not really a police matter we are discussing, this is a case history in abnormal psychology. A case history that unfortunately did not come to light until too late. He needed, not policemen, but a doctor."

"My revolver was the doctor," Belmonte said, hardening his eyes.

"Yes, the best, and by that time, the only possible one."

"How can anyone like that be detected?" Belmonte wondered aloud. "Could a person tell just by looking at him?" Then he answered it himself, "No, I suppose not."

"Sometimes you can," Manning mused. "If you're smart, if you know what it means when you do. And you usually don't. Sometimes you'll catch an unguarded gleam in the eye for a moment, a glitter, a fervor, where you wouldn't in anyone else's. Oh, nothing much, and you're not expecting it anyway, you're trustful, you say to yourself you imagined it."

"Did you ever see a telltale look like that in anyone's eyes?" Belmonte asked him curiously.

"Yes, once, I remember now that I did. It was in a room at police headquarters. A room crowded with people. They were questioning a suspect. I was fiddling away with a file, listening. I hurt myself, here—" He ran a finger thoughtfully over a cicatrice still visible in the bulge below one thumb. "I came forward into the light, close to the suspect. All were repulsed by the bleeding, messy sight. But in the eyes of one man, and one man alone, I detected a certain unhealthy interest, a look that was almost an ogling. I thought I was mistaken at the time, and like a fool I let the impression go; it left me. But that was it, that was it, then and there, if I'd only realized."

"And who was it, the suspect—of course?" Belmonte asked interestedly.

Manning took a moment to answer. He turned his empty brandy jigger upside down. "No, the man who was there to question the suspect. Police Inspector Robles."

Belmonte's face was a pucker of sudden white shock.

"And now you know," the American said quietly. "As you're entitled to. But that look on your own face right now is the look that will be on everyone else's, when they hear it. It'll be bad for the police, and worse for the public. So I think it's better if we keep it where it is now: just between you and me and the shovelful of hot coals."

He stood up and stretched himself in the healing, cleansing sunlight slanting down under the café awning.

His voice trailed off as if he didn't want to talk about it any further. "Something that will never be mentioned again —but will always be there—between you, and me, and the bad dreams of our nights."

"It's beautiful now!" she exclaimed. "Come over here and look."

He came up behind her, where she was standing, before the open full-length windows. She was gazing out with all the rapture attending a first discovery. And it was a first discovery in every sense of the word; she had never seen this place before, a cloud had darkened it until now.

They stood looking out in silence for a while, he at her shoulder. The lucent evening sky, the wavy black hills against the hidden blue gas flares left behind by the sunset. And nearer at hand, those streaks of luminous talcum, stretching away in narrowing perspective, that were the streets and bright cafés poor little Clo-Clo had known so well.

Her ghost must still be ambling along them right now, down there; but a pert, friendly sort of ghost, not a terrifying one, smiling and flipping her handbag jauntily at the passers-by she met.

"So you're going back?" he said finally.

"I guess so. On the next boat. But that's not for thirty days yet. What're you going to do?"

"I don't know. Stay down, I guess. Things seem to be opening up a little more for me now, since that happened. Belmonte and I are to share that reward offered by the municipal council, I told you that, didn't I? And His Nibs the Commissioner has even offered me a job as a sort of special investigator without portfolio on his own immediate staff. And just to round out things full circle, I had a letter this morning from my old client, Kiki Walker, hinting that a little misunderstanding shouldn't stand between friends and she'd be very glad to have me do publicity work for her again. What I'll probably do is open a little agency of some sort, now that I've got capital. Typewriters or shaving cream or something very undramatic like that."

"You should get yourself a girl and settle down."

"I have already, but she doesn't know it yet."

"When are you going to tell her?"

One of his four or five cumbersome hands made vague motions behind her back, but without actually touching her. "Pretty soon now. Sometime within the next thirty days, before that boat leaves."

12   TA-51